BRENNEN

BOOK ONE IN THE ROYAL DRAGONS SERIES

HELEN JOHNSTON

BRENNEN

THE ROYAL DRAGON SERIES
BOOK ONE

HELEN JOHNSTON

Copyright ©Helen Johnston 2021 all rights reserved.

BRENNEN
THE ROYAL DRAGON SERIES

HELEN JOHNSTON

This book is a work of fiction. Names, characters, places and incidents are either the product of the author's imagination or are used fictitiously, and any resemblance to actual persons, living or dead, events, or locales are entirely coincidental. This book contains sexually explicit material and is not intended for anyone under the age of eighteen.

No part of this book may be reproduced in any form or by any electronic or mechanical means, including information storage and retrieval systems, without permission from the author, except in the case of a reviewer, who may quote brief passages embodied in a review.

All requests should be forwarded to: hjohnston35@yahoo.com

OTHER TITLES BY HELEN JOHNSTON:

The Innocence series:

Innocence Lost Innocence

Reclaimed Innocence Reborn

Jarryd's Journey

Ravage

The Eternal series:

Eternal Hunger

Eternal Cravings

Eternal Desires

Work in progress:

Lyle's Legend

My Molly

Due Christmas 2021:

Wishing upon A Christmas Star

NOTE FROM AUTHOR

Hello everyone,

Here we are at the beginning of a brand new series, with new characters to fall in love with. I'd like to take a moment to thank my wonderful editor, Stephanie, at Farrant Editing. This book wouldn't be what the final product became without her!

To Patti Roberts who is my fabulous book cover artist. She takes my ideas and makes them a beautiful reality.

To all my friends who share my books on Social Media, I luvs ya all!

To Helen's Hellions on Facebook, thank you for all the encouragement you gave me. Especially when I wanted to give it all up. You rock ladies!

I hope you enjoy Brennen!

Helen xx

CONTENTS

Prologue	1
Chapter 1	5
Chapter 2	13
Chapter 3	22
Chapter 4	27
Chapter 5	33
Chapter 6	39
Chapter 7	47
Chapter 8	53
Chapter 9	58
Chapter 10	62
Chapter 11	68
Chapter 12	74
Chapter 13	79
Chapter 14	85
Chapter 15	90
Chapter 16	98
Chapter 17	103
Chapter 18	107
Chapter 19	114
Chapter 20	118
Chapter 21	124
Chapter 22	129
Chapter 23	137
Chapter 24	146
Chapter 25	154
Chapter 26	162
Chapter 27	170
Chapter 28	177
Chapter 29	185

Chapter 30	191
Chapter 31	196
Chapter 32	205
Chapter 33	212
Chapter 34	217
Chapter 35	220
Chapter 36	227
Chapter 37	232
Chapter 38	240
Chapter 39	248
Chapter 40	257
Chapter 41	262
Chapter 42	268
Chapter 43	274
Chapter 44	280
Chapter 45	286
Chapter 46	292
Chapter 47	301
Chapter 48	307
Chapter 49	314
Epilogue	318
About the Author	321

PROLOGUE

Finally, I'm home. The long walk was made worse by the terrible storm that's been raging all day—usual weather for England during the middle of winter. While on my journey, one kind citizen decided to drive straight through a giant puddle and gift me with a cold shower. And as if that wasn't enough to make my day miserable, I'm exhausted after an incredibly long twelve-hour shift. Being on my feet all day is wearing thin. I have no idea how others do it year in year out.

Opening the heavy front door, I holler, "Macie, are you home?"

"In the kitchen," I hear her soft voice call out.

I hurry inside and close the door firmly behind me so the rain can't splatter the fancy wood flooring in the entrance hall. After dumping my rain-soaked jacket and waterlogged shoes in the cupboard, I make my way to the kitchen, seeking the heat I know will be coming from the Aga.

"How was work?" Macie asks, handing me a strong mug of tea.

I hum a sound of pleasure. "Thank you."

It's just how I like it: hot, dark, and sweet. I smile, inhaling the steam and wrapping my hands around the mug, warming my numb fingers.

"Work was… well, work." I shrug. "You know that new manager?" She nods. "Well, she's making waves." I roll my eyes. "I don't think I can stay there much longer. It's zapping the life right out of me."

"Well, I might be able to help with that," Macie informs me with a bright smile, taking a sip of her own tea.

I raise an eyebrow and place my mug on the marble countertop. "I think you've done enough to help me."

"Just hear me out, okay?" She waits until I nod for her to continue. "As I've said before, you did me a huge favour when you moved in. Who else would have looked after Gertie and Bettie while I was working?"

I let out a very unladylike snort. Gertie and Bettie are her houseplants.

"It's true." We laugh, because in the short time I've been Macie's tenant, I've already killed Gertie and Bettie's predecessors. I haven't got a single green finger. Perhaps mine are the fingers of death— to houseplants, at least.

I lean against the countertop. "So, what's this way you can help with the job situation?"

"I have to go into hospital. No, it's nothing serious," she adds when my shock and worry become apparent. "I've finally got the date for the operation on my dodgy knee." She stirs her spoon around her mug, not quite looking me in the eyes.

She's got a dodgy knee? I had no idea. She certainly didn't show any pain when she dragged me along to her latest HIIT class at her private gym. Macie is highly active, and it shows. She has a banging figure, which is complimented by her height and blonde hair. I'm not gay, but she's a perfect specimen of womanhood in my eyes.

"I didn't know you had a dodgy anything. You should have told me. I would have done more to help around here." I wave my hands around, indicating the house, feeling guilty for not knowing this basic information about her.

"It's not that bad, honestly." Her aqua eyes stare into mine as she waves my comments away. "But here's the thing: I won't be able to continue my cleaning of the church. So, I'm thinking you could drop your hours at the supermarket and pick up my cleaning job in the evening. You'll be a lot better off as the church pays very well." She's smiling at me, knowing full well I won't turn down the chance to reduce my hours. It really is becoming unbearable.

The staff—most of them, at least—are a great bunch of colleagues, but no matter where you work there will always be a few who take great delight in making life hard. So, I'm not going to kick a gift horse in the mouth.

I take a sip of my tea, unable to stop the grin forming on my face.

"Do you think the church will accept me—me being a heathen and all?" I laugh.

She laughs with me. "You are no heathen. You've just lost your way for a while." She gives me a knowing smile.

I place my mug down and give her a hug. We've not been friends long, but she's become a sister to me. A 'sister from another mister' as they say. She found me when I was at my lowest point, picked me up, and shook me off. Now I'm living in her home, working hard to get together a deposit for my own flat.

    I pull back and give her a bright smile. "Okay, I'll do it."

CHAPTER ONE

A few months later.

For fuck's sake! my mind shrieks, as my ankle twists and I fall to the ground with all the grace of a baby gorilla— though to be honest, I'm sure they're far more graceful than I. Looking around, I'm thankful no one is here to spot how uncoordinated I am. It's usually quiet this time of night; just me and my trustee cleaning equipment.

People ask me why I don't find it creepy to clean the old church, especially during nights like this, when it's thundering and blowing a hooley, as my mum often said. I usually tell them to just look around. It's such a beautiful old building, full of history. Faded tapestries of brave warriors going off to battle on their fearsome steeds hang from the ancient, arched windows, and charmingly worn parquet flooring greets you when you enter. I'm not religious in any way, shape or form, but I can appreciate the history and architecture of this building. It's seen so many people come walking through its doors. If only the walls could talk; I bet they could tell an interesting story or two.

Macie had her operation a few weeks ago and is now recuperating at home, but it will see her out of action for a further six months or longer. Every night, I make sure she's comfortable before leaving her to come and clean this church. After everything she's done for me, I want to help her. Plus, the money is really good.

I couldn't afford to say no, not if I wanted to leave my job at the supermarket at some point in the future. Not when I was in a mountain of debt, thanks to Giles, the pig spawned from Hell. He just upped and left after deciding we were over, saying he'd fallen in love with his secretary, who was more 'his type'. I remember the night in the pub when he pulled the rug right out from under me. His eyes had travelled up and down my body contemptuously, a sneer firmly in place as he grimaced and told me, "I really don't know why I've been with you. It's a mystery how someone like me could be with someone like you in the first place."

At the time, I wanted to scream at him, but then again, I wasn't sure why he'd stayed as long as he had either. We never had sex. He always worked late, and I was asleep by the time he got in. At the weekends, he always preferred to spend his time at his private gym rather than with me.

In hindsight, Macie and I guessed he had probably been banging his perfectly groomed secretary the whole time I'd been with him. I roll my eyes every time I think about how cliché it all is.

The only thing that worked out in my favour was we

weren't married— not that he'd ever shown any interest in being married; at least not to me. After our breakup, however, his friends took great delight in informing me his secretary was sporting a rock the size of a small country on her finger.

I hobble to stand and wince at the pain shooting up my right leg. That's going to leave a bruise. I chew my lip, something I tend to do when I'm in pain or worried about something. I plonk my ass down on an old, worn pew and tug my jeans up, then remove my trainer and sock, both of which have seen better days. Yep, my ankle is already starting to swell. Luckily, I'm about finished here anyway, so I'm going to call it a night and walk home—very slowly.

Home is still a rented room at Macie's place. I moved in with her because I could no longer afford the rent on the lovely flat I shared with the pig spawned from Hell. Not that I was given the option of keeping it. After Macie took me home with her on the night of the dumping, I received a phone call from his lawyers, who asked where my belongings should be sent to. I never thought I'd be here— alone; a lodger in someone else's home at the age of twenty-six.

Feeling sorry for myself, I decide to go ahead and lock up, when a door loudly slams shut somewhere in the church. My skin prickles. No one should be in here at this time of night. I've been doing this shift for a few weeks now and haven't spotted a soul. I hurriedly shove my foot back into the sock and trainer, then stand, crying out when I put weight on my ankle.

"Who's there?" a man shouts from within the vestry, his rich, baritone voice carrying a thick accent, as if English isn't his first language. It's not one I recognise, and it makes the hairs on my arms stand on end.

My eyes pop wide when he stalks into the main part of the church. He stares at me with an unblinking gaze that travels up and down my body, assessing me.

I feel like a bug under a microscope. It's a tad disconcerting to be studied so intently, especially by a stranger, and one that's so large.

My brain suddenly catches up with what I'm looking at. Bloody hell, he's huge. My mouth falls open when he strides confidently towards me. I back away the best I can on a busted ankle, but even if I could run, I suspect he'd catch me without any trouble. When he shows no signs of slowing down, I turn and try to run anyway, but cry out when his hand lands on my shoulder. As heavy as an anvil, it almost knocks me to the floor.

"Well, aren't you tiny, but I dare say a tasty morsel to welcome me?" he informs me, his gaze unwavering as I slowly sit. I have no choice really, not when his hand makes me move that way.

Oh my God. Really—who is this big? And tiny? Who's he kidding?

"Who the hell are you? Let me go!" I demand, showing more bravado than I feel as I struggle to get free of his vicelike grip. I'd find this funny if it weren't happening to me. It's just like a corny, old horror movie. Am I about to become the main character that ends up dead; in a church, of all places?

"You joke? Of course you know who I am or you wouldn't be here," he growls at me, his midnight blue eyes narrowing. "Now come on, the vortex will be shut in a few more minutes.

You know the drill." He hauls me to my feet and hefts me over his shoulder, oblivious to the extra curves my body carries. Giles, the pig spawned from Hell, would have been panting and faking a heart attack by now.

"Now just a bloody second. What's a vortex? Where are you taking me?" I yell, but he remains silent. "I have a family. They will be wondering where I am," I lie frantically. My parents passed away suddenly a few years ago, in a car crash, and since then my life has tumbled into a spiral of one shitty moment after another. And here I am, having another shitty moment.

By this point, I'm well aware I'm in a dreadful plight, so using all my strength, I hammer my fists down on his back. But it doesn't make the slightest difference.

"Don't be silly. All the females we take from this planet are single, with no living family. They know what they are going to be used for and they come willingly. What is the matter with you?" he snaps, as if all this should make perfect sense to me. He comes to a stop and pulls me off his back to take another look at me.

"I—I just clean the church. The lady who usually does it isn't well and asked me to cover her shifts." I try to pull away again. I'd kick him if my ankle weren't hurting so much.

He rolls his head as if trying to release some tension. "Your friend… is her name Macie, by any chance?" He raises an eyebrow at me, waiting for my answer.

I chew my lip nervously and stare into his midnight blue eyes, which are framed by eyelashes I could only dream of owning. Damn if my abductor isn't mouth-wateringly delicious. Totally swoon-worthy. His face is all angular lines, with a strong nose and sleek cheekbones. His lips are a perfect cupid pout and make me wonder if they kiss as good as they look like they do. I shake my head, telling myself sternly that no matter how gorgeous he is, he is still trying to kidnap me!

"Yes, that's her name. Why? What's going on?" I demand. A moment later, I realise I shouldn't have admitted my friend was meant to be here instead of me.

My hands go to my hips as I glare at him, but I feel an icy shard of terror sliding down my spine. This isn't going to be good.

He glares right back and then rubs a frustrated hand down his face.

"You've got to be fucking kidding me. You're really not Macie?" he asks, his accent becoming even more pronounced as he walks to lean on the wall a few feet away. It could be Russian? Latvian? Something far away, I reason with myself.

"No, I'm really not." I edge ever so slowly towards the exit, watching him intently. For a mad man, he is an exceptionally fine-looking specimen.

"Stand still!" he barks, once again striding towards me. "This is my one shot. My female is meant to be waiting here for me. For four hundred years this moment has been waiting to happen." He grabs me once again and throws me over his shoulder, leaving me to bounce around like a sack of potatoes as he continues his walk with long determined strides towards the vestry, where he came from. "You'll have to do," he growls under his breath.

"Wait! Please don't do this," I plead, hitting his back—not that it makes a blind bit of difference; it's like hitting a steel wall. "Hold on—what do you mean, *four hundred years* and *you'll have to do?"* I demand. I'm furious, utterly fed up with the men in my life making do with me. Like I'm never bloody good enough.

"Fuck you!" Using my good leg, I boot him in the stomach —only for my foot to bounce off. Damn, he's hard all over. I keep kicking, lashing out in any way I can. He grunts when my foot collides with something sensitive, and I mentally high-five myself.

His hand lands on my ass, and a hard slap echoes around the church. My eyes widen and my mouth falls open. He spanked me. He actually bloody spanked me. I'm horrified.

"Be still! I don't want any trouble from you." He leaps into the air, and I squeal. Landing on the small stage, he walks towards the back, and I hear a strange whooshing noise.

Twisting my head, I try and see what's going on, and my jaw drops. I must have fallen asleep. Yes, that's it. I'm in the middle of a horrifying nightmare. There isn't really a silver and black gaping hole that's moving and swirling in a mesmerising way. I pinch my arm in an attempt to wake up, but nothing happens.

"Take a deep breath," he tells me, before he steps towards whatever it is. "The vortex won't stay open for very long, and I don't want to become trapped here on Earth."

"What do you mean, *take a deep breath? Here on Earth?* Where are we going?" I yell at him, resuming my assault on his body.

I'm in full panic mode, and my anxiety is through the roof, but before any sound can escape me, we are falling through the swirling black and silver hole—vortex, as he calls it—and spinning out of control. I tightly clamp my eyes shut, my screams filling the void. His hands smooth down my ass, as if he's trying to comfort me, but it does nothing to help.

I'm suffocating.

I'm going to die.

I don't try to stop it; I rush headlong towards it, irrationally praying that once I'm dead, I can start breathing again.

CHAPTER TWO

*S*ometime later—who the hell knows how long—I hear distant voices and feel someone petting my hand.

"What do you mean this isn't the one?" a male voice asks. I don't recognise it, but why should I—I have no idea where I am. "She looks human enough." He has a similar thick accent to the man who took me. English can't be their first language.

Human enough? What the hell does that mean?

"Shh, Hunter, in case she can hear you," another voice pipes up. This time it's a female's voice with a slight Scottish accent.

I really should open my eyes, but I have no strength, not even for such a small thing. Instead, I slip back into unconsciousness once more.

. . .

"Come on, Little Flower, it's time to wake up." This voice I recognise. This is the deep tone of my abductor's voice.

I feel a hand stroking mine again, and this time, I fight to open my eyes.

"That's it. Welcome back." The man who abducted me is grinning at me, his incredible midnight blue eyes flashing interest in my direction. "You had us all quite worried." He sits his huge frame down next to me, and I shrink away from him, pulling the thin blanket that's covering my naked body up until it's under my chin. *I'm naked?*

"I'm not going to hurt you," he states calmly. I glare at him.

"Then take me home," I rasp. My throat is sore, burning, as if a thousand fire pokers have been shoved down it.

Upon hearing my plea, he smiles sadly, regret shining in his eyes. "I'm sorry, Little Flower, the vortex only opens the once."

I close my eyes and lose the battle to keep them open any longer.

Round three of waking up and my eyes stray to the doorway. There's a commotion outside.

"Hunter, you can't stop me. I'm going to see her. She needs friends here, and I'm going to be that for her." The hushed but urgent female voice reaches me just before a petite woman comes barrelling into the room. Her bright red, unruly hair falls in waves down to her waist, which, for some reason, makes me instantly and irrationally jealous. I've only seen hair like that in shampoo adverts, glossy magazines, and on TV. She skids to a halt, her warm smile lighting up her grass-green eyes.

But it's not her gorgeous eyes that hold my attention. It's her skin, which is a pale creamy colour, littered with pretty freckles. Her arms make me gasp as I stare at them. It's hardly noticeable, but when she moves, I can see white markings. It's as if she's been branded and these are the scars left behind. I know I'm staring, but I can't help it. The marks are incredible; intricate swirls and dots. I'm sure there must be some sort of meaning to them all. I feel rude for staring, but I'm intrigued as to why she would do this to her body. Or did they do it to her without her permission? After all, *he kidnapped me*!

Impatiently brushing her hair out of her face, she stops by my side.

"You're awake, lass." She beams. Her very slight Scottish brogue is soft and like a balm on my shredded nerves. She politely ignores the fact I was rudely staring at the markings on her arms.

I raise an eyebrow.

"I know, there must be so many questions. Brennen." She glances at the brooding man still holding on to my hand.

So that's his name. Brennen.

"Why don't you go and grab some food? I can feel Hunter lurking in the corridor. Take him with you and let me have some time alone with her?" She tilts her head in the direction of the wide doorway, just as another man walks in.

Hunter. I have no idea what they feed them here but talk about colossal. His short black hair highlights his chiselled facial structure and full lips, which are supported by a square chin that would make him the perfect candidate for a G.I. Joe advert. His eyes match Brennen's in shape and colour.

The woman takes in my wariness at the new arrival.

"Ack, don't fret, lass. Hunter is as soft as a teddy bear. But don't tell him I said that," she whispers, then winks at me before swivelling around at the exact second he reaches for her. He pulls her into his arms and kisses her soundly.

Wow, get a room. I'm not the least bit jealous of their obvious passion. Nope.

The markings on her arms stand out even more against his black t-shirt. They are raised and look like brail running up and down her skin.

What the hell is going on?

The woman gently untangles herself, looking into Hunter's eyes. "Take Brenn and get some food. He's not eaten since getting back, and she's skittish enough without the pair of you glaring and looming over her." She laughs softly as she pushes him away.

He nods and kisses her forehead, before beckoning my abductor to join him. Just before the men leave, Hunter does the strangest thing: he runs his fingers lightly down her arms. The savage look of lust he gives her has me blushing on her behalf.

"I won't be far. You're perfectly safe, and Alish is staying with you," Brennen, my abductor, tells me, diverting my attention from the couple. Then he's heading out with Hunter. The pair are an impressive sight. That's when I realise I'm not dreaming—my imagination isn't that well developed. I know my fantasy life can get a bit kinky, thanks to all the erotic romance books I love to devour, but even my imagination couldn't possibly come up with such hulking males.

"There we go. Peace." Alish sighs, smiling at me. "So, as Brennen said, I'm Alish. The other male is Hunter. He's my mate and one of Brennen's cousins. What's your name, lass?" She makes herself comfortable on my bed, tucking a stray lock of hair behind her ear. I try very hard not to stare at her markings.

I take a moment to answer, not sure I want to talk to this woman. I've been taken from my home and she's here trying to be all nicey, nicey. But she sits and gives me time.

I roll my eyes and huff. "Araline. My name is Araline."

"That's such a pretty name. You must have royal French ancestors. It suits who you've been paired with." She smiles as if it should all make perfect sense to me.

"I don't think I have." I try and think back to my family and if they'd said anything about having a French side. I can't remember them mentioning it. But more importantly, just what the hell does she mean by *paired with*? "I didn't know it was French," I mumble.

"Oh, yes, lass. It means French nobility, and as I said, it's perfect, because you've been paired with Brennen, and he's royalty here," she informs me, a look of pride flooding her features.

"Royalty?" There, she said it again: "Paired with Brennen?" I shake my head, not wanting to know right now. "So, exactly where is here?" I ask, taking in the room. It's enormous and luxurious, all white marble with gold thread running throughout. But all I can think about is: what is the easiest way to escape. I glance back at Alish, and for the first time since she entered the room, she looks apprehensive.

"Just spit it out," I rasp, clutching at my sheet, wondering if I'm in Scotland. Though so far, this Alish is the only one I've heard with that accent.

"It's going to sound farfetched, but believe me, I tell you the truth," she says, faltering slightly before taking a breath. As I watch her, my heart hammers against my chest, and my apprehension builds.

Just where the hell are we?

"You aren't on Earth any longer." She stares at me, her eyes unblinking as I gawp at her. She holds up a finger as I go to interrupt her. It's then that I notice her hands are covered in the markings also. "Hang on; let me give you a brief explanation. There's a vortex between this world, Mertier, and Earth: the black and silver… well, tunnel, for want of a different word, that Brennen took you into. Here, tragically, no females are born. Only males. Hundreds of years ago, the then ruler of this planet came to an agreement with some of Earth's rulers. They would send their more advanced technology in exchange for Earth women of childbearing age."

I'm flabbergasted. Truly, I have no idea what to think at this point. I'm supposed to believe I'm on a completely different planet, and it's called Mertier?

While I stare unbelievingly at her, I feel at a slight disadvantage, what with being naked and lying on my back. I wriggle to sit up, yanking the sheet with me. I wince when a sharp pain shoots up my lower leg, and I'm reminded that my ankle was sprained before all this madness started.

"Why the hell am I bloody naked?" I growl. "As to the rest, I really don't know what to say to being on another world, but my ankle's killing me. Have you got any pain meds?" I ask, trying not to dwell on the revelation about not being on Earth. As if I can be anywhere else? Perhaps I fell and banged my head on a pew in the church and I'm safe in a hospital bed and this is all just a dream. Yes, that must be what happened.

"The vortex burns off Earth material, I'm afraid. When the males go through, they wear clothes with a special coating on them. Let me get you something for the pain." Alish sees my wince as I try to get more comfortable and leans over, pressing a button on a control pad by the side of my bed. "I can't imagine what you're going through, lass. My clan in Scotland prepare and educate the females that have been handpicked to leave and join their chosen mates here on Mertier, from a very young age. To just arrive here with no prior warning or education must be daunting, to say the least." She pats my hand.

"Yes, daunting," I murmur rather sarcastically. That's not how I'd describe it. Not in the least.

A young male arrives and walks silently into the room holding a silver tray with bits and pieces on it. I watch as he smiles warmly at Alish.

"Good morn to you, Lady Alish." He places the tray on the little table beside my bed and smiles shyly at me.

He looks to be about twelve; at that age where he's all gangly legs and arms. He has a shock of blond curls and the same eyes as my abductor and that other man, Hunter.

"Good morn. How are your studies going, Tallith?" Alish

enquires, picking up a jug of what I presume is ice-filled water. It shimmers silver as she pours some of it into a glass.

The boy's face falls.

"Okay." He stabs his toe sullenly into the marble floor tiles, his eyes anywhere but looking at Alish.

Alish tries to hide her smile, her green eyes merrily dancing before she tells him, "If you need extra help, you must ask. These are important lessons if you want to go to Earth and explore."

"I know, Lady Alish. I know." He huffs sullenly. "I don't know if I even want to go," he tells her, his eyes wide with shame, as if what he's blurted out is a terrible secret.

He eyes me warily, then nods and scurries away before she can answer him. She sighs gently and hands me the glass and a couple of brightly-coloured pills.

I examine them suspiciously, rolling them around in my palm.

"What are they?" I ask.

"Just simple herbs that will help with the swelling and pain. I promise you they aren't harmful. I wouldn't do that to you, or Brennen. He's waited far too long for you," she states, smiling.

I swallow the pills—what other choice do I have at this point? The water is delicious; the cleanest, most pure water I've ever tasted. Damn, you could bottle it and sell it for a fortune. I drink every drop, and she kindly refills the glass. I can feel the soreness of my throat start to ease. Once the second glass has been drunk, there are so many questions I want to ask her: What are her arm markings? Why does she genuinely believe we are on another planet? Who is this Brennen that she says I'm to be mated with, and what exactly does mated mean?

All these questions and more buzz around in my mind. Until finally, I lean back and close my eyes.

CHAPTER THREE

I must have drifted off again, because when I wake, Brennen and Hunter have returned. I stare at the two men and gulp. Only me—getting abducted in a church could only happen to me.

"Brennen, let me introduce you to your Araline." Alish does the introductions, and his face breaks out in a wide grin.

"It's an honour to have you here as my mate, Araline," he states, and my eyes widen.

Mate? What the fuck is this 'mate' business?

"So, let me get this straight. This place," I wave my hand around, "isn't Earth. I'm on a completely different planet, whose men go down to Earth every few years and steal women?" Both of the men's eyes flare.

"We don't steal them; they are educated. It's their choice to join us and they always know what's going to happen to them. They are welcomed and treated like the princesses they are," Hunter says, frustration flashing in his eyes. I get the feeling they aren't used to being questioned about their way of life. Alish tugs his hand until his arm goes around her waist, and I watch as he visibly relaxes.

"Oh? I must have missed my education. Or did the fucking memo get lost in the post?" I glare at them all. I'm pissed off now. "Oh, but hang on, I'm the *'you'll have to do'* woman, aren't I, Brennen? I'm not even really wanted here." I fold my arms over my chest and raise an eyebrow at him, daring him to lie.

There's a sharp intake of breath by both Alish and Hunter. Alish tightens her lips, glaring at Brennen. She is clearly unhappy with him. I shake my head while Brennen looks decidedly uncomfortable.

"I'm sorry if I hurt your feelings, Araline. That was said in the heat of the moment." He stares at me, his midnight blue eyes boring into mine.

I ignore him and turn to Alish. "I need some clothes, please. And shoes. I'm not staying naked in this bed any longer."

Alish watches me, and for the first time I really scrutinise her. Her clothes aren't too different from what I would wear but are obviously of a much higher quality than I could ever dream of affording. I glance at the men, and their clothes look like they're ready for some sort of combat; tight black tee-shirts that stretch across their muscles, showing them off to perfection, and multi-pocketed black trousers tucked into what I'd call army boots. I can see what I presume are weapons strapped to their boots, belts and chests, and I'm almost positive there are more that are hidden.

"I will bring you some shortly," Brennen informs me. "We

had the measurements of your friend who was meant to be coming here; you look about the same size." He looks me up and down as if mentally measuring me.

I stare at him, dumbfounded. We really aren't the same size at all. *Men!*

"I don't want someone's cast-offs, thank you very much. It's bad enough that I'm stuck here with a man who doesn't want me. I don't want her unwanted clothes as well," I growl, my eyes filling up with tears, but I angrily brush them away.

Brennen takes a hurried step back, as if I've slapped him, and Hunter's eyes are wide with shock.

"It's okay, Araline. I will go and find you some clothes," Alish says softly. She grips Hunter's hand and begins to drag him away. It looks like he's about to say something to me, but she shakes her head, and they leave me alone. With *him.*

"You have no idea what I'm feeling," I tell him before he can utter a single word. I have to take a breath because I'm slowly losing my shit here. I stare into his eyes. "You've removed me from my home, my life, and stuck me on a strange planet. Where I know no one. I have no job or way of looking after myself. WHAT THE FUCK AM I SUPPOSED TO DO?" I scream at him. God, if I could reach him, I'd hit him.

He steps towards me, but I yank the silk sheet around me and hop off the bed, cringing at how my ankle throbs. I wobble and feel as if I'm about to pass out, when I hear him swear violently before his arms wind around me. For such a large man, he is completely gentle with me as he scoops me up and places me back on the bed.

Oh, for fuck's sake, I can't even run away. I close my

eyes, feeling pitiful, and turn my head away from him, finally allowing the tears to fall. I feel the bed roll as he climbs in next to me, wrapping his arms around me. I have no energy to tell him to piss off, so he just holds me while I cry.

"Little Flower, I am so sorry for how I acted back in the church." His voice is low, and I don't want to admit it but I kind of like his accent. His chin is resting on top of my head as he tucks me into his chest. "This has never happened before. In all the hundreds and hundreds of years we've had this agreement with your Earth, there hasn't been a single female that has been taken by mistake. I know that won't make you feel any better in the slightest, but we will work this out. I promise you. Just give me a chance."

I don't answer. I've never felt so drained in my life. It must be the drugs Alish gave me or that vortex we came through. That's *if* I believe I'm really here and not in some drug-induced coma brought on by some freak accident.

"Let me tell you a bit about Mertier." His deep accent is relaxing, and I nod slowly, feeling powerless to do anything else. "It is quite different to Earth, but I'll keep it brief for now. You will soon discover all it has to offer."

I lay still with his arms around me, and how stupid is it that I feel safe? I sigh. I haven't got the energy to worry about it at the moment.

"We have two suns, and two moons, one of which is inhabited by the Rumos, which you'll soon learn about. Obviously, that means it's hotter here, but we do have two distinctive seasons. They are similar to Earth's summer and winter. But with two suns, even our winter is still warmer than your summers. That's the only time we have our heavy rains. Have you ever been dancing in warm rains, Araline?"

I shake my head again, and he carries on. "We will go dancing in the rain, I promise you. Our technology is highly advanced, and again, I will point it out as we go. I don't want you to worry that you have to learn it all today. We have the rest of our lives to figure it out. Together."

He sounds so sure that all this is real. It does sound wonderful, to be honest. But I have a feeling that when I wake up, I'll be lying in a sterile hospital bed, hooked up to beeping machines.

My eyes close, the pills finally kicking in, and I can't stop myself; I fall asleep in his arms. I wouldn't admit it to a soul, but for whatever fucked-up reason, I feel safe knowing he is here with me.

CHAPTER FOUR

Brennen

"Is the lass sleeping?" Alish whispers to me as she walks back into the room.

"Yes, she finally dropped off. She's exhausted." My hand gently strokes her cheek. It's incredibly soft.

"I have some new clothes for her." She hangs them up on the rack behind the bed, then turns and looks at me tentatively. "Can I make a suggestion, Brenn?"

"Of course, your council is always welcome," I tell her.

"Before you take her home, have Ta remove anything you bought for Macie. Araline won't want it. And strike that name from your memory. Never mention her again."

I nod in agreement. "What a fucking cock-up. How do I explain about Ta to her? Has anyone notified the Council as to what's happened?"

"I'd leave Ta out of it until you get home and have the

privacy to explain our ways." She sighs. "Your father visited the Council this morning. I don't think they are happy about it, but what can they do? They're not about to go up against him, are they? We can't send her home now. You know how that'd turn out. You have to make this work, Brenn," Alish implores me, running her hands over the clothes as if to get rid of any creases.

"I've been expecting Mother and Father to arrive." I grimace at the thought of the king and queen joining us here before I manage to talk more with Araline.

Hunter walks in, kissing his mate before staring at me. "Cousin of mine, you never do things the easy way, do you?" He grins, pulling Alish into his side. "Your parents will come and see you once you have her settled in your home. They won't want to overwhelm her at this point."

"I really don't think she could be any more overwhelmed. Do you? I made it clear I took her only because the other woman wasn't where she was supposed to be. I told her that she'd have to do and threw her over my shoulder like someone possessed. She's petrified of me, and I can't say I blame her. I would be too." I have to glance away so they don't see the look of utter anguish in my eyes. "How do I make this right? How can she ever fall in love with me and want to mate with me after all I've done to her?" I rub my face in frustration. "I've snatched her away to a life she has no idea about."

"I don't know, Brenn. But you have to. You have to find a way to make her realise life here will be infinitely better for her than on Earth," Alish says softly, smiling sadly. "I had such a different arrival than she is experiencing. I hate that she's hurting."

"She's the only one who's gone through this. It's unprecedented," Hunter says gruffly. "Can I make a suggestion?" he asks, watching me warily. I doubt he's ever seen me so emotional. Warriors on Mertier are taught to hide their feelings. When I nod, he carries on. "Take her to your home and get her settled. If she sees what her new life is about, she might thaw towards you a little."

"Yes, I think you're right. I won't even mention the fact that she's to be Queen one day. I don't think that will help our cause. I've completely fucked this one up," I tell them, shaking my head. I turn my attention back to my mate.

My mate... I feel exhilarated and a little fearful that perhaps all this has been too much for Araline to cope with. What if she never comes round to loving her mates? I must somehow make this right. But to be honest, I have no idea how.

"Take it slow with her, but, yes, I think it's best not to mention the queen bit for a while. It'll only spook her more. She's been looking at my arms. She didn't ask about them but I know she's curious. I should have covered them until everything had been explained to her. Dragons might be more than she can handle right now." Alish shakes her head, brushing her long hair over her shoulder and twiddling with the ends. "We're going home, Brenn. It's been a long and interesting day. Do as I say: take her home so you and Ta can spoil her."

Hunter puts his arm around his mate, and they head out the door.

"See you tomorrow, Brenn." Alish gives me a little wave before they disappear.

"Come on, Little Flower, it's time to get you home." I reach and press a button on the control pad beside her bed and wait for someone to come and help transfer us home. I'm excited about the prospect of getting to know her. My mate. Fuck, I love saying that. I've waited so many long years for her. She's a fiery little thing, which I have to say I didn't think I'd enjoy, but I do.

I smile wide as she wakes, her pretty topaz eyes staring straight into mine, but it doesn't last long. She's out cold before I can talk to her some more. I glance up when I hear footsteps approaching, and Tallith comes bounding into the room, skidding to a stop and smiling happily when he spots me.

I know he admires me a little, but a lot of the younger males do. After the boy's father passed away in one of the skirmishes when Tallith was only an infant, I felt a little responsible for him as his father was a proud and strong warrior, and a good friend of mine. I put him through warrior camp training to see if he wanted to follow in his father's footsteps, and made sure he had everything he'd need to succeed in life. I have a feeling he's more of a scholar than a warrior, though, and that's just fine.

"Prince Brennen!" Tallith cries out with excitement, before remembering his manners and bowing formally to me. "It's good to see you. I watched you in the last bout of games. You were marvellous." He blushes a little, dropping his gaze, embarrassed by his outburst.

I grin, remembering what it was like to be young and overenthusiastic about most things. The games are held every five years on Mertier. The royal dragons are pitted against

Mertier's best within the non-dragon army. It may sound as if it's all one-sided against the army, but these males are the elite group that have enormous skill in defence and fighting. They don't go down easily.

"Tallith, it's good to see you again." Standing, I hold out my arm for him to grip, keeping my face serious when Tallith smiles happily at being invited to greet in the way of the warriors. "You have a good, strong grip."

Tallith nods enthusiastically. "What can I get for you, my prince?"

"I'm taking Araline home and need transport. Can you arrange a carrier to be here?" I ask gently, running a finger down her cheek.

Tallith looks warily at me. "Are you sure you want to do that? She didn't look too happy at being here earlier with Lady Alish."

I know we can't have gossip about the royal family starting. No one can know about Araline being the 'wrong' female yet. I want her settled and happy before we deal with the rest of Mertier.

"Yes. I'm sure once she's in her new home, she'll be much happier. So, I need the royal transport, please. Do you think you could arrange that for us?" Allowing some impatience to reinforce my wishes, I hide my amusement as Tallith nods vigorously.

"Of course I can. It'll be waiting for you whenever you're ready to go. Congratulations on finding your mate." Tallith beams at me before he leaves me alone with Araline.

While she sleeps, I take my time studying her. Picking up her hand, I discover how much smaller it is compared to my overlarge one. It makes me feel incredibly protective of her. I gently touch her messily cut, inky black hair. It's shorter than the women here wear it and looks as if she hacked at it herself with some sort of blunt instrument. I grin. I kind of like it. It makes her unique.

Her eyes flash open, topaz blue glaring into mine. She's a fierce little thing. But I don't like how she pulls her hand out of mine and shrinks back against the wall. It's regretful that a few words spoken hastily by me has made her afraid of me.

What should have been a joyous occasion for us has turned quickly into a shit show. All because of my selfishness in needing a mate so desperately I snatched this remarkable woman away. And now she has no clue as to the life she will now lead. Instead of taking her home to Ta and making her ours in every way possible, we now have to take our time and bring her into our way of life at a much slower pace.

CHAPTER FIVE

"Are you ready to come home with me, Little Flower?" Brennen asks me gently. Taking my hand back, he strokes my palm. "We have use of transport. I could show you around your new home, if you'd like?"

He watches me as I nibble the inside of my mouth. It has to be obvious to him that I'm undecided about what I want to do next.

"Why can't I stay here?" I demand. I know I don't want to travel anywhere unless it's to go home, back to Earth.

"Because this is one of our hospitals, Araline. Wouldn't you like to see some of the world that is now your home?" he asks, before walking over to some clothes that are hung up on a rack. "These will be far more comfortable to travel in than just a silk sheet. Though I have to admit, the thought of you naked under that sheet makes my body hard."

My jaw drops. Is he flirting with me? I'm already angry with myself for allowing my eyes to track him walking away.

Damn, his body... Even concealed by clothes it looks exceedingly inviting.

"Put the clothes on the bed and go and wait outside," I demand. Like hell am I getting naked in front of him.

He doesn't look happy at that request. When my eyebrow rises as if to question why he's not moving yet, he grumbles, "I'm your mate; your body belongs to me, as mine does to you." But he does as I ask and waits outside.

"My body belongs to me, pal," I murmur as he stomps away.

Only when I'm certain he's not coming back do I climb out of bed and quickly pull on the clothes. I almost moan at how soft the underwear is, and it fits perfectly. I try not to wonder how Alish got the correct size. The jumper feels like it's cashmere and hugs my more than generous curves. I wouldn't usually wear something so figure-hugging as I like to try and hide my body, but there's no hiding here. The trousers are not dissimilar to Brennen's: cargo, with multiple pockets. Functional.

My ankle is still tender and swollen, and I really don't fancy putting shoes on, but I spot a pair of black ballet pumps. The soft leather-like material isn't like anything I've worn before. I've never been able to afford quality clothes. I usually buy from the cheapest of shops, mostly second-hand ones.

"Okay, I'm ready," I call out to him, though I don't think I'll ever be ready to face this new world. Before I can voice my concerns, however, Brennen marches in. He has such a sexy stride; he owns the space his body inhabits with a confidence I've never experienced.

I'm struggling to get my foot into the damn shoe. Once

he's in front of me, he bends down on one knee and takes the shoe from me, then helps my foot into it. His touch is so tender I can't help but wish I'd met someone like him on Earth. But let's get real here; a man on Earth who looks like him wouldn't even glance in my direction.

"Next time you're struggling with anything, call me." His eyes travel up my body and dance with approval at my clothes. "Whether you like it or not, Araline, we are a partnership. You're stuck with me, I'm afraid." He grins at me, and my heart stutters. He's way too good-looking.

"Just like I'll have to do for you, you mean?" I ask him, not willing to let him forget that slight. If I let my guard down, I just know he's got the power to destroy me.

He sighs and turns his head away, but not before I see the flash of sadness flit across his face. He takes a deep breath before saying, "You look beautiful, Araline."

I feel his eyes all the way to my bones as they work their way first down my body, then up. Before I have a chance to reply, he sweeps me up into his arms. The squeal I let out is less than ladylike.

"I can walk," I splutter, as my treacherous arms wind tightly around his neck. My reasoning is that it's an awful long way to fall from up here.

"Not on your ankle, Little Flower. It would look very bad if I allow my mate to walk when she is injured," he tells me.

To be honest, I couldn't hope to keep up with his long, powerful strides if I wasn't hurt, never mind that my ankle has started to throb again. He walks down a stunningly crafted staircase, and I have to admit, my eyes are wide with wonder. The entire building seems to be made of the white marble with gold veins, which glistens in the suns. Yes, this world has two suns, just like he told me. I have to close my eyes against the fierce blaze once he steps through the doors, but it's not as hot as I'd expect from having two stars.

"Here, take this visor. It will help to protect your eyes." He pulls something black out of one of his trouser pockets and passes it to me as he puts me on my feet. I quickly put them on, and they make an immediate difference in helping against the harsh glare of the suns. They have what feels like putty that moulds to my nose, holding them securely in place without the need of arms like the sunglasses on earth. I give my head an experimental shake and they stay on. They are incredibly light and comfortable.

"Thank you. You don't need to wear them?" I ask, and he shakes his head. I feel the weight of his stare as I catch my first glimpse of this foreign planet, and that's exactly what it is. "Bloody hell." I try pinching myself to wake up but nothing happens. My stomach drops as it becomes crystal clear that everything he said is true. Indeed, we are not on Earth any longer. I'm not lying in a hospital bed, experiencing some sort of drug-induced hallucination.

I'm not sure what to look at first. It's not so dissimilar to Earth in that the sky is blue, though a darker shade than I'm used to, and for that I'm thankful as my nerves are stretched rather thin. The buildings are fantastic though; very grand. An architect's wet dream. They're all built with that marble-like substance. It's everywhere and glistens and sparkles beautifully in the suns. The street is exceptionally clean, with no rubbish or graffiti like you find in every city on Earth.

The air feels heavy. I can't explain it. It's like when you

get off the aeroplane in a hotter climate than you're used to for the first time and whoosh, it hits you. The heat makes the air feel as though you can touch it. I wave my hand around as if the air is a tangible thing, but nothing.

"It's hot," I tell him, fanning my hands in front of my face. Not that it does much. "Tell me you have air con in the buildings." The hospital felt nice and cool, so I'm praying all the buildings will feel that comfortable.

"The buildings are cool because of the material they are built from," he informs me while I'm still taking in all the sights.

The ground is a pale cream colour, dry and arid-looking. Something I always thought countries on Earth that have very little rain, like the deserts, might look like. But where they have very little vegetation, here, overlarge, extremely colourful plants surround each marble building in abundance. They fill the warm air with a sweet-smelling fragrance.

"They are stunning." I gesture towards a plant climbing up the side of a building. The roots are a deep purple, the petals on the large flowers fuchsia pink.

"You see the flowers?" He points to the wall of flowers. "Most are edible. We don't have anyone hungry here, but there is always food available for those who need it, growing everywhere." He grins at me. I can see how proud he is of his home, and from what I've seen so far, I fully understand why.

"That's a bloody fab idea. We could use that system on Earth." I smile at him. "So, where are we?"

"On Earth you have countries, cities, towns, villages. Right?" I nod, still enjoying his accent as he talks. "Here on

Mertier, we have Districts. We are presently in District One. Districts are then split into sub numbers."

I must look like it's going straight over my head, because he laughs. "It'll get easier the longer you're here. I promise, Araline."

"So, District One is like your capital?" I wonder aloud. "And then your sub numbers are like your towns?"

"Yes." He beams at me. "For example, we are in District One, Sub Five. Five is the medical and wellbeing area. We are heading to District One, Sub One. That's where your new home is. No other District anywhere on Mertier has a Sub One, only here in District One.

"It is the Royal District, home to all the royals of Mertier."

CHAPTER SIX

As I try and process all the information he's telling me, a small flying vehicle approaches us, and my breath catches in my throat. It's not a plane, but it's not a car either. It's a mash up of the two. It's silent as it descends a few feet in front of us, stopping just before touching the ground. Two small, colourful flags attached to the front flutter in the warm breeze.

Without a thought, I grip Brennen's hand tightly and try to back away.

"What is that?" I point a shaking finger at it, my stomach dropping. I fear I already know. He's going to tell me we are about to take a flight in it.

I feel him chuckle before answering, "It's how we travel on Mertier. Don't be afraid. I drive expertly."

I jump at hearing his voice. My nerves really are frayed.

When a glass gullwing door swishes open and up,

glistening silver steps slide into place, and the young man, Tallith, jumps out.

"I have it ready for you, my prince, just as I promised." He's smiling wide, and the look of hero worship is plain to see.

"I don't want to fly," I whisper to Brennen, hoping we can find another way to get to his home. The fact that he was just addressed as a prince is something I picked up on, but I have far more pressing matters to worry about. I bite on the inside of my mouth as I try and get my anxiety under control.

"Now, Little Flower, you have to trust me. I wouldn't put you in any danger." He grins down at me, before turning to Tallith. "Thank you. I will be informing your tutors of how helpful you've been."

I watch as the younger male blushes and quickly scampers away.

"He worships you," I tell him. "Does everyone treat you like that?" I scowl at the thought of women fawning all over him but then remember no women are born here, so at least I won't have to contend with any exes. *Whoo hoo, a first plus for this world.*

"Of course they do," he says in all seriousness, and then winks at me before stepping onto the hovering transport. He holds out a hand to me, waiting patiently for me to take it. After a few deep breaths, I grip it tightly and we slowly progress towards a row of seats. Windows surround us, giving us a three-sixty panoramic view.

The driver turns and grins at Brennen. "You want to fly yourself home, my prince?" Brennen nods. "You've always been happier in the air than on the ground." He manoeuvres out of the driver's seat and nods to me. "Welcome to Mertier. I saw Brennen the night he went to Earth to bring you home. He was the happiest I've ever seen him."

Before I can tell him I'm not the girl he was excited about, he leaves us. There's an awkward silence, and I can't bring myself to look at Brennen. I close my eyes and massage my temples, feeling the beginnings of a migraine. I slump down into the nearest seat, feeling utterly sorry for myself.

"If you'd like to sit up with me, you'll get a better view," he says softly, but I still can't look at him. After a few seconds, he sighs and straps me into the seat. His hands are gentle but clinical as the soft leather harness pins me in place. It's a little disconcerting to be strapped down, unable to move. My anxiety rises, and my teeth gnaw at my lip. I can tell he's dying to talk, but I just can't.

He leaves me and moves into the cockpit, so he's able to take control of the flight instruments. There are buttons and dials he competently operates. It's obvious he knows what he's doing. He smoothly ascends, and my stomach drops as the glass allows me an uninterrupted view of this alien planet. I close my eyes. I've lost all interest in where I am. All I want to do is curl up into a ball and cry.

I hate feeling so out of control of my life; it's been happening a lot the last few years.

I don't hear Brennen until I feel his hands on mine. My eyes pop open.

"Who's flying this bloody thing?" I demand loudly, franticly looking at the now empty cockpit.

"I programmed it so it will take us home without incident. I give you my word. Do not worry, I will never allow anything to happen to my mate, Araline." His smile is genuine, but it quickly vanishes when I say, "But I'm not your mate. Your mate is lying in a hospital on Earth. I'm just the poor substitute."

Though my words were spoken in a soft whisper, he jolts as if I slapped him.

"And if it takes lifetimes for you to fall in love with me, then so be it. I'll never give up on you," he growls, his hands stroking mine.

"Why can't you just go down to Earth and bring her back up here? I could go back with you, we swap, and everyone's happy," I beg him, my eyes pleading with him. All this talk of love has me even more unsettled.

"The vortex doesn't work like that. It only opens when one of our males reaches maturity and their mate has had sufficient training in our way of life. We don't get a choice. We are told when to go, the name of our mate, and where she'll be waiting. And we eagerly wait for that precious moment. Earth women are wanted. They are treated with the utmost respect and will never be harmed. That is what I can offer you if you give me a chance, Araline." Before I can answer, the flying vehicle drops down and hovers a few inches above the ground. "We have arrived. Welcome to your new home." He quickly unbuckles me, which I'm happy about because I was beginning to feel like a bondage victim. He lifts me up into his arms as the gullwing door opens and the steps to the floor glide effortlessly into place.

I glance around. This isn't a home, it's a bloody palace. It's surrounded by a high stone wall for privacy, and the driveway is a sweeping, cobblestone affair that's complimented by lush, green, grass-like verges. Strange-looking trees with purple trunks and colourful flowers, which are similar to what Brennen pointed out earlier, are growing here in abundance, and odd-shaped alien fruit is growing throughout the grounds.

The palace is stunning, and I feel my mouth gape open in wonder. It's made from the same white and gold marble substance and has large columns with intricately carved writing and symbols, which at a quick glance look similar to Earth's hieroglyphics. I fleetingly wonder if the conspiracy theorists were right and the Egyptian pyramids were, in fact, the work of aliens.

Dotted around the grounds are huge dragon statues, once again made from the white and gold marble. They glisten in the sun, each in their own unique pose. They are fearsome and look as if they are ready to spring to life at any moment.

"You live here? Alone?" I croak, feeling way out of my depth. I've only ever seen large places like this on *MTV's Cribs* or in posh magazines at the dentist's office. I never dreamed I'd have the chance to enter one. I feel like I'm too dirty to go inside, never mind live in it.

"Not exactly alone, no." He approaches the front door and ducks down a little when a screen appears from a hidden slot in the wall. A red light flashes brightly, as if taking a picture, and after he straightens, the heavy metal door slides open. It doesn't open like a normal door but swishes sleekly into the wall.

"Let me down, please," I murmur as he enters. He places me on my feet, and I quickly remove my visor so I can get a good look, but I don't really know where to start.

The marble is carried on throughout, and inside the

temperature is cool, which is welcome after the heat from outside. He says it's not too hot, but he's obviously never had to live in England. We're lucky if the sun graces us with its presence.

"Where are all the guards? Your servants? If you're royalty, I'd expect this place to be guarded like Fort Knox," I ask, looking around for some sort of security.

"Oh, we have them, but they are exceedingly good at their jobs and remain unseen unless we need them," Brennen tells me, and before I can think of a reply, someone else demands my attention.

"Welcome home, Araline." I hear another man's deep voice and swivel around to face whoever is talking. Damn, the water here must have steroids in it. I wonder if all the men of Mertier have perfect bodies. His body is leaner than Brennen's, more of an athletic physique rather than bulk muscle, and is shown off to perfection in his tight black tee-shirt. He's leaning against the wall, his arms crossed, and his vivid blue eyes are twinkling mischievously. His thick, silver-blond hair is cut in a very swanky skin fade, with swirls cut into the scalp, leading down to his neck.

"Araline, this is Ta. He's your second mate," Brennen tells me.

My mouth drops open again.

"Second mate?" I'm sure I must have misheard. "Why do I need two?" *What the hell will I do with two of them? How do I get myself in these situations?*

"No women are born on Mertier. We have no idea why. We've had our top scientists working on it for centuries. Each woman brought from Earth can have up to five mates. You have only two, I'm afraid. Due to his royal bloodlines, we need to keep mates at a lower ratio," Ta informs me matter-of-factly as he walks over to us. Walk is a soft way to describe his movements. He prowls, like a sleek panther before it pounces on its prey.

I'm shaking my head. It's all too much.

Like an utter girl, blackness greets me, and I pass out.

Ta moves with lightning-fast reactions and catches me before I hit the floor.

Brennen

"Well, that went well. This is why I said you should have told her, or at least given her some warning, before bringing her home." Ta looks at me, his frustration at the situation making him sound harsher than he usually is. But I notice how tenderly, almost reverently, he holds our mate. "I didn't even mention your dragon, and that's the reason she will only have two mates. I have a feeling he will become extremely territorial over her. How the hell are we going to make this work, Brennen? She will be totally untrained in how to take us both, and we are both highly dominant, sexual males."

"I don't know. She doesn't even know about the dragons yet." I sigh, rubbing a hand down my face. "It's not an ideal start, but we can do this. We have to do this, Ta." I stroke my hand down Araline's face. "Let's get her into bed. Her ankle is still going to give her pain."

Ta carries Araline to our bed, and we tuck her in.

Frowning, I wonder how the hell she will react to my inner dragon. If discovering having two mates rendered her unconscious, my hope for the situation isn't high. Uneasiness swirls in my gut.

Will we be able to make this work?

CHAPTER SEVEN

When I wake up, I find myself in the most elegant bedroom I've ever been in. My eyes are wide as I take in the high-vaulted ceiling made from tinted glass, which keeps the glare of the suns to a minimum. It's in the shape of a cathedral spire and points elegantly towards the stars. The bed is huge. I've seen super-king sizes on Earth, but this has to be double that size. It has the softest mattress and pillows that mould to my body shape. It's all covered in a thick, white, silk material. I bring up the top sheet and rub it over my lip. So smooth.

The wall facing the bed is again made of the same tinted glass as the roof spire, allowing the room to be flooded with light. I hope it's got some sort of covering, otherwise I'll never get any sleep at night. All the walls and the floor are made of the same white and gold marble they favour here.

Sitting up, I shuffle over to the side of the bed, which I find is on a dark, mahogany-like plinth. The actual bedframe is a similar style to a slay bed and is made from some kind of silver metal. It's tremendously grand and imposing.

The double doors slide open quietly, and Brennen and Ta walk in looking absurdly gorgeous. My nipples tighten under the white silk, and I become very aware of my nakedness. I wrap the sheet tightly around my body, trying to hide the affect they have on me.

"How is your ankle, Little Flower?" Brennen asks, looking concerned. When he sees my knuckles turning white from my grip on the sheet, he explains, "If you're wondering why you're naked, it's due to the bed coverings. They have micro technology to keep your body at the ideal temperature."

I just stare at them both, not sure what the hell to say.

"Let me see it," Ta demands, walking over to me, and for a moment I wonder what he's wanting me to show him. Not waiting for an answer or my permission, he lifts my leg and places his large hands over my swollen ankle.

I'm about to protest, when his eyes flash silver, and then I feel heat.

"What...?" I ask, feeling my eyes widen with shock. Looking down at what he's doing, I see his hands glowing white. *Well, that's not normal.* I don't feel any pain; if anything it makes the ache dissipate. I can't help but smile. "Thank you. That's a handy gift to have, Ta. Can all the males on Mertier do that?"

He releases my ankle, and I gingerly move it. The pain has gone. I'm so relieved I'm tempted to kiss him, but instead I shrink away from my wayward thoughts. I don't kiss strange men I hardly know—unless a few glasses of gin have been consumed.

"You're welcome. I can't have my mate in pain." He grins at me, and oh boy is it mischievous— naughty even. "And no, some males have other gifts, but I think I'm the only one who can heal through heat." He tilts his head to the side, his gaze assessing me. "We've had food arranged if you feel up to joining us?"

Brennen presses a button on the wall behind the bed, and to my surprise, the wall slides to one side, revealing a second room. A dressing room, full of empty wardrobes. "These are for you. When you're feeling up to it, we can take you shopping for everything you'll need." He has a smile on his face, but it fades when I don't show any excitement. "Don't you like shopping for personal items? We are told that women from Earth love nothing more than to go shopping." He glances at Ta, seemingly at a loss for what to say.

I sigh, feeling my cheeks warm, and look anywhere but at them. I'm not comfortable talking about my image hang-ups with strangers, no matter how much they believe we are mates. It makes me feel self-conscious. And to make matters worse, these two fine hulks of perfect male specimens could never understand how having a few extra inches on my boobs and hips makes shopping for clothes unpleasant.

"It's not that I don't like to; it's just I'm not comfortable with how I look," I mumble. "There are parts of me I wish I could change." I drop my head, my cheeks burning now. I feel like a dumpy little thing, not the graceful, lean Macie they were expecting.

I glance up nervously when I hear an animalistic growl. It's coming from Brennen. I shrink back as he stares at me, looking utterly pissed off.

"Your body is bloody perfect. I don't know what crap you've been told, but don't ever put yourself down in front of us." I look at them both and gulp.

Okay then, that told me.

"I have to agree with Brenn. I had the pleasure of undressing you and putting you to bed earlier. It made my body hard, and I ached in all the right places. Your body is lush, and I can't wait to play with it," Ta says with a roguish grin and a wink. His accent is deep and sexy, and also hints that English isn't his first language.

I don't know what to say to that. I must admit, I get a thrill from knowing they both seem to like my body, even if I'm not ready to acknowledge that.

I've been programmed to try and starve myself in order to achieve the figure women on Earth are told is the sexiest. Well, according to the glossy magazines, anyway. I've had a love/hate relationship with food for as long as I can remember, following one fad diet after the next, but nothing was successful. I'd lose a few pounds, but they'd go straight back on with the next chocolate bar or ice cream.

Gripping the sheet closer, I stare at them.

"If you think I'm walking around here with only a sheet on, you're going to be sorely disappointed." I feel at a huge disadvantage with only a sheet covering my body. When they don't acknowledge my words, I sigh. "I need clothes. I don't feel comfortable in only this sheet. Surely you have something I can wear?"

"Here, take this." Without hesitation, Brennen removes his black tee-shirt and hands it to me.

I try very hard not to gawk at his chiselled muscles, before pulling it over my head. The material is one of the softest things I've ever felt, and it's still warm from his body. It smells of him; a dark, spicy scent that screams manliness. I stand and wriggle out of the sheet before hastily pulling the shirt down, which almost reaches my knees. For the first time in my life, I feel petite.

"You'd look sexy no matter what you were wearing, Araline," Ta informs me. His hand engulfs mine as he gently tugs me in the direction he wants me to go.

"Thank you for the shirt, Brennen." I look up and find him right by my side. I can feel the heat coming off his body. It's like I'm hemmed in by two sex gods. I don't even want to think of them both being my mates. I'm so not ready for that conversation.

He looks down at me and smiles, and it's a real humdinger. He's beautiful. "You are very welcome, and please, call me Brenn."

I nod and try to rein in my wayward thoughts, but fail miserably.

The men bring me to a room with numerous intricately carved mahogany tables and large, multi-coloured cushions. I follow their lead and sit on the cushion they point to.

Suddenly, one of the marble walls opens, revealing a secret door. A few younger males walk out, holding several silver serving platters heaped with delicious-smelling food. They silently place them on the tables and nod respectfully before leaving, the door closing seamlessly behind them. If you didn't know it was there, you wouldn't be able to find it.

I eye the food suspiciously. It looks and smells

scrumptious, but to put it bluntly, it's alien food. I'm sat with two aliens on another planet.

I start to gasp for breath, pulling at the neckline of the T-shirt. *Is it getting hot in here?* I jump up, my ankle finally not hurting, and frantically move away from them, looking for an exit. But I can't find one, and my anxiety hits an all-time high.

Oh fuck! I'm trapped in here with them. I can't breathe. There's no air. I close my eyes and silently scream, *Help me! God, someone help me.* Leaning against the cool marble wall, my legs give out and my bum hits the floor.

CHAPTER EIGHT

*B*rennen and Ta move quickly and silently, sitting on either side of me. Their arms go around my neck, supporting my head.

"Breathe, Little Flower," Brennen says softly, smoothing my hair out of my face and stroking down my neck. His featherlight touches are about as non-threatening as you can get.

Ta takes my hand and places it on his chest. "Feel my heartbeats, Araline. Breathe in time with me."

"Heartbeats—as in plural?" I whisper. Eyes shut, I concentrate on his heartbeats. He has two hearts? I mirror his breathing, and after a few minutes, my panic dies and my heart slows.

"Yes. The non-royal males of Mertier live far longer than the males on Earth. We have organically formed—or grown, if you like—hearts and have surgery after we are born, where the medical teams insert the second heart. Also, our water has special properties which helps to keep us alive longer. Brennen's body is also different to males on Earth, but don't worry about it now. We don't want to swamp you with all the little details. We can explain about the differences as we go," Ta tells me, as he places a soft kiss to the top of my head.

"I'm really on another planet, aren't I?" I shudder and feel large fingers grip my chin, manoeuvring it until my eyes open and I gaze into Brennen's dark navy ones.

"Yes, you are, but you have us to help you with anything you need. You really can have your heart's desire. Whatever dreams or desires you had on Earth, you can have them and more here with us," Brennen informs me.

I take a couple of steadying breaths and nod. There's really not a lot I can do about my predicament. I'll have to go with the flow for the time being. I seriously can't believe—won't allow myself to believe—there's no way off this bloody planet. I will bide my time and plot my escape.

"Okay, let's eat." Just as I say that my stomach lets out a loud rumble. I want to die of embarrassment.

The two men grin and help me to my feet, and we make our way back to the cushions. Once sat, they pile our plates with food. Brennen hands me an overfilled plate, which I tap with my fingernail, listening to the *ting*. It reminds me of the Waterford crystal glasses my parents had when I was younger.

They take the time to explain what everything is to me. The food is brightly coloured with lots of vegetables and a meat substance that's been shredded. I hesitantly try some, and to my amazement it actually tastes exceedingly good. As I tuck in with gusto, the fresh flavour explodes across my tongue. It's been such a long time since I've had a decent meal. I usually have to live off the cheapest food I can find, often having to resort to the reduced section in the supermarkets.

My plate is soon empty, and I can't stop my smile.

"That was delicious. Is the food always that good?" I rest my hands behind me and stretch my legs under the table.

"Of course. Brennen is royalty here," Ta informs me, before he stacks our empty plates on another table.

"Yes, Alish mentioned it. So, you're a prince?" I ask Brennen. He looks nothing like the princes I've seen on the TV, who have been pampered all their spoiled lives. Brennen is all hard lines that scream he's not a rich, lazy member of royalty.

I watch as his gaze flits to Ta's, before he takes a deep breath and replies, "Yes, Araline, I am a prince—the next in line to the throne." He watches as my eyes widen. "I will be the next king of Mertier." He tacks on the last bit to make sure there is no misunderstanding, I'm sure.

King. I've been kidnapped by a damn future king.

Staring at Ta, I find my voice and ask him, "So, what are you? If you share women here and he's the next king, what are you? Another prince?"

He chuckles. "No, I'm afraid not. Brenn and I have been friends since we were born. We shared everything together, like schooling and training. So, Brennen thought it was a natural choice to have me share his Earth woman."

"How very accommodating of him," I answer surly.

Before I can carry on, the hidden door re-opens, and the young males come in to clear away our plates and leave more covered in sweet-smelling goodies. I catch one staring at me and smile. He blushes and rushes out before I can say hello.

"Try some of these. They are seeds we harvest and dry out. We've found Earth women have a sweet tooth and thoroughly enjoy them. I believe it's not dissimilar to Earth's chocolate." Brennen hands me a couple of small white seeds, and I follow his lead as he pops one into his mouth.

Oh my God! He's right, it is similar to chocolate—if chocolate was on steroids. I would never have believed anything could taste better than chocolate. I scoop up a handful of seeds, closing my eyes as the flavour pops across my tongue, making me hum with happiness.

I sigh. "That's better than sex."

"Better than sex?" Ta gasps, and I almost laugh at the horrified look on his face.

Brennen raises an eyebrow. "What kind of crappy sex are you used to?"

I look down, wondering how to explain my almost non-existent sex life with my ex. It's not a polite conversation to have.

"Well, um… it's not been great. Let's leave it there, shall we?" I glance away, not willing to talk to them about it. All the books I read and loved waxed lyrically about having screaming orgasms, and a few of my girlfriends enjoyed sex. But I didn't get it. As long as the pig spawned from Hell came, he wasn't too bothered about me.

My eyes are downcast. I feel like a proper loser as I think about how long I put up with him.

Ta and Brennen bristle with anger. Brennen scoots over and wraps his arms around me, holding me tightly. I'm rigid within his arms, but he holds me nonetheless. After a while, my body relaxes, and I can't stop the pleasure I feel from the simple act of being held. It's been way too long since I've had a man's arms around me.

I allow myself a few blissful minutes in his arms, the heat from his chest going a long way to thaw my anger at this whole mess of a situation. But I can't let my guard slip.

Looking at them both, I see their smiles are full of sincerity, but I say, "You say the vortex we came through won't work to take me back, but I'm the first woman to be brought here against her will. Maybe the rules might be different for me? There must be a way— a failsafe, should this happen? Someone must have made contingency plans." I look at Ta, who sadly shakes his head.

"I'm sorry, Araline. I would give you this whole world if you asked, but that's the one thing I can't give you. Can you not give us a chance?" he asks, picking up my hand and brushing his velvet lips across it.

I stare into his bright blue eyes, trying to process what he's said. Could there really be no way home? I start to tremble and feel my eyes welling up with tears, but before Brennen can utter a word, an alarm goes off, making me jump and cry out.

CHAPTER NINE

"It's only the front door. We must have callers." Brennen stands, taking me with him, as Ta strides across the room to see who it is. His confident walk does funny things to my insides, which I'm not ready to confront. It's then I remember I'm only dressed in Brennen's tee-shirt. I hear heated, muffled voices and unconsciously edge closer to Brennen. I'm not ready to meet anyone new yet.

The door to the room glides open and a slightly older version of Brennen marches confidently inside, a beautiful, petite woman hastily trying to keep up with him.

"Father." Brennen smiles down at me but falters when he takes in his mother's expression. She looks sad.

"So, you had to bring home a woman not meant for you. A woman who knows nothing about our world, our ways. One, I've heard, who isn't happy to be here." The king's eyes, which are the same midnight blue as Brennen's, are cold as they slide to my face. I shrink back as he looks me up and down and takes a steadying breath. "She's meant to be our next queen. Male, what were you thinking?" he growls.

"Kyanite, please. Let's not do this here." The woman smiles at me. "Araline? Welcome to Mertier. I'm Sha, Brennan's mother. I'm sure you have thousands of questions. We will help in any manner needed. You've already met Alish?" When I nod, she carries on. "Good, she will make you an excellent friend."

I keep quiet. These people are extremely intimidating. I suppose as King and Queen of Mertier they must be. Do I have to curtsy? I don't know the proper etiquette for this situation.

"I was told any problems with the council were smoothed over by you, father," Brennen stated, pulling me closer to him as if to shade me from the other man's stare.

"Of course I did. You're my son and will be the next king; I couldn't allow them any leeway. But if this woman won't accept you and Ta, then she will be put up for bidding and whoever bids the most for her will be her new mate."

My gasp silences everyone, and then all eyes are on me, scrutinising me.

"You're fucking kidding me? You're barbaric. I will not be handed off to another stranger. I didn't fucking ask to be brought here," I shout, past caring who the fuck he is. *How fucking dare they?*

Brennen and Ta hurry to my side. To protect me? Their expressions are furious as they glare at the king, whose face, I must admit, is priceless. I bet no one has ever dared to talk to him like that.

"Araline, let's take a walk outside," the woman politely

suggests. She takes my hand out of Brennen's and gently but forcibly tugs me out of the room. When Ta starts to follow us, she holds her hand up, "No, Ta, you are not needed."

He looks unhappy with the dismissal, and to be honest, I'd prefer him to be around while I'm with this formidable woman, but with a curt nod, he does as she orders and turns back to Brennen and his father.

We walk in silence until we are standing outside. The two suns are low in the sky now, and I stare at them both. The sky looks so different with two suns instead of just the one. The soft pink glow they are leaving as they set is pretty breathtaking.

"It's so different here, but in some ways just the same," I say softly.

"I'm sorry about the way you've had to see it all for the first time, Araline. Usually, arrival day is a celebration." She smiles at me, and I find it to be odd. She's Brennen's mother but only looks slightly older than he does. Her skin is unblemished, and her thick, glossy, chestnut hair is hanging in waves down her back.

"How old are you?" I blurt out rudely. "How old is Brennen?" We sit on some elegantly carved marble steps before a large pool, which is filled with water that has a silver hue. There are brightly-coloured fish whose scales sparkle as they dance in and out of the water, putting on a show.

As I stare at them, I hear something that astounds me.

They are singing—the fish are singing as they break the surface of the water.

I can't stop my smile as I watch and listen to them. They are enchanting.

Magnificent birds with plumes of all colours decorate the sky as they fly around, singing their own songs. They perch on the trees surrounding us, giving a never-ending background of gentle music. I must admit, it's a glorious space.

I'm brought back to the here and now as Sha tells me, "I am over seven hundred Earth years old."

I gasp. She only looks to be in her thirties.

"Brennen?" I breathe.

"He's four hundred and fifty."

CHAPTER TEN

I hear the words and close my eyes. *Over four hundred years old.* My mind can't comprehend it.

"Once we are brought through the vortex, we stop ageing —or rather, age at a much slower rate than we would have on Earth. The properties in the water here help with that. I won't lie to you, life here is different than you are used to, especially with having more than one mate," she says, picking a bright blue, ornate-looking flower and smelling it with obvious delight.

Her arms are bare and have markings on them similar to the ones on Alish's. Unreadable symbols and dots and swirls. Beautiful but strange. They completely cover her arms and hands, and I spot them on her legs, beneath her flowing dress, as well. I finally realise what they remind me of: Indian henna body paintings. But instead of dye, it looks like it could have been burned on? Brands. I wonder if they cover her whole body but feel it would be rude to ask.

Pulling myself together, I answer her honestly. "Yes, that's something I'm not sure I can handle." Of course, I've heard of polyamorous relationships, but it isn't something I've ever contemplated trying.

"Yes, I'm sure that was a shock. But you only have Brennen and Ta. And if you give them a chance, they will give you the world. They are good men, Araline. Honourable." She passes me the flower and I take a sniff. Wow, the scent is strong.

That's the first thing I noticed about this world: everything is brighter, more alive somehow. I feel like I've been colour blind my whole life, that everything has been muted, and now I can see everything in technicolour and hear all the different, distinctive sounds.

"I don't want to talk out of place, but Brennen wasn't honourable when he snatched me from where I was working to bring me here, was he?" I stare at her, daring her to try and dismiss it.

"No, that wasn't his finest moment. But he..." She looks into the distance and takes a steadying breath. "The problem with Mertier is that the women here can't give birth to females, and we have no idea why. We have the most amazing minds trying to figure it out, but nothing so far. So, the men have no hope of having a wife, or daughter. A long, long time before I arrived here, the then king found the vortex that led to Earth. He went through it many times, silently watching Earth. Long story short, he struck a deal and here we are. But before a male here can go and claim his mate, he has to meet certain criteria's before he reaches six hundred years old, and then he has to go before the council to present their case for why he should be deserving."

I look at her, my mind latching on to her words. "So, if the old king could go back and forth, then why the hell can't I go back?" I demand, my mind already planning on leaving here. If I'm honest, I have no idea why I want to go home so badly. I think about it for a while as we sit in silence. I have nothing back there. No family, no lover, not even my own place to call home. I have friends, but we only get together now for events like birthdays and weddings. I have nothing. Looking around at this beautiful planet, I realise I could have it all.

I just need to be strong enough to give it a go.

Sha takes hold of my hand, and again I find myself staring at the patterns.

"I'm sorry, Araline, once females come through the vortex, going back isn't possible." She holds up a hand to stop me from interrupting her. "At the beginning, a few didn't fit in and wanted to go home. They missed their family too much to stay, so were granted their wish. But as soon as they stepped through the vortex, their bodies disintegrated. It was too horrendous for the men to witness. All kings since then have forbidden another female to try. They found out it has something to do with different levels of oxygen in human's blood."

I slump back, closing my eyes.

"There simply isn't a way for you to go back to Earth," she says softly. "The females who come here have known all their lives they were coming. They have been schooled in all our ways and look forward to meeting their mates. Could you not be happy here?" She turns to face me, smiling. "I'm sure you will love it once you have adjusted to us."

"What about what Brennen's father said: if I don't take Brennen and Ta for my mates, I'll be put into some sort of bidding war? What's all that about and how long do I have?" I wince at the idea of just being handed around from man to man like an unwanted puppy.

"A few weeks, I believe. I know it must seem all kinds of wrong to you, but you have to understand that no women are born to us. The men are offered little hope of getting a mate unless they are worthy. It's only happened a few times, but if a female didn't or wouldn't tolerate their chosen mates, then she would be found some more. At the moment, you have only Brennen and Ta for mates. If you refuse them, you could end up with far more."

I blanch at the picture forming in my head. *A few weeks?*

"You demand I fall in love with two men I've only just met, or risk having to try again with possibly more than two? You can't just will love to happen. I have no trust in them, no love, or any kind of feelings. I'm trapped on another world with no hope of ever going home. I've lost the ability to have a daughter just by being here. Tell me, Queen, why would I choose to stay?" Closing my eyes, I feel tears run down my cheeks. I'm not usually a show my feelings in front of others kind of girl, but I can't seem to stop it.

"I'm so sorry, Araline." She pulls me into her arms and hugs me. "I can't say I know how you're feeling because I don't. I can only offer our help in getting you acclimated to our ways. You already have a friend in Alish, and there are more females waiting to meet you. You can own the world here. Please give those males time to prove themselves to you."

I sniff and pull myself together, wiping my eyes.

"They scare me," I admit. "They're so big; they overwhelm me. I have no idea what I'm meant to do with them both." I blush, knowing I shouldn't be having this conversation with Brennen's mother, of all people.

She laughs softly. "That will come in time, and they know to be extra gentle with you. Get to know them; let them show you our world and what you could be if you accept life with us." She tilts my head towards her. "You are so wanted, Araline. These men will give you all you could ever want for as long as they live." She smiles and stands, holding a hand out to me.

Taking her hand, I stand. "But I'm not wanted, am I. How would you feel, Sha? I'm not even meant to be here. Not in any way. The one they really want is still on Earth. I'm not the one promised to Brennen and Ta. What happens if another male brings her through, and then my males decide they don't want me any longer and want her instead?" I look away, not wanting her answer. My look must say a thousand words because her eyes sadden and her skin pales. Shaking my head, I start walking back to the house, and she quickly follows.

Grabbing my hand, she pulls me to a stop.

"Don't you believe in fate? I don't believe she was the one for them and neither do they. Whatever her reason was, your friend—she sent you to us. You are the precious gift for my son. You, Araline, were meant to be in that church at that exact moment to meet my son. That's what I believe. Have a little faith. I promise you it will be worth it." She squeezes my hand and nods as we enter the room, where the men are talking in low voices. They fall silent as soon as they spot us.

CHAPTER ELEVEN

*S*till feeling uncomfortable wearing only Brennen's shirt in front of the king and queen, I watch as Sha hurries over to her mate. His fingers trail over the markings on her arms, just as Hunter did to Alish earlier. I watch his actions, intrigued again as to the story behind them. After he's traced down her arm, he engulfs her in a hug and kisses her so passionately I blush. I've never experienced that kind of desire in my life. I wonder what it feels like to have a man hold you in such a way it leaves everyone with no doubt about who you belong to.

"Get a room," Ta jokes, smiling at me. I can't stop the shiver sliding down my spine when I see need shining in his eyes.

I pull at the hem of the shirt as they pull back from one another. Sha is smiling happily and the king growls at Ta, but he's grinning. He turns to Brennen.

"Sort this out, male. Make it right." He nods at me, and I

watch as they both leave. He leans down and whispers in her ear. Whatever it is, it has her giggling.

Brennen approaches me, and I can't help but admire his rippling muscles as he approaches. *He's sex on legs.*

"I'm sorry for how abrupt he sounded, Araline. This isn't your mistake; this is all mine. But I want to make it right. Will you give us a chance?" He pulls me into his body, and I rest my head on his chest. I can't help but snuggle closer. Really, I don't know a female alive who wouldn't.

I feel Ta move in behind me. His arms wind around my waist as he rests his head on my shoulder and whispers, "Araline, let us prove to you that you're the one for us. The only one we will ever desire."

I feel his lips trace featherlight kisses down my neck and can't stop the tremble of unrepressed awareness of how close these males are. Anxiety blooms, and I pull away. Good to their word, they quickly let go of me. I stumble away, immediately feeling chilled. Their bodies feel hot, as if they are my personal heating systems, and I realise I'm craving their heat. I'm always cold.

Staring at them, I bite my lip, and the coward in me has me saying, "I need clothes. Can we go somewhere and get some? I feel at a disadvantage not having anything here that's mine."

"Of course," Brennen informs me. Taking my hand, he leads the way upstairs with Ta following.

"I'll get us some transport and alert the places we will call into so they can prepare," Ta says, pulling out a device. He sees me raise my eyebrow, silently asking what it is, and chuckles. "Araline, this is our way of communicating with others on the planet. I believe you have something similar on Earth?"

He hands it to me to check out. It's lightweight and made out of shiny black metal. The same lettering I saw on the columns by the entrance of the building are etched into the metal. I hand it back and he flips it open, leaving me to enter the bedroom with Brennen.

Brennen takes me over to the walk-in wardrobe and hands me the clothes Alish got for me in the hospital.

I motion with my fingers for him to give me his back, and he rolls his eyes but does what I ask. Once he's facing the door, I hurriedly pull on the clothes.

"You couldn't have given me these before we ate?" I wonder aloud, as I put the clothes on.

"You will have to forgive me, Little Flower. I must admit to preferring you in my shirt or, even better, naked." I can hear laughter in his voice. Tricky man.

"Okay, I'm dressed," I tell him. He turns and reaches for the tee-shirt I hold out to him.

"Mmm." He smells it before pulling it on. "It smells of you. I like it." He grins at me and holds out his hand, patiently waiting for me to put mine in his.

I desperately want to huff, roll my eyes, and scream like a toddler having a terrible twos tantrum, but his hand feels warm enveloping mine. We meet Ta by the open, ornate front door, and I realise it's night-time and we're off on a jolly, but then I spy the flying vehicle waiting for us. My stomach tells me I don't think I'll get used to flying everywhere.

Ta scrutinises me. "Do you not enjoy flying, Araline?" he

asks as we walk up the steps. They automaticity retract, and the door closes behind us.

"Not really, no," I whisper as I sit down. They take a seat either side of me.

"Are you ready, Your Lordship? I have the coordinates Ta requested all programmed in," the driver enquires.

I glance at the cockpit and see the lights and knobs, which shine brighter than in a Boeing 747.

"Yes, we are." Brennen grins at the male while taking my hand again.

I've never met a man more touchy-feely than him, nor Ta. I kind of like it.

"Do you always go shopping at night?" I ask, trying to take my mind off where I am, but before he can answer, the vehicle moves into motion, and my stomach drops.

Without thinking, I grip both of their hands. I miss their smiles of triumph because I'm too busy looking through the glass roof. I spot two moons. It's a bit freaky to see two, but they light this world up far more than the one that orbits Earth. Plus, they are pink. They glow a gorgeous pale pink that bathes the night sky in a softer light than the moon I'm used to.

"We generally do as it's too hot during the summer. As Brenn is a prince, they open whatever time we desire." Ta smiles as we pass buildings. They look different in the pink glow of the moons, as if the harsh white has been dulled.

I'm amazed at how many people are milling around. They stop what they're doing to bow their heads as our vehicle flies by, and I wonder how they know who is inside. I answer my own question when I look through the front window and spot the flags blowing in the wind.

"Is that the royal flag?" I wonder aloud, admiring how the deep purple dragons emblazoned on the silk-like material shine under the moons' lights. I must have missed it on the flight here, but to be honest, I wasn't in a take-in-the-details kind of mood.

"Yes. The dragons represent the royal house, as they are our inner animal," Brennen explains, and I look at him sharply.

"Inner animal? You mean you channel the strength of a dragon, right?" *That's what he must mean. Not where my foolish mind is taking me to!*

Brennen rubs the back of his neck before meeting my eyes.

The pause tells me everything I need to know. *A dragon. I'm mated to a bloody dragon?*

"All royal males are shifters. We share our bodies with dragons. We have done since the first king of Mertier stumbled into the cave where the dragons lived. The longer you're with us the more you will learn of our history. Don't panic, Little Flower. We are with you. We will always be with you," he explains, like he's reading out a recipe for how to boil an egg. As if turning into a dragon is an everyday occurrence. Obliviously it is for him.

I shrink back against Ta, my mind boggling at what my life is becoming.

"My dragon will never hurt you, Araline. He will protect you, put you above all others, and eventually, when you're ready, he will fall madly in love with you," Brennen says softly, his midnight blue eyes shining with sincerity.

Ta doesn't let go of my hand, and the warmth is welcome at the moment. If only Brennen had kept his gob shut in the church about me *having to do* because Macie wasn't there. Lust is a dangerous thing. I've never had any man, especially hunks like these two, make me feel like I'm the centre of their universe. I have a feeling the longer I spend with these two, the more I will crave what they are offering. It could turn a girl's head. *Could.* I'm not sure I'll ever feel good enough for them though.

Do I stay with them or take my chances with this bidding draw I'll be forced to attend in a few weeks?

"I can't think of you being a bloody dragon at the moment," I tell him honestly.

"I'm about to land in District Four, Your Lordship," the driver informs Brennen, then makes a smooth decent. The door opens silently, and I see we are hovering a few inches above the ground. "I'll be here when you've finished."

"District Four is the shopping area, Araline." Brennen nods and smiles at the driver while explaining to me. He holds his hand out for me to take, and when I grip it, I'm pulled effortlessly to my feet. Ta follows me, and soon I'm wedged between the two males as we make our way to God knows where.

CHAPTER TWELVE

I squirm, trying to gain some personal space. I'm beginning to doubt these men know the meaning. Their body heat is far higher than mine, or what I'm used to, and damn it, I need some space. I stop dead and they do the same, turning and looking enquiringly at me.

"You need to move over a bit. You're suffocating me." I see their faces drop before they quickly mask it, and I hate that I feel like a bitch for asking for a little room. "Look, I promise not to try and run away, okay?" I smile as they move over— a smidge. I sigh and shake my head. I have always craved a man who wants me desperately, but I didn't bank on finding two of them.

Not that they want you, my mind screams at me.

Brennen takes my hand as we enter a shopping centre and Ta walks behind me, gently resting his hand on my shoulder.

It looks quite similar to the ones back home, but on a much grander scale, like the upmarket designer ones I stayed away from. The height is impressive; it must be spread over a few floors. There are actual walls made of the tinted glass and colourful plants cover the vast majority of the external walls. The scent from them fills the air and it feels like a welcoming space.

"Araline!" I hear my name and twist around to see Alish hurrying over to us with Hunter following, who's holding some brightly-coloured parcels and the hand of a small child. He's the spitting image of him, only with Alish's red hair and grass green eyes. "It's good to see you up and about, lass, and you're not limping. Ta must have worked his magic on your ankle?" Her smile is wide and carefree, and her eyes sparkle with merriment as she pulls me in for a hug.

I'm not used to their easy displays of affection, and I'm a tad overwhelmed.

"Yes, he did. It was a bloody shock when Brennen took me to his home and I found Ta waiting for us. Another male I'm meant to be mated to. A bit of warning would have been nice." I look at her, so confident, her man obviously totally in love with her. The little boy smiles at me. He's is such a cutie. I return his smile and he grins. He's lost a couple of front teeth and looks utterly adorable because of it.

"This is Steel, our son," Alish informs me, picking him up.

"Hello, Steel, it's good to meet you. Oh, he's a cutie, Alish." I laugh as he wriggles free to come and give me a cuddle. I'm not used to small children, but I kneel down so I can hug him. He stares at me, unblinking, as if sizing me up. It's quite unnerving.

"Hello, Araline, are you Prince Brennen's mate?" he enquires softly.

I'm shocked. He looks to be about four, but he's far too articulate for a child of that age.

I look at Alish and raise an eyebrow.

"They age faster here— mentally," she tells me with a smile.

Okay then.

"I am, Steel," is all I can think to say, before Steel returns to his father. Brennen joins them, and I watch as he interacts with the child. While they are occupied, I whisper to Alish, "Do you have more mates?"

I glance up at Hunter, hoping he doesn't hear and praying it isn't too rude to ask, as he's a formidable-looking man. I wonder how they really feel at having to share their females.

"I do. Only the one other, like you. His name is Brogan; you'll get to meet him soon. Your arrival yesterday wasn't exactly textbook standard. I'm sorry we didn't have time to prepare you." Her eyes are full of emotion as she looks up at Hunter, and his hands automatically stroke her shoulders as if to comfort her.

"So, I take it you turn into a dragon as well?" I blurt out.

"Yes, I do." He smiles at me, turning to Brennen. "You've told her about our dragons? Has she seen him yet?" Hunter asks, grinning. "How'd that go down, cousin?"

"They really turn into dragons?" I whisper to Alish. "For real? Dragons?" I step backwards, hoping she'll follow me so we can talk about this in more depth. But she stays firmly in front of her male, and my back hits a wall of muscle as Ta steps in behind me. I almost roll my eyes again.

"We've not had time to fully discuss it, but we will," Brennen answers. "Mother and father paid us an unannounced visit. He dropped the bombshell about the bidding draw. You can imagine my Araline's response." I stare up at him and find him shining with pride.

Hunter barks out a laugh, pulling Alish into his body. It's as if he can't bear for her not to be touching him. Steel is held by both of their hands. "I wish I had been there to witness that. Your father isn't used to anyone standing up to him."

"They really do, and so does Steel." Alish smiles down at her son, as she answers my earlier question "I keep forgetting you've not had any training before arriving." She shakes her head. "You've so much to learn and enjoy. I'd love to see this world through your eyes. It must be like waking up from a dream and finding out it's true."

"I'm not sure about that," I tell her morosely, biting my lip.

She grips my hand. "You will. In time, you will see the benefits of being here with us. It was your arrival day yesterday."

I look at her, not knowing the significance of that date.

She must see my confoundment because she hurriedly explains, "That's the date you celebrate each year from now on. We don't have birthdays for the females as we aren't born here. We arrive. It's a day of huge festive celebrations where you get utterly spoilt. My arrival day is in a few weeks, so you'll see how we celebrate it." I nod at her, not knowing what today is, let alone yesterday's date. Do they even have the same calendar as Earth or is that yet another thing I have to learn?

"We should leave you. I'm sure you have lots to buy. Have fun, Araline; allow your males to make this transition time everything it should be for you. I'll come and see you in a few days, if you'd like? Have some female time. I could bring a few of my friends for you to meet?" Alish asks, flicking her long braid over her shoulder. Her grass-green eyes sparkle as Hunter nods at us before turning them away.

"Bye, Araline," Steel calls out and waves to me.

"Bye, Steel." I wave back. "That sounds nice, thank you, Alish. See you soon," I call out, and she gives me a little wave before they disappear. I make a mental note to ask her about the markings on her arms the next time I see her.

Glancing around the building, I see it's a hive of activity. Everyone seems happy and their chatter fills the air. The shopfronts are lined with brightly-coloured wares and the clothes are just beautiful.

Obviously, everyone's decided to come shopping tonight, I think.

"I see word has gotten out that the prince is here." Ta snorts, taking my hand and leading the way through the throng of people. Everywhere we walk, people stop and bow reverently at Brennen, smiling at him and us. And it slowly sinks in just how important he is to them. I stare at the women and notice none of them have the markings Alish and Sha have, and I wonder what the significance of that is. I really need to question Alish the next time I see her.

CHAPTER THIRTEEN

One thing vastly different between Mertier and Earth is that no one is snapping pictures; there isn't a single camera to be seen. If he were a royal on Earth, we would be overrun with the dreaded paparazzi. It's refreshing to see he can go out and about without being mauled by strangers.

I watch Brennen as he smiles politely at them all, but he doesn't stop. He keeps my other hand firmly in his as we make our way to wherever Ta is headed.

"Don't you have internet shopping here? It'd be far easier to do our shopping, and have it delivered to your palace," I ask, hating the idea of having to try clothes on. The fitting rooms I'm used to have those blaring white strip lights that never make my body look good in anything.

"It's our palace now, Little Flower." I bite my lip at that. He smiles at me before continuing. "We saw what internet shopping was doing on Earth. It seems a good idea, but we watched as your towns disappeared, as the local shops were put out of business while more and more chose the quickness and ease of shopping online. We decided we didn't want that for Mertier. We encourage our smaller enterprises to succeed and try our best to help them keep making a profit. A happy shop owner means they will give first class service, and that will bring in more customers and more money. Earth has fallen foul of the top few percent owning all the wealth, and the middle and poorer people are the ones struggling."

I understand and agree with everything he said. Earth is failing so many people in the twenty-first century.

"Okay, I get that," I say, bumping into Ta when he halts abruptly, making me almost bounce off his rock-hard muscles. Brennen steadies me, and I have to wonder if he needs to hold me against himself that long. I am literally sandwiched between them both. I gulp, my heart beating erratically at their nearness.

"Sorry," I murmur to Ta, as my hands brace on his back. Even through his black shirt I feel the heat his body gives off, and I have to mentally tell myself to remove my hands and not allow how good he feels to seep into my awareness.

He turns around, grinning. "If that's what I need to do to have you put your hands on my body, then I will have to keep doing it." He winks before ushering us forward and into a well-lit boutique.

A woman scurries out from another room and bows formally. She's stunning. Of Asian descent, she has gorgeous hazel eyes and a petite, trim figure.

"You're Lordship, it's an honour to have you in my shop. I am Lizza, and it's a pleasure to serve you." She beams at me.

"And you must be Araline." She laughs at what I guess must be a look of shock on my face. "Word travels fast between the Districts, even more so where our beloved royals are concerned," she tells me, and I guess it's true. Everyone loves a good gossip, whether they're from here or Earth.

"It's a pleasure to meet you, and happy arrival day for yesterday. I hope you find something you love. Please take your time looking. If you need anything, anything at all, just give me a call." She seems friendly, so I give her a smile.

"Thank you." I want to confide in her that everything is a little overwhelming at the moment, that I don't understand where I belong now and I'm worried that if I can't form a bond with Brennen and Ta that I'll be put into this bidding thing and could end up with up to five males. I keep silent though, as I'm not sure who I can and can't trust here. So I just tell her, "Your shop looks amazing, Lizza." I can't help myself; I look at her arms. They are mark free. So, it's only Sha and Alish who have them. I give myself a mental shake and listen to what she's saying.

"Thank you. Please take your time. We will stay open for as long as you desire." She has a very calm demeanour, which just adds to her charm. "We have free refreshments here for your pleasure. Please, help yourselves." She nods and leaves us to it.

"She seems very nice," I whisper, as Ta hands me a glass of ice cold, silver, shimmering water. Seriously, this water is amazing, and I quickly gulp it down while I take in the shop.

The boutique is light and airy with a wide richness in colour splashing from the many varied flowers that are artfully dotted around. I leave the males and walk over to one of the many racks of clothes. They are superbly made from expensive cloth that on Earth I'd only ever wistfully admired from afar. I run my fingers over a few cashmere jumpers. I can't deny that I have always longed to own clothes such as these, but it just hadn't been possible on my meagre salary. I walk on, admiring what the shop had to offer.

"Take your time, Little Flower," Brennen calls out as they find a rich purple, velvet sofa with numerous cushions on it and make themselves comfortable, their eyes following me around the shop.

"There aren't any prices on the clothes. How do we know how much anything is?" I whisper, a little bewildered, all the while thinking that my mother always said, *'If you have to ask the price, you can't afford it'*.

"It doesn't matter how much it is. If you like it, it's yours. The royal estate will pick up the bill." Ta grins at me. "And you'd look stunning in that." He nods toward a dress, and I head over to where he is pointing. It's silk, sapphire blue, with a handkerchief hem, cold shoulder sleeves and a plunging neckline. It's still decent but would no doubt hint at what it's covering.

I run my fingers over it lovingly. It's a beautiful dress. I've never owned anything so feminine. Ta moves quickly, and I feel his hands running over my body. A breathy sigh escapes me.

"I want to see you in this. Better still, I want to be ripping it from your body so I can get to what's beneath. Try it on for us?" His silky-smooth voice with its accent makes my nipples hard. It's dark, spicy and full of carnal promise.

I don't trust myself to speak and can only nod as he hands

it to me and leads me towards the dressing room, which he ushers me inside of.

"We'll be right here," he promises, and swishes the heavy curtains closed. I find myself facing a huge mirror.

I hear footsteps and know it's Brennen joining Ta. I quickly remove my clothes and pull on the silk dress. It's glorious. It melds to my body, perfectly displaying the curves I've hated for a lifetime. I tug at the neckline. It's lower than I'm used to. Turning, my eyes ping open wide. The back of the dress isn't there. There's a strip of material going across my shoulders but then nothing until the very base of my spine. I gape at it. I've never in my life worn such a provocative piece of clothing. *Well, that's different.*

"Are you ready?" Ta asks, moments before the curtain is pulled back. I stare at them.

I'm way out of my comfort zone in this. All my insecurities are screaming at me to cover up, to not wear something so revealing. I squirm under their heated gaze.

"Fuck!" Ta exclaims.

"Fuck indeed," Brennen manages to grate out.

Taking my hand, Ta leads me out of the changing room and twirls me around.

"You are so fucking beautiful, Araline," he whispers against my ear, as he pulls me closer. "So very beautiful, and all ours." He passes me over to Brennen, who grins at me as his hands run over my exposed skin. A slow caress that has my skin erupting in goose bumps.

"I would love for you to dress this way from now on," Brennen says, as his eyes rake over my body. "We'll take this dress in every colour it comes in," he tells Lizza, as she makes her way over to us.

"Of course, you're Lordship." She smiles at me, "Wow, Araline. It's as if that dress was made for you. You look stunning."

"Don't you all think it's a little tight? Or revealing?" I ask them. Turning back towards the mirror, I nervously yank at the dress, tugging it as if that will hide all the imperfections, all the lumps and bumps I see.

"You're not on Earth any longer, Araline. The females of Mertier wear less clothing as it's hot here all year round; the suns can be unforgiving. And why hide that sexy body? Look in the mirror and see how your males look at you in this," Lizza tells me with a friendly smile.

I dare not point out at this moment that they aren't exactly my males. But I keep quiet and turn, facing the mirror again, and gaze into Brennen and Ta's eyes. They look at me as if they want to devour me. There is no mistaking their desire. After that, I give up trying to protest and we spend a few hours trying on one thing after another.

CHAPTER FOURTEEN

By the time I announce I'm tired and hungry, there are piles of clothes we have chosen.

"Okay, that's enough!" I protest, but I'm laughing at the same time. I can honestly say I've not had this much fun buying new clothes in... well, ever. But then, I've not had a bottomless purse before. Everything I've tried on has made my body look better than it's ever looked on Earth.

I fall into the chair between them both. Looking around the shop, there's a few others shopping in here now, and I smile at a woman who is twirling for her male. The happiness and the love she feels for him is obvious, and I silently wonder if I could ever feel like that for Brennen and Ta.

Brennen holds out his fingers, and in them he's lightly gripping a seed like the ones I ate earlier. I spy the silver tray Lizza placed on a desk, holding a mountain of them for people to enjoy. I dutifully open my mouth, and he pops it in. I suck on it and the tip of his finger, and his eyes flare and darken, but he doesn't remove it. My tongue flicks against it and he shudders, just before it pops free from my hold. I've never had this reaction from a man before. It's quite heady.

"I think, Araline, you are a little vixen," Ta whispers against my ear, before nipping the lobe and making me jump.

I turn to look at him, still sucking on my sweet. I could eat these sweet treats all night.

"Maybe." I delicately shrug a shoulder at him, then stand. "Come on; show me around a bit more. Please."

I'm dressed in one of those dresses they seem to love so much. I feel a bit self-conscious in it, but their reaction, which was so genuine, has me going along and wearing it for them. My new shoes have gems on them, which are the same colour as my dress, and they sparkle as I walk. The heels are a tad higher than I'm used to, but I fell in love with them and just had to have them.

I'm a bit of a shoe whore but have never been able to afford the designer brands I coveted.

Brennen and Ta stand as one, and I take a step backwards as their imposing height and extra-large bodies throws me for a moment. I shiver, feeling a little threatened. No idea where that came from, but they catch it.

Brennen takes my hand and whispers, "We could never hurt you, Araline." He brings my hand up to his mouth and brushes his lips across my knuckles.

It's such a tender kiss that my breath hitches for an entirely different reason. I have to watch myself; they could wreak havoc on a girl's sensibility.

"No woman on Mertier has ever been hurt intentionally. We are brought up to cherish them and love them," Ta tells me, taking my hand and leading us out of the shop. I have time to quickly wave to Lizza and mouth a thank you. She's happily tallying it all up and calls out that it will all be delivered to the palace tomorrow.

"You're telling me no woman has been hurt?" I ask them. It seems a bit farfetched that not a single one has been hurt in all the years they've been going to Earth and collecting them. I watch as they glance briefly at one another but stay silent. I let it go. We're having such a great time I don't want to spoil it. I will question them or find out at a later time.

I'm walking between them, each holding a hand. I can only imagine what the reactions on Earth would have been, but here, I look around and see many women with multiple men and not one looks unhappy. In fact, it's the complete opposite. Every single one looks utterly loved and adored.

We end up at an indoor fountain that's trickling the same silver liquid the pond had. It's beautiful and shimmers under the lights. Sitting on the edge, I can people-watch from here. It's one of my favourite pastimes, and it soon has me smiling. To be honest, it's hard not to smile at this world. What I've seen of it, anyway. It's almost too good to be true.

"So, we know Brenn is a prince. Ta, who are your family? Will I get to meet them?" I look up into his eyes, and he smiles.

"My father's name is Azure, and he's a good friend of the king. Which is a good job, since he is his advisor. That's how I grew up with Brenn. My mother passed away when I was young, so my father used to bring me to Court. I was put in the nursery with Brenn, and they soon realised we were inseparable. He was always getting me into trouble with our tutors." Ta laughs at the memories. "They would never believe me when I told on him. Oh no, not sweet, angelic-like Brenn."

Brennen rolls his eyes. "Don't you believe him, Little Flower. He's the rebel. I used to follow him everywhere, from one hair-brained idea to the next."

No matter what they say about one another, there is clearly a lot of trust between them. I realise I'm relaxed, happy and content. It's been a long time since I've felt that, and I smile.

But before I can bask in the moment, it's shattered when a deafening, wailing alarm goes off. I hurriedly put my hands over my ears.

"What's going on?" I shout over the din.

"Now?" Ta demands incredulously. He's furious "They chose now to attack?" Before I know it, he's on his feet and lifting me into his arms. And then he's running. Yes, running.

All hell has broken loose. People are running, and panic is etched into the other women's faces. Guards appear and swarm around the three of us, and we are ushered into one of those flying vehicles. We are airborne before I'm even strapped in.

"What's going on?" I demand, louder this time. I watch Ta take a deep breath while Brennen is talking on that black metal device Ta showed me earlier.

"We have enemies, Araline. Every so often they like to make their presence known to us. But don't worry, you are perfectly safe," he tells me. All the while, I can see he'd been keeping an ear open to what Brennen is saying.

We soon land back at the palace, and I'm ushered inside. I scream as the ground beneath us shifts and shakes. There are guards surrounding the palace, inside and out. Large men, the most intimidating I've ever seen, and they have heavy-looking weapons drawn, awaiting orders.

After giving them their orders, Brennen turns to Ta and shouts, "Take her down and keep her safe!" He looks as fierce as the other guards as he pulls me into his arms and kisses the life right out of me. I've never, ever been kissed with as much desperation and desire as this. My legs go weak, and I slump against his chest, desperate for it to continue. But all too swiftly I'm pulled from him.

"No! Let me go!" I shout unthinkingly at Ta, needing more of that kiss. Heaven help me, I want more.

"He needs to go and do his thing, Araline, and I need to keep you safe." Ta bundles me up into his arms once more, and I watch silently as Brennen shifts into his dragon.

CHAPTER FIFTEEN

"Oh, my God!" I shout. My eyes go wide as I take in the colossal black dragon, which stands where the man who just kissed me like no other was stood.

"Ta! He's a bloody dragon!" I know— I know they told me. But fuck! That's a real puff the magic dragon standing right in front of me. His effervescent eyes swivel in my direction, and I ram a fist into my mouth to stop the horror bubbling from me. Hysteria is clamouring to be set free as I stare at it.

All the noise— the shouting; the sounds of weapons going off; even Ta, who is trying his hardest to calm me— fades into the background. All I can focus on is the colossal black beast standing just a few feet away from me.

The dragon snorts black as night smoke from his nostrils, and I watch the tendrils curl upwards, towards the ceiling. His tail swishes this way and that as he slowly makes his way over to us. Fear claws its way from my stomach until I can't help the whimper that escapes me. I dare not scream. I don't want to piss him off.

"He won't hurt you, Araline," Ta reassures me.

But I don't think I'm ready to see if he's right. I try and break his incredible hold on me, but I get nowhere. The dragon stands within inches of me, so what's the point of trying to run anyway? I close my eyes, taking a deep calming breath and count to twenty. Upon opening them, I stare into his, trying desperately to see the man I know is still in there, somehow.

He huffs, his heated breath making my hair flutter as he moves back. Opening his tremendous wings, which have alarmingly sharp talons on the end, he flaps them as the roof to the palace slides back. I watch in awe and silence as the dragon lifts his great hulking body into the air and flies upwards, away from us.

I turn and stare at Ta.

"Where's he going? And who is attacking us?" I ask, as he turns and stands me on my own feet. We hurry further into the palace. The roof is once more closed, and all the windows have now got black metal shutters covering them, which plunge us into darkness. I close my eyes, trying to slow my heartbeat. I'm scared. It's just my luck that I get kidnapped to the Garden of Eden, only to find out there are things trying to destroy it.

After a few long minutes of following Ta, he stops and uses a keypad to open heavy metal doors. It reveals a metal box-like room with large monitors so we can see what's happening in every room in the palace. He holds my elbow, shows me to a comfortable couch and sits by my side, taking my hand, trying to reassure me.

"This is our panic room, Araline. It isn't used very often and is well stocked with all amenities, if need should ever arise. Brennen is trained in battle. All the royal dragons are."

"But, if he's the next king, then why aren't others sent? It doesn't make sense that the future king would be allowed to put himself in any danger," I say, and I have to admit, my voice holds a hint of hysteria.

"Every royal is born with a tremendous gift, Araline. They are the only ones equipped to fight the Rumos, who want what we have— the vortex to your world. They know our dragons will demolish their attempts. I don't really understand why they keep continuing to attack."

"Tell me more about them, these Rumos," I ask him, sitting back against the cool marble.

"Many moons ago, about the same time the vortex was discovered between Earth and Mertier, they lived here with us. We lived in complete harmony. But they wanted to go to Earth and conquer the planet and enslave the humans. Our king and council of the time banished them to one of the habitual moons. We think, though we have no proof, it was them who did something to the water or soil that prevents us from being able to give birth to females." He looks serious and gives himself a shake, then smiles at me, which makes my insides turn to mush. "When they attack, one of the men in the mated families will stay with the female, to make sure she is safe. As

Brenn is a royal and dragon, he will go to fight, and I will keep you safe. If there was another male with us, then we would take it in turns to guard you. Every male on Mertier is trained to be a warrior."

I can't suppress a shudder as the palace rocks above us, but the panic room holds. I nervously glance at the TV monitors that show what's going on in the grounds, and whimper. I watch a few dragons as the night's sky is illuminated by them spewing bright white fire upon the intruders, these Rumos. They fly with a graceful ability that belies their massive bodies, which must be a couple of double decker buses in size. It's as well choreographed as any ballet and I can't help but be amazed as they duck and dive and weave in and around until they reach their enemy.

Bloody hell, I've never seen anything as powerfully beautiful and graceful as the dragons. The Rumos, with their pale skin and even paler hair, who remind me of people with albinism, don't stand a chance, but they put up a valiant fight. They have spears with metal looking barbs on the tips that they jab towards the dragons once they come within close proximity. Their clothes, as I watch, seem to be fire retardant, but only for a few good blasts. It's a suicide mission and I can't help but to wonder what they hoped to accomplish. Ta draws me closer to him, wrapping his arms around me and resting his head upon mine. I look away as bodies are set ablaze. It's macabre watching the burning bodies twitch until they fall to the floor.

"I promise you, Araline, Brenn will be perfectly safe," he tells me, but I can't form an answer. My eyes keep trailing back to the monitors. The dragons may have huge body mass, but they are agile beings. The intruders don't stand a chance. There are wailing alarms going off all over the Districts as Ta points out different places, and we watch as Mertier's warriors brutally attack the enemy. They don't muck around and soon have the ones left alive lined up and handcuffed. They're marched off somewhere I really don't want to know about.

"I told you everyone would be fine. We have dealt with the Rumos many times over the years. They aren't equipped to mount an assault that would harm us. Once they were banished from Mertier they left with no modern technology. They are lightyears behind even Earth," he tells me, as we walk out of the panic room and through the palace until we are outside.

The suns are coming up, and I realise it must be very early morning.

"If they stand no chance, why would they do it?" I ask him. The clean-up has already begun. They may not have the power to cause any fatalities, but the damage was extensive to the gardens, and I just bet a few Districts were hit with all they had.

"I think they are that desperate to gain control of the vortex," he answers, as a great dragon lands at our feet. I hurriedly take a step backwards before Ta takes my hand. "It's Brenn, Araline."

I take a breath, pull up my big girl panties, and walk over to him. I hesitantly lay a hand on his scales. He's so warm. I walk around him, my hand stroking him as I move, and I feel his great body breathe in and out. His tail twitches as he raises it so my hand can reach it. The five deadly spikes that are evenly spaced out down the thick muscle of the tail are unforgivably hard and as sharp as a razor's edge. All the way around I walk, until I'm facing his head, and his wicked fangs that are as wide as my forearm. I place my hand on his snout and find it's incredibly soft. His hot breath as he huffs is laced with black smoke, and it reminds me of the burning people the dragons set alight earlier. I pull away, but he follows me, nudging my hand to resume stroking.

"Demanding much?" I manage to laugh, and just like that, my fears vanish. "Can I sit on you?" I ask. Feeling very daring, I walk around to his side again. He crouches down until I can grab his mane, and with Ta's help, I hoist myself onto his back. My legs are spread wide, and I keep a firm grip on his glossy mane but squeal as he stands, spreads his wings, and flaps them.

"Oh my God, no... no... no!" I shout as he lifts off the ground, and then we are airborne. Thankfully, he doesn't soar high or go too fast. We keep low to the ground with Ta running alongside. *I'm flying! I'm actually flying!* My fear subsides and I bubble with laughter. Flinging my arms wide, I do a Titanic moment. Never, ever in my life had I envisaged riding a damn dragon! We head back and he lands softly, and Ta helps me dismount. My arms go around the dragon's neck and my face rests on his cheek. I'm totally not scared of him now. He nudges himself free, and with a bright flash he's human again and as naked as the day he was born.

Wow! My eyes trail over his impressive set of pecs while he stands with his hands on his hips, enjoying my appraisal of him. Dragging my gaze further down his body, I follow his happy trail, all the way down to his cock. My eyes widen and I choke as I see he has two cocks. One is a lot smaller, protruding from the base, but it's still visible. I hastily look away, thinking, *that's never going to fit and what the hell do I do with two cocks?* I'm blushing. *It's not like you've never seen one before. Get a grip!* I give myself a little mental shake. *But there are two cocks!* I'm not going to think about *them* now.

Ta chuckles. "That's one of the differences between the dragon's bodies and the men of Earth. They have an extra, smaller cock that is there purely for the female's pleasure." My eyes go wide with the thought. "Put some clothes on, Brenn." He leans down, grabbing some clothes that he brought with him from the safe room and chucks them at Brennen.

"Why? I like her eyes on my body," he replies huskily, but pulls them on. "Did you like what you saw, Little Flower?" He walks over to me, and I'm all tongue-tied as I look helplessly up at him.

I'm no shy virgin. I have a healthy sexual appetite. But he makes me feel vulnerable. I take a step back and hit the chest wall of Ta. His arms trail around my waist, holding me in position as if he's offering me to Brennen. At the same time, his lips feast on my neck, making my eyes roll to the back of my head. Brennen's soft fingers gently stroke my cheek, before I feel his velvet-soft lips brush across mine. God forgive me, but I moan into his mouth as he deepens the kiss, and for a moment I forget where I am and what's happened in the last twenty-four hours of my life. All I want is to forget, and I have a feeling that if I allow them, these men will do a damn good job of making me forget my own name, let alone what's happened to me.

A soft moan escapes me, before I feel Brennen tear his lips from mine and growl. Ta immediately stops and withdrawals also, and I'm left dazed and bewildered as to why they've pulled away. That is, until I open my eyes and see four more dragons watching us a few yards away.

CHAPTER SIXTEEN

"They are Brennen's brothers," Ta whispers in my ear.

"What do you want?" Brennen demands of the dragons, and one by one they shift back to men.

I blush and turn my head away, as they are all naked. But I didn't miss how their bodies were as colossal as Brennen's, with as well-defined muscles, and they aren't in the least bit self-conscious about being naked.

I hear a few chuckles.

"Brother, she's a bashful little thing," one states. I can hear the mocking laughter in it.

I wrench my eyes around and stare at him.

"What I am is none of your business, is it?" I challenge him, daring him to argue with me. I've just about had it with bossy, overbearing dragons.

"I do like her spirit, though," another one announces with a grin.

"Araline, let me introduce my brothers." He points from left to right. "Ragen, Ace, Zane, and Raide." They all bow their heads to me as their names are called out.

"You've not mated her yet, brother?" It wasn't a question though. Somehow, he knows. They all know that Brennen and Ta haven't fucked me.

I watch as the brothers take an appreciative sniff, as if scenting me. Four sets of eyes that match Brennen's in colour drift over my body. I feel it like a soft caress, and I take a step nearer to Ta, feeling a little unsettled as the males keep staring at me.

"What do you think we were about to do when you lot turned up? Uninvited, I might add," Ta growls at them, bringing me into his arms.

"We've never had to be invited before," Zane points out. His grinning face tracks Ta's hands as he wraps them around me, hugging me closer to his body.

"Well, now you will wait until you are," Brennen informs them, standing on the other side of Ta, bringing my hand up to his lips to kiss my knuckles.

"You lucky bastards," Ace says softly, before turning and calling out to the rest of them, "Come on, let's give them their privacy. I don't think Araline's prepared to be shared with us." With wistful and longing expressions, they nod, saying goodbye, and shift once more to their majestic dragon forms before flying off.

I release the deep breath, and then my brain catches up with what Ace just said.

"Just what the hell did he mean by, *'I don't think Araline is prepared to be shared with us"?"* I twist so I can stare into both of their eyes.

"In the non-royal families, if they have a lot of males, like Brenn's obviously has, some of the females enjoy the attentions of the other brothers before they get mated. But as the dragons are born only to the royals, it doesn't happen in Brenn's family all that often, as dragons are usually far too territorial and overprotective to share with more than one male," Ta explains, while Brennen watches me.

My mouth drops. "So, hang on, you pass your mates around your family, so they have the chance of a fuck before they bring their own females, their mates, to this world?" I take a step away from them. *Bloody hell!* Brennen's brothers had flown here to see if I'd allow them to fuck me?

"I need a drink. Do you have anything like alcohol here?" I stalk past them and stomp away, heading back inside the palace, but they are soon at my side.

"We do. Come this way." Brennen takes my hand and guides me into the room where his mother and father first met me. The bright cushions and low tables are lit with flickering lights, and I sink into one. The materials used are scrumptious in rich, vibrant colours. Running my hands over one, I can't fail to notice the work that's gone into the tapestry of dragons in full flight, blasting objects with their white fire. They have the dragons down right to the very intricate details.

I watch Ta sit next to me as Brennen walks further into the room. He pulls the door open and one of the young serving boys hands him a tray before closing it behind him. The heavy tray has a cut glass decanter with bright, almost florescent yellow liquid within, and three small glasses. He sits, handing

Ta the tray, who quickly fills up each glass and passes them to us.

"To our Araline. Our unexpected blessing. To a beautiful woman I hope comes to love us as much as we love her already," Brennen states, before swallowing the liquid down in one gulp.

"To our mate, who I wouldn't change for anything." Ta winks at me, grinning, before he swallows. They both look at me expectantly.

"I don't really know what to toast. My life has changed irrevocably. It's only been twenty-four hours for me, and you have to appreciate this world is completely different to Earth. So, I'm just thankful I'm still alive." I know I must sound a little sad, and I am. I have no idea what's to become of me. What if I can't mate with them? Well, I know what. I'll be put into some lucky dip, bidding thing, and the next group of males will get to enjoy me. My body. I throw back my head and swallow the liquid.

"Bloody hell!" I hoarsely whisper. "What the hell is that?" I splutter and cough, trying to clear my burning throat. I look at the tiny glass, thinking that at any moment I'm going to start breathing fire like Brennen's dragon. My eyes are watering, and I brush the tears away. "You could have given me a little warning." I slam the glass back down and shudder. That was foul. "I don't think I'll try that again," I say, and feel my eyes droop. My co-ordination is totally out of whack. "I may be a bit pissed." I take a deep breath and sway on the cushion. "You did this," I say, though it only sounds vaguely like what I'm trying to say. I waggle my finger at them. Bloody hell, I've not been this drunk in years. "You did this to have your wicked way with me." I giggle, and then slam my mouth shut.

"I didn't expect her to swallow it all in one go." Brennen laughs as I try to focus on his face.

"You are way too damn good-looking." I huff, and then slap my hand in front of my face to try and shut myself up. "You both drank it in one go." I lean back, forgetting I'm on a cushion, and fall backwards with a squeal. Ta, with lightning reflexes, is up out of his cushion and catching my head before I hit the marble floor.

"My saviour." I giggle at him. "Now take me to bed or lose me forever." I quote the line from my mother's favourite eighties movie, Top Gun, but of course, they don't have a clue what I'm talking about. I see them look questioningly at each other—before I pass out.

Brennen

Ta looks at me. "Well, she did say…" He grins, picking Araline up.

"No, Ta. Not like this." I also stand, putting my hand on Ta's shoulder.

"I know. Only kidding. But, Brenn, look at her. She's so beautiful," he whispers, before we both walk out of the room and up the grand staircase to take our mate to bed.

CHAPTER SEVENTEEN

Waking up, I feel overheated, and no wonder. I turn my head and see both Ta and Brennen in bed with me, fast asleep and holding me securely between their bodies. I mentally check my clothes and breathe a sigh of relief. Okay, all still on.

I gently pull back the covers and gasp. They are totally naked. Glancing at their peaceful faces, I decide it's safe and feast on the sight of them. They are glorious. Hard muscles from years of training; perfect, lickable bodies. My mouth waters, and I wonder if I'm still drunk on that drink. I don't feel hung over—the opposite in fact. I feel alive. Whatever was in that drink has rejuvenated me. I feel almost high. My inhibitions are at an all-time low.

I'm in bed with not one but two sex gods. Do I really want to pass up this opportunity to study them? *No, I really don't.*

I don't know who to look at first. I chew my lip, contemplating which one to ogle first.

I compare their bodies. Brennen is an enormous male. His body is a wall of hard muscle. It's a fighter's body. He's covered in scars, as if someone has taken a fine knife and sliced him with it. *It must be the battles he gets into*, I reason. He makes even me feel small and dainty and that's saying something. His cock is, well, how do I put it into words how utterly mouth-watering it looks? My eyes open wide as I take in the extra bit that's sticking out from it, just above his actual cock. Like a smaller cock, not as wide or long. Thinking about it, I realise just what it'd rub against if he were fucking me. Like the ears of a rampant rabbit vibrator! Wow.

I turn and study Ta's body. He's leaner than Brennen, more of an athletic build, and not an inch of fat mars his beauty. He's tall, with large hands that I remember lighting up like a Christmas decoration when he healed my ankle.

I turn back to Brennen and feel a little giddy as my hands stroke down his chest. He moans in his sleep as I take my time running my fingers over his hard muscles. My mouth drops open in amazement, when just under his skin, I watch his dragon scales shimmering, and I have to remember he's not a man. He's not a human man at all. He can shift into a ferocious dragon, for fucks sake.

He sighs in pleasure, but I turn to Ta and repeat the touch to his naked body. I take my time, enjoying this new feeling of daring. I really don't know what's come over me. I've never initiated sex before in my life, as I found it utterly boring, a complete waste of time. Not that that's what I'm doing now. *Absolutely not!* All I want to do is touch them a little.

All the books I read waxed lyrically about how amazing sex was. Hell, even a few of my girlfriends happily told me how divine it was. I have a feeling it would be anything but boring with these men.

Ta's vivid blue eyes flash open, making me jump, and he winks at me, grinning. I gasp and go to pull my hand away, but he gently grips it and places it back on his chest.

"I like your hands on my body, Araline," he whispers. But I feel like a perv for touching them while they were sleeping and blush wildly to be caught doing it. I hastily pull my hands away.

Ta follows me as I lay back down, closing my eyes, as if I can block out the fact that I'm in bed with not one but two men. His lips brush sensually over mine as if daring me to kiss him back, and I feel Brennen start to undress me. I should stop them. I should—

My breathing is erratic. This kiss is slaying me. My arms rise as if on autopilot, while Ta breaks the kiss so my dress can be tossed, uncaring of the beauty of it, to the floor.

As soon as I'm free from the dress, Ta is back and his lips continue to fan the flames of my desire, higher and higher. I have to break free. I can't think. All I can do is feel how my body is responding to their touch. A moan leaves my mouth as my bra and panties are removed, and I'm as naked as they are.

Their lips and tongues leave scorch marks wherever they touch me, and my back arches when they each take a nipple in their mouths and tease the extra sensitive peaks. Brennen leaves my breast and kisses his way to my lips, then whispers against them, "This is just for you, Araline. Today we show you how much your body turns us on and how yours responds to us. Don't fret about doing anything; let us show you how your body was made just for our touch."

Opening my eyes, I stare into theirs, but soon moan as Brennen kisses his way down my body. He makes himself comfortable, and his wicked, naughty tongue dances its way to my fevered clit. At the same time, Ta sucks my nipple and his hand plumps my other breast. I'm lost. I've never had this kind of attention paid to my body. They are 'learning' me. Every time I moan and show them I love something they do, they repeat that touch, over and over, until I'm mindless with desire. Until I scream out my releases so many times I almost pass out with the passion.

I have no idea how long they carried on their dark, erotic seduction. It was unlike anything I have ever experienced. But true to their word, they don't fuck me. They show me undeniable pleasure until my throat is hoarse with screaming my ecstasy. I try unsuccessfully many times to touch them, as they are hard and needy, but they keep saying today was for me, and we had the rest of our lives for me to touch and learn their bodies.

CHAPTER EIGHTEEN

I must have passed out at some point, as waking up, I have no idea what the time is, the date, or even what planet I'm on. Closing my eyes, I remember the weird but provocative dream I had last night. I dreamed I'd been in bed with two men at the same time. Scandalous! However incredulous that may be, my body aches in all the right places, and I feel utterly sated in a way I never have before. Turning my head, I see a vivid blue pair of eyes on the most gorgeous face staring at me, and then I quickly turn and… OMG! There he is. The man who abducted me. I am in bed with two men!

It wasn't a bloody dream. *I'm a slut,* I groan silently. Wiping a hand over my face, I pray that when I re-open my eyes, they'll be nothing but a figment of my overworked, undersexed mind.

"We're still here, Little Flower." I can hear the laughter in Brennen's voice as he leans in for a nibble on my earlobe. When did that become so erotic?

I'm glad he finds this funny.

"We've had a bath made ready as you may be a bit sore." Ta's voice is strong, unrepentant, and undeniably sexy. Both of their accents cause me to shiver wantonly.

It has my lady bits all in a tingle again. *Hush you,* I shush my bits. The last thing I need is round two. Well, I need it like the air I breathe, but I'm unwilling to admit that to myself just yet.

Brennen's talented tongue is causing goose bumps to erupt all over my body as his lips journey down my neck, and it isn't me who sighs all girly-like and leans my head over to allow him more access. Nope, not me at all.

Just as Ta's fingers brush across my oversensitive nipples, I sit up, dragging the silk sheet over my body. I know subconsciously I'm trying to hide; I'm not ready to think about how they made me feel last night. I'm really not trying to be a prick tease, but other bodily necessities need dealing with.

"Okay, show me the bathroom. I need, um, something." My eyes cross when they step out of the bed and wait for me to join them. I have to take a moment just to admire their physiques. They are highly aroused, and I have to drag my eyes away from their straining cocks. I huff and ungainly roll off the bed, clutching desperately at the sheet.

I spy Ta groaning silently as I put an end to more sexy fun and games, but being the gentleman he is, he doesn't push for anything.

"After all we did last night, Little Flower, you surely can't be bashful around us still?" Brennen grins at me.

It only makes me grip the sheet tighter.

He leaned down, whispering in my ear, "I licked and sucked every inch of your sexy body. It was the most—"

"Oh, shush you!" I moan, and I know I'm blushing a lovely shade of red, but I almost sway on my feet as the memories flash behind my eyelids. These men are insatiable.

"I loved how you tasted, and I can't wait to do it all over again," Ta reminds me as he takes my hand and leads the way to the bathroom.

Their words have me trembling. I love how dominant they are with me. They don't ask if what they are doing is good for me because they knew damn well it is. It is the best I've ever felt, and we didn't even have sex. I now crave to have them fuck me with every fibre of my being. I stumble as my mouth goes dry with want, and Brennen hauls me into his arms. I gasp, as no one but him and Ta has ever carried me before. Pervious guys had always moaned that I was far too heavy and that I'd put their backs out.

But not these men.

He walks into the bathroom, with Ta following. This room is breathtakingly beautiful. I'm beginning to think they don't know the meaning of ugly architecture. The same white marble with the gold running throughout is everywhere; even the bath is made out of it. After he shows me where the toilet is, and I figure out how it works, I wash my hands and walk back out to where the bath is.

The bath is unlike anything I've seen in my life. It's more like a sunken pool, but bloody massive. It has a graduated entry, and I watch Ta walk in and keep walking until it's deep enough for him to float on his back. Brennen keeps hold of the sheet I'm wearing, so I have no option but to walk into the pool naked. As I run my hand into the liquid, I realise it's not like Earth's water. It's silver. I take a breath and sink underneath, and when I come up for air, my skin is glistening with a silver glow. I look at Ta and Brennen in fascination. The silver liquid shimmers on their skin, and they rub themselves, making it disappear into them.

"This water is reserved for the royal family. It has healing properties for the dragons. My dragon is desperate to come out. Are you ready to meet him again, Araline?" Brennen asks me. I can see his dragon scales shimmering under his skin, as if he's trying to push his way to the surface. There's a definite fight going on between Brennen and the dragon.

Do I want to see his dragon again? Yes! No! My mouth goes dry while I try and calm my thoughts.

"He wants to see you again, Araline. He loved feeling your hands stroking him," Brennen says gently, as if he's aware that I really don't know if I want to meet him again or not.

Ta walks up and stands behind me, wrapping me in his warm embrace.

"You're always so warm." I sigh, snuggling back against him. "Much more than I am. Do your body temperatures run higher than humans'?" I wonder, stroking his arm, admiring his muscles that cocoon me against his body.

"We do. Now, stop stalling. You have a dragon that you have already seen and already touched, who wants to meet you. To do so again won't be so frightening, will it?" Ta demands.

I nod silently, and then tell them, "Okay then." At this point, it's highly doubtful my brain's firing on all cylinders. It still feels befuddled from what they did to me last night.

BRENNEN

I stiffen as I watch Brennen's body start to shimmer and morph into the beautiful but terrifying black-winged dragon.

"Breathe, Araline, he won't hurt you. He's no more likely to hurt you than Brenn or I," Ta whispers in my ear, as I realise I'm holding my breath.

"He so big," I murmur. "And just look at those fangs." I look at the long white fangs and remember what the dragons were capable of and what they had done to the others while Ta and I had been in the safe room. They are brutal creatures. How would it know the difference between me and an enemy? Its mighty tail swishes as if it's impatient. Taking a deep breath just as Ta releases me and takes a step back, sinking into the water.

"Bastard," I mutter, but my legs are moving me towards the dragon. I have to deal with this. I've met him before, now it's time to get a grip. This is really happening. I'm in a pool with a dragon. I can do this! "You are so damn big. Please don't eat me." My hands reach out, and I stretch up so I can pet his velvet muzzle. He lowers his head towards me, and my eyes widen. But I keep still. He huffs and black smoke clouds around us as he nudges me. It's a gentle nudge— well, gentle in his mind, I'm sure, but it still knocks me off my feet, and I'm plunged into the water. I come up spluttering and gasping for air to see the body of the dragon shuddering. I look closer and realise the damn thing is laughing at me. Without thinking, I splash water at it. "It's rude to laugh at people you knock over," I growl at it.

"Oh dear." Ta laughs. "You've done it now, Araline."

I only have a few precious seconds to comprehend what he's talking about, before the dragon's tail whips through the water and returns the favour. The splash lands on me like a damn tidal wave, knocking me over again. This time the current his tail whipped up spins me and sends me flailing, my legs and arms trying to push me out of the water, though with little luck. I start to panic, before I feel large claws capture me. They close around my body gently, so as not to cut me, and lift me out of the water. He releases me, and while I'm coughing up water, his face moves within inches of mine.

He's damn well laughing again.

"Well, I'm glad you're having fun!" I tell him, a little peeved. I stand up, and he comes even closer, until my hands can stroke his long, glistening black mane. The hair is utterly soft and silky. Beautiful. He rubs his face up my body, and I giggle as his scales tickle me. I'm not scared of him. Yes, he's a huge dragon, and yes, I know he can be deadly fierce, but I know deep in my bones that he won't hurt me. No idea why I know this, but I do. I climb up onto his neck and walk down his back until I lower myself and lie back. His body is warm and is a lot softer than you'd think.

The dragon lowers himself until he's submerged under the water, his snout hovering above so he can breathe. This pool must be deep. Ta pulls himself up and joins me on the dragon's back.

"Do all dragons love the water?" I ask Ta, as we are taken for a turn around the pool.

"This water, yes. It replenishes them, heals their wounds. A dragon could have died, but as long as we can get him to a pool like this one, he'll be saved. It will also keep you as young as you are now. Think of it as our fountain of youth. Once you arrive on Mertier and have access to our water it will freeze you your body, so you'll forever be young and beautiful. The people of Mertier use the public baths that has water like this but not as potent. It'll allow them to not age, but it's only the royals who get the full strength of it."

I can only imagine what my face looks like. I'm gobsmacked. *Bloody hell!* My only wish is that if I'd known this would happen, I'd have gone on a diet to end all diets. Now I'll be stuck this way. I can feel my eyes welling up and angrily brush the first tears away.

"What are you thinking? I thought all women want to be young and gorgeous forever?" His eyes drift to the dragon and he raises his eyebrows. Ta pulls me into his arms, holding me as great, heavy sobs wreck my body.

CHAPTER NINETEEN

After everything that's happened to me over the last couple of days, hearing I'll never be a slim Jim, for some reason, has pushed me over the edge and I'm wallowing in self-pity. Unbeknown to me, as I'm far too gone on my pity wagon to pay any attention, the dragon has walked out of the pool and Ta has me in his arms whilst the dragon shimmers and becomes Brennen once more.

"What's she upset about? What did you say this time?" he whispers, while sitting down and stroking my back, his lips pressing soft kisses across my shoulders.

"I've no idea. I told her about the powerful elements in the water and she lost it." Ta kisses my forehead, and I take gulps of air to try and steady myself.

God, I feel pitiful. I'm in the arms of a sex god, another is kissing and nibbling my shoulders, and I'm ugly crying.

"Tell us, Little Flower, what is going on? Who do we need to kill to make you happy?" I feel his lips against my shoulder and giggled-hiccupped which ended up sounding like a pig snorting. Very appealing. Not!

"No one," I whisper against Ta's chest.

"Then, what is wrong?" Brennen asks again.

I swivel around to face him. "You mean, apart from being kidnapped and brought to a new world, and being told *'you'll have to do'*? What about being told I have two mates, and finding out I've lost my chance to have a daughter? Or maybe it's the fact I'm now to stay in this fat body for-fucking-ever?" I would have carried on but the scary growl that erupts from each man has my eyes flaring wide.

Ta places me on the floor and jumps up.

"Get up. Stand the fuck up!" he shouts at Brennen. "I don't give a fuck if you're our next king, you don't deserve Araline!"

He's furious, his eyes flashing to silver as Brennen stands.

"I know. I was, to use an Earth term, a dick. I'm so very sorry, Araline. I wasn't thinking straight, and I was frustrated, but that's no excuse. Please, forgive me?" He looks at me, his eyes darkening. He sighs, his teeth clenching as if he's trying to keep his emotions buried deep inside.

But before I can answer, Ta draws back his fist and let's rip. It lands squarely on Brennen's jaw, and his head whips to the side as he stumbles back.

"You should be on your fucking knees, begging for forgiveness. You—" He breaks off and glances at me, then softens his voice. "Araline, what's the foulest insult on Earth at this time for someone?"

I think for a minute, knowing what word he is thinking of.

"Cunt," I whisper. I hate that word. It's vile. But at times, I've come to realise it's the only word that will fit.

"Yes, that's it. You, Brennen, are a fucking cunt!" Ta yells at him, folding his arms across his vast chest and glaring at him.

Brennen squares his shoulders, his face a mask. I have a feeling he wants to hit Ta back. He's probably not used to being shouted at or punched. But he doesn't. He bows his head, roughly exhales, and falls to his knees. I'm astonished. This huge sex god is on his knees before me.

Taking my hand, he kisses each knuckle reverently, then stares into my eyes, his own full of anguish. "I am sincerely sorry, Little Flower. Going through the vortex distorts much of our brains. It's incredibly hard to think rationally. It's usually just a quick grab for your mate. I wasn't myself. I can only tell you that you are more than enough. I could never envisage a mate I'd want more than you. If you really don't think you can forgive me, then I'll understand if you would prefer to find new mates." He lowers his head as Ta shouts at him in a language I don't understand. Perhaps Mertier's native language.

"So help me, Brenn, if you've ruined this for us, I will kill you," Ta growls, and gets onto the floor behind me. He hugs me tightly to him. "I'm not willing to let you go, Araline."

With my hands still clasped tightly in Brennen's and Ta's arms wrapped around me, I whisper, "It's not entirely your fault, Brenn. I have little self-confidence. You see, on Earth, women are, supposed to look a certain way. When you don't, you can sometimes get ridiculed and can be made to feel bad, I especially had a horrible time at school, about how I looked.

It's awful. So, you just hit a nerve. The men I've known before you two never made me feel like you did last night. It was a revelation that sex without the, um... actual penetration, could be that good. I want it again, and more. And no, I don't think I want to be with anyone else but you two."

The delight on Brennen's face is instantaneous. He grins wide, and I turn to see Ta is mirroring it. Brennen leans in and kisses me sweetly, his palms cupping my face so gently I sigh and lean in for more. One of my hands runs into his hair at the back of his neck, holding him to me. The other is behind my back, and I reach out and grasp Ta's cock. I smile into Brennen's kiss when Ta groans in pleasure as I stroke him intimately.

Before we can take it any further, the door alarm goes off, and I jump.

"Fuck them. They'll leave," Brennen says against my lips.

"Yes, don't stop, Araline. Oh god, your hands!" Ta moans into my neck from behind me. His teeth scrape against that sensitive spot I love so much, making me tremble and gasp into Brennen's mouth.

But it goes again, and both men growl. There's a knock at the bathroom door, and I squeal, "Don't let anyone in here!" I can feel my skin blushing a bright red from being caught in such a compromising situation. Then I remember, every woman is in this situation. It's the norm here.

CHAPTER TWENTY

They pull away from me, snarling out a few profanities as they stand. One of the staff silently enters, keeping his eyes fastened on Brennen and Ta.

"My Lord, Lady Alish is here to see Araline. I have made her and her friends comfortable in the gardens. They are sheltering in the shade. We have put out refreshments and food for them all." He nods, bowing stiffly, and leaves, closing the door softly.

"I forgot she said the other day that she would pop round with a few of her friends," I say happily, as they help me to my feet. "I need to get dressed. I don't want to keep them waiting." With my hands in theirs, we walk out of the bathroom. It's strange and I've only just noticed, but as soon as we exited the water, we were completely dry.

My body is still tingling with the erotic need these two make me feel. We head to the huge walk-in closet I saw yesterday, and I smile as I see that while we were in the water, what we bought at the shops had been delivered and unpacked. I stroke my hands over the beautiful rack of clothes. They are the most expensive I've ever owned, and I'm in love. "If I'm just meeting friends, should I dress casually?" But looking at the clothes, I realise there isn't anything casual there.

"No, you always want to make an entrance, as one day you will be their queen." Brennen smiles at me, removing a dress from the rack. The vivid blue matches Ta's eyes to perfection. It's stunning, but I've always wanted to disappear into the shadows, not stand out like some damn peacock. I obviously make a face as he quickly puts it back. "Or this one?"

I nod. I can work with that. He lifts it over my head, and I realise it has an in-built bra, which I'm glad for. My boobies are the kind of ones that need scaffolding to keep gravity from taking over. The handkerchief hem flutters around my thighs. It's a tad shorter than I'm used to but I must admit, while I'm twirling around like a right girly, it looks good. I wonder if I have any panties, before Brennen hands me the most miniscule pair of panties I have ever seen. They will just about cover my modesty and I roll my eyes at the way they are both grinning. Really? I raise an eyebrow, silently questioning them. But they only laugh as I slip them on.

Another member of staff walks in with a large container and sets it on one of the marble sides and opens it up. I peer in. It's make-up.

"I'd be honoured if you'd allow me to make you up." He smiles at me. He's about my age, but hey, that could mean he's about five hundred here.

"I don't really like a lot of make-up on, but if you can make me more presentable, that would be nice. Thank you."

I'm ushered into a nearby chair that's seated by a huge freestanding mirror and a floor lamp, which he switches on. I'm illumined in a soft white glow. He gets to work, telling me to look up or pull a weird face with my lips. I'm trying to watch while he works but don't really see much. When he's finished, I view myself in the mirror and gasp. I run my hand through my hair, it's so short that it soon falls into style. I cut it myself just after the pig spawned from hell dumped me, I took a pair of scissors to it and hacked it all off until it was close to my head. I think in posh salons it's called a pixie cut.

"Wow! That looks amazing. Thank you." I stand and hug him, I'm that surprised by what he's managed to do. He blushes and mumbles his reply, before hastily packing away the makeup and heading out, bowing to Brennen on the way.

"Shouldn't I have hugged him?" I ask, panicking that I'd just made a major no-no on this world.

Brennen takes me in his arms, hugging me tight. Ta, from behind, holds me tightly. "No, you've done nothing wrong, Little Flower. The males here are starved of the female touch, so when they receive it, they may not know how to act correctly. It's our failing, never yours."

"Now, give us a twirl," Ta demands, and they both let me go and take a step away. Their eyes hungrily trail over my body, and it blooms for them, my nipples peaking to hard little points.

"Fuck, you are perfect, and we will be the only ones knowing that you have those daring panties on." Ta's guttural growl has my heart speeding up. The utter dominance of the timbre obviously hits the spot with my girly bits.

Brennen's eyes travel from my toes, all the way up, until they caress my breasts.

"He's right, Little Flower. You are perfect. All you need is a pair of shoes." He leaves and returns with a pair of shoes that are covered in brightly-coloured stones. They look like rubies, sapphires and diamonds. I look at Brennen questioningly.

"We have an abundance of gems that would otherwise be precious on Earth, here on Mertier. We mine them so we can make our mates pretty things as women from Earth seem to like them," Brennen explains, slipping the shoes on my feet.

I have to admit to having a Cinderella moment. They aren't too high and fit perfectly. They are exquisite, and the gems sparkle in the light.

"I love them. Thank you." They seem happy with my response, and each take a hand and head to the door. "Hang on, you need to dress," I tell them, staring at their still naked bodies.

They look amused but hurried pull on clothing.

"We are taught that Earth women are not used to such nakedness." Ta laughs when I roll my eyes. "But you will get used to it. Around the private residences and some public ones, most are naked because it's hotter than on Earth."

"Well..." I'm not quite sure what to say. I'm not a prude but sometimes feel uncomfortable being naked in front of people. Being on the larger side, some people are so judgmental that I find it hard to bare all at times. I grip their hands as they lead the way downstairs and out to the grounds, where a group of women sit, chatting happily away. I slow, feeling nervous, as I know how bitchy a group of women can be towards one another. I've always hated being the new girl.

"What happens if they don't like me?" I whisper to the men, biting the inside of my mouth.

They stop and shield me from the women's gazes, lifting my chin up.

"They are going to love you," Ta tells me with a firm kiss to my forehead. Why are those kisses somehow more toe-curling good than a good, long snog sometimes?

Brennen brushes his knuckles down my cheek. For someone so large, he can be so gentle at times.

"And if they don't, tell us, and we'll have them killed," he says with a straight face that has my eyes widening with shock. But I see he's laughing, and I join in.

"See, once they see that pretty smile, they'll love you," Ta says, and they turn and walk me over to the women.

Alish stands, bows her head to Brennen, and gives me a huge smile. "Thank you for having us in your home," she tells us. "Araline, lass, come sit with us." Her gentle brogue washes over me, and I nod.

"Have fun, ladies," Brennen says, before looking me directly in the eye. "Remember what I said." He pulls a finger across his throat, which has me shaking my head as I try to keep the laughter from bubbling over.

"Enjoy," Ta tells us, before leaning down and kissing my neck. It's really a nuzzle, and I blush as the women look knowingly at us.

"Go, now," I mouth at them, and gently shoo them away.

Turning back towards the ladies, I smile and say, "Hi, I'm

Araline." They all smile back and shift over so I can join them.

"Araline, let me introduce you. Ladies, this is Araline, our future queen of Mertier. Araline, this is Petra, Simone and Zara."

The women smile and say hello. They are certainly a beautiful bunch and a mix of races.

Petra is of Chinese descent, with gorgeous deep hazel eyes, a petit, trim figure, and a long wave of ebony black hair hanging in a long rope down her back. Simone is French, and her elegant, polished look is totally a Parisian thing and something I could only envy but never quite achieve. Zara informs me she comes from Africa. Her weaved hair with multi-coloured beads swings as she talks. Her ample figure is covered in an ethnic tribal robe, and the intricate embroidery is breath-taking.

After all the introductions are finished, Alish asks, "How are you settling in?" She pours me a drink into a large glass goblet. This is encrusted with gems as well. *They must be using the good crockery.*

Taking a long sip, I think about my answer. Am I actually settling in? I sigh, looking at the ladies. They look polished, confident, and a world away from how I've felt all my life.

CHAPTER TWENTY-ONE

I watch the ladies. They are waiting expectantly, and I wonder just what they've been told about me. Can I trust them? I can't help it; my gaze lingers on their arms. Petra and Zara have the same markings Alish and Sha have, but Simone doesn't. I really need to know why some have these mysterious markings and some don't.

"It's not exactly where I saw myself this time last week," I murmur, more to myself than to them. Placing the goblet back on the table, I glance around the perfectly manicured garden. The splashes of bright colours of the overlarge flowers alongside what I presume might be fruit growing from the trees with purple roots. They are pretty spectacular. Earth seems muted in colour compared to this world.

Simone eyes me suspiciously but quickly covers it with a smile— a false smile that no one can see but me.

"Where did you expect to be? You are our next queen. You have been in training all your life for this, non?" She raises a delicate eyebrow and haughtily looks down her nose at me. Alish scrutinises her.

So, it's not been made public that Brennen brought me back instead of Macie. Perhaps I should make it known to everyone that it isn't me who is supposed to be here, that I'm not really their next queen. I feel like an imposter. I'm just about to pour my heart out when Alish comes to my rescue.

"I remember my arrival day," Alish tells us, patting my hand. "I think, no matter how much training you receive, you'll never be completely ready, and Araline has the added stress of knowing she's our next queen." She smiles at me encouragingly.

"Indeed." Simone drew the word out, as if she knew I've had no training whatsoever.

This is all I need; some petty, vindictive woman. I look at the others and can see what Simone is saying is mirrored in Zara's eyes, but thankfully not in Alish's and Petra's.

Petra leans over the table, gripping my hand. "I have a feeling about you, Araline. You will find your place, as we have all had to do." She glares at Simone, who stares right back, but the other two drop their eyes and nod in agreement.

"Okay, I have a question. What's with the markings on your arms? I've noticed some women have them, like Alish, Sha, Petra and Zara, but when we were shopping, I noticed others don't, like Simone. What's with that?" I watch as Simone turns her head away, muttering something about how I should have been educated about that before I arrived. I ignore her.

"I knew you had noticed mine at the hospital," Alish answers, a small, secret smile forming as she strokes her markings. "When we are mated to our males and the dragon has accepted you as his, the dragon marks us. It's a very magical moment in our relationships, and only women mated to dragons ever receive the marks."

"They are all different," I state, studying their arms more closely. I'm itching to touch them, but I'm guessing that would be rude and intrusive. Each one is beautiful and intricate, and I can see by their expressions that they love having them.

"The markings are personal to each mating." Petra smiles. "Each dragon will mark his mate to his individual taste."

"Does it hurt?" I ask. That's what I'm worried about. I don't do well with pain of any kind. I'm not a masochist.

"It's not pain, as such. It can be uncomfortable, but it's over in the blink of an eye," Alish says, her gaze flicking to Simone.

Simone delicately sniffs, plucks a better-than-chocolate seed from one of the crystal servers, and looks away.

I think it's time for a change of topic. Simone obviously doesn't like talking about this.

"I'm looking forward to exploring this world. What do you think I should look at first?" I try valiantly to save this afternoon. Sitting here and being scrutinised as if I'm some sort of bug under a microscope, feels like I'm in a school exam.

"Oh, I'd make time to visit the Seven Pools of Serenity." Petra closes her eyes as if remembering a special memory. "Book in advance— though saying that, if Prince Brennen just arrives, I'm sure they'll give him the day or the night for just you, him and Ta." She waggles her eyebrows at me, and I can't help but laugh.

"And just what are the Seven Pools of Serenity?" I pop a sweet seed into my mouth and almost moan, but manage to refrain, not wanting to look like a heathen in front of these sophisticated women. Even in this posh dress and shoes, I don't look as polished as these ladies, and I never will, no matter how hard I try.

The ladies laugh and glance at one another as if they were about to reveal a fabulous secret. I lean forward, biting my lip in expectancy.

"It's a magical place, lass, steeped in myths and legends. We believe it's where the dragons first came into being. When a dragon returns, it unlocks their more sensual side," Alish informs me. "I highly recommend you go with Brennen and Ta."

They are all smiling at each other, except for Simone. She's scowling at them all and turns it to me. *What the hell have I done now?* I brace myself for her catty remark.

"I hear it's wonderful for those mated to dragons. For us mere mortals, it's a special place for rejuvenating oneself." She huffs, facing me I see her eyes sparkle with anger, even hatred. "Not all of us have the privilege of being mated to a dragon." She sighs, looking away. "It might help if you were mated, Araline, before you set off for such a hedonistic place. And as you've not mated your males, yet... What's wrong with you?"

Well, now I understand why she didn't want to talk about the markings on the other ladies' arms. Petra and Zara shift uncomfortably and look anywhere but at me. I sigh, wanting to punch her in the gob, but clench my fists under the table, willing myself to behave. Alish bristles and is about to speak, but I raise my hand, wishing her to remain silent. She nods and settles back in her seat.

Staring Simone straight in the eyes, my resting bitch face firmly in place, I tell her, "I wasn't aware there was a timeframe in which to fuck them. Thank you for pointing it out. Now, why don't you piss off, and I'll get straight on it." I am fucking fuming. How dare she talk about my sex life, or lack thereof, as if it's up for common discussion.

Her face is a picture. She's obviously not used to being put in her place. I can't stand bullies. She's chosen the wrong opponent. *That's right, bitch, I bite back!* Sitting back, I watch her and raise an eyebrow, silently begging her to keep going.

"Well..." she spits out, "if I'm no longer required, *Your Majesty,*" she sneers, "I'll do as you suggest and piss off." She stands stiffly, waiting for the others to join her. When no one moves and it's clear she will be leaving alone, she tilts her head upwards, squares her shoulders, and stalks off. But I hear her mumble, "This isn't over."

CHAPTER TWENTY-TWO

To be honest, I'm a little shook up by it, so I take a healthy gulp of my drink.

Alish takes my hand, giving it a friendly squeeze. "I'm glad you stood up to her, lass. It's about time someone did. But a word of advice: watch your back. She's a nasty little viper."

"Then why the bloody hell did you invite her here?" I ask her, aghast that she would think someone like Simone would be nice to me.

Alish lowers her eyes, clearly upset about what's happened. "I keep trying to involve her, to bring her into our circle. But after all this time I should have known better." She looks sad and shakes her head. "I am sorry, Araline, lass. Forgive me. She won't be invited again."

Petra puts her arms around Alish. "You have got to cut her from your life. She's a jealous, mean little woman."

Looking at me, Alish continues, "She was promised to a

dragon warrior, one of Brennen's brothers you see, but he was killed in battle just a few days before her arrival. The Council decided to send another male to collect her but before she had the chance to go into the bidding, she was snatched by Talon." She closes her eyes and takes a deep breath; I'm holding mine as its gripping finding out why Simone is like how she is. "Who happens to be another cousin, but this one is from the king's brother who we don't talk about a lot, was put to death for treason, Talon and his brothers ran for their lives and created a camp which is now known as the Outsiders Camp, this is where she lives. We aren't allowed to socialise with them, but I feel such pity for her that I see her whenever I can. It was very wrong to bring her here. I see that now." Alish's face was full of anguish. "She took the knowledge of the fact that she was going to be put in the bidding very badly, as she was trained to be with a royal dragon, and one other ..." She closed her eyes as if reliving what had happened.

Petra gripped Alish's hand tightly. "But it's how she dealt with the news after she realised she was to be placed with a normal Mertier male and not a royal. She became rather bitter and angry with everyone," she whispers.

"So, she doesn't even live as you all do?" I know Alish's explanation is a simplistic version of what's really going on, but I save my questions for a later time. "I've heard of this bidding thing. I've been told I'll be put in if I don't mate with Brennen and Ta," I say in a hushed voice. I pity Simone, and can kind of understand why she's unhappy.

"Yes, and when Talon snatched her he gave her to five males. The total amount you can have," Alish says, her eyes wide with unshed tears.

"Bloody hell," I utter, shaking my head and refilling my goblet.

"She came from a royal lineage on Earth. She was trained to enter the royal court here, thinking she would have a dragon and one other male. The Council sent another male to bring her here and then Talon stole her. She had to be sedated for many months, according to the rumours. She hated everyone and everything, still does." Petra's eyes glaze over as she remembers, she gently dabs at them with an elegant handkerchief.

"Why is this Talon allowed to snatch women? Why aren't these Outsiders dealt with?" I question. I know I'm not up to speed with the laws here, but damn it, it sounds like he's a danger to everyone. "I'm surprised she's not committed suicide," I say. "I mean, if she's that unhappy."

"She has tried, many times," Zara informs me, she looks away, taking a sip of her drink, her brown eyes soft with tears. "They keep all weapons hidden and watch her every single hour of the day. She's been here over fifty years and is yet to be with child. If she were only to fall pregnant, I feel it would help her. Ground her in a way her males can't seem to."

"God, that's appalling. Why can't she just live by herself? Why does she have to live with all those males? It's barbaric and beyond inhumane," I ask the women. It's incomprehensible to me why their males' sexual needs seem to forfeit the women's.

"I know it seems wrong, but it's what works here and has done for many, many hundreds of years," Alish says, she grips my hand and her eyes will me to stop.

"Just because something's been done for forever, it doesn't

make it right." I'm angry. I feel so sorry for Simone, even if she's a bitch. I can understand why she's like she is.

"You have to remember, Araline, we knew this was to be our life, from infants. We accepted it. We welcomed it. If we had expressed that we didn't want it before we were due to come here, we wouldn't have arrived. Not a single one of us is forced into this life. But we did arrive, and we love our lives," Petra said thoughtfully.

"I get that, Petra. I can fully appreciate that you've been trained all your lives prior to arriving, you know and are happy with your lives. But how has Simone been treated by these other five? What happens to women put into the bidding? Do they just spread their legs willingly?"

They gasp their eyes wide as I take a deep breath. These women have lived a completely different life to me. I know I have no right to tell them it's wrong, because to them it's perfect, and to be completely honest with myself, it's a hell of a lot better than the one I've known on Earth. But I do know how Simone feels. I will have to find her and talk to her some more, but not right this second.

Zara continues, "Simone is ..." she taps her long fingernail, which is painted brightly to match her dress, on the table, "let us just say, difficult at times. There are already a few stories floating around about you, Araline. Not very flattering ones. That seems to have unhinged her further, because it's said you don't want to be with Brennen and Ta, and that's what she's craved since she was a child. If I can be so bold as to offer you some advice?" Her beautiful smile is aimed at me while her warm brown eyes evaluate me. She tilts her head questioningly, and I nod for her to carry on. "They say you aren't really Brennen's mate. They say you've not mated with him and Ta fully yet. The unmated males, if they find out— and sadly they will— will demand your name be put in the bidding draw for up to five of them to win you. I don't know the full story and I don't need to, but be warned, Araline: Simone, I think, will only fuel the fire if she can."

Well fuck! I fidget in the seat. I already know what she says is the truth. But can I really trust her and Petra?

"How many mates do you two have?" I ask them. I'm curious as to how this poly lifestyle works. Is there truly no jealously between the males? Do you keep a diary dictate who you're going to be with on what night?

"Both Petra and I are mated to dragons, as you can see by our markings. Every dragon will only accept one other male to share their woman with. The dragons can become very territorial once they are truly mated. You will understand more once you, Brennen and Ta are mated," Zara says, taking a sip of her drink.

"I'm confused. If what you say is true and the dragons become territorial of their women, why would Brennen's brothers, *all of them*, come calling to see if they could fuck me?" I ask, and it was only after looks of amazement from the other women that I wish I'd kept my gob shut.

The three women stare at me, and it's so silent that I can hear the brightly coloured birds, chirping away in the trees and the vermillion leaves fluttering in the warm air.

After an awkward pause, Alish comments, "We've not heard of that happening? I mean, we know it happens with non-royal households. The brothers are, sometimes, invited to share the woman for the first few weeks until she joins her mated males." She glances at Petra and Zara, who both shake their heads.

"We can't answer that for you, I'm afraid, lass. You'll have to take that up with Brennen and Ta. Perhaps it was because they could scent you've not mated yet? But I really don't know." She delicately shrugs her shoulders.

"So, basically, I have to fuck both men, otherwise in a few weeks I'm going to be in a bidding draw, and whoever ends up with me, maybe more than the two I've already got, I'll have to fuck them? That's about the gist of it, right?" I ask. "What about my choice? My rights? Or do I not have any here? It seems to be all about the men and their sex drives and demands."

Before anyone can answer, a booming male's voice fills the garden. "Where's my mate?"

My head swivels until I spy a colossal male. He is standing with his hands on his hips, with a sexy, brooding smile aimed at Zara, who stands and walks over to him. His hands run up and down her arms, tracing the intricate patterns before lifting her off her feet. She squeals happily as he spins with her in his arms.

"I have missed you. You've been gone far too long. Larz sent me to drag you home."

"Ryth, put me down. I need to introduce you to Brennen and Ta's mate— your future queen," she tells him. He allows her to slip down his body until her lips are at the right level, and then kisses her. Wow, what a kiss! I'm blushing on her behalf. Turning my head, I make a grab for my drink. I'm so not used to so many public displays of affection and it seems the males of this world don't know when to stop.

I glance at Alish and Petra. They are smiling wide as they watch the couple stroll over to us hand in hand.

"Are all the men oversized here?" I whisper, wondering if it's something in the water that made them so overpowering.

"Araline, let me introduce you to Ryth, one of my mates. He's a cousin of your male, Brennen. He's also one of Brennen's personal guards," Zara told me with obvious pride, as she ran her fingernail down Ryth's muscular shoulder. His low growl of pleasure had me swallowing hard. *Damn these dragons!* He's dressed in a skin-tight, black, sleeveless shirt, which only accentuates his muscled body, and black trousers matched with heavy-looking black combat boots.

"Another dragon, I take it?" I ask him, as he turns his attention to me. His dark blue eyes twinkle with mischief.

He bows low, and then stands to his full height. I look up and wonder when I had ever felt petit around men. But then, these weren't your run-of-the-mill human men. No, these were dragons. Ryth takes my hand and brings it up so he can lean down and rest his forehead against my knuckles.

"My lady, it's an honour to meet you. I did actually see you when Brenn joined us to fight the other day. But I was in my dragon form, so you probably don't remember me." His voice is a low cadence, and I can't help but smile.

"I don't, sorry. So, just how many cousins and other family members does Brennen have? They seem to be popping up everywhere," I ask.

"I'm one of seven cousins, and only three of us have our mates. You've met his brothers, so I'm told?" I nod.

"Araline, Ryth is Hunter's brother. They have two more brothers, Shade and Darius, from Brennen's father's brother,

Onix. The other brother, Jet, has three sons; Jovian, who is Petra's mate her second mate is Logan, then Stellen and Calix. There was a third brother, Talons father who we told you about earlier but we don't talk about him if we can help it." Zara laughs at my look of confusion. "Don't panic. Over time, you will become used to who is who." She smiles and waves just before they fly away.

Before I can ask Alish more about Talon's father, I hear the flap of wings and look up. There are two ginormous dragons landing in the gardens.

"There's my ride. Jovian," Petra calls out, sounding excited as she stands. She almost vibrates with longing as she stares at one of the dragons.

I follow her lead and stand, and she kisses my cheeks. "It was lovely to meet you. You must all come to ours next? I will introduce you to more of Brennen's cousins." She laughs, tucking a strand of hair behind her ear, a pure girly gesture, before she nods to us. She walks with such grace— something I'll never manage in a million years— to the two magnificent dragons. One bows his head and moves away, while the other lowers its great, hulking body to the floor so she can climb onto his back. His black eyes stare into mine and he snorts. I take that to be a hello of sorts and nod back. His wings unfurl and flap, and the great *whoosh* of sound has my breath stalling until he was up and flying away.

CHAPTER TWENTY-THREE

"I don't think I'll ever get used to that sight," I murmur to Alish, sitting back down, my eyes tracking the flying dragons.

She laughs and rises from the seat. "It was lovely to see you again, lass, but Hunter is becoming restless, and I know Steel will be home from training soon. We'll come and see you soon, or you and your mates could come to us?" She takes hold of my hands, smiling. "Trust in your mates and everything else will sort itself out. I promise you."

I see the happiness shining in her eyes. This woman is loved and loved well. I am more than a tad jealous. As I watch her walk over to Hunter, I think about how I want to feel that hunger of love, to know I was utterly accepted for who I was and all I could become. Hunter blows black smoke from his nostrils, and Alish giggles as his tail curls around her and sweeps her onto his back. He flies off, and it's incredible to watch. And then I'm all alone.

It's so quiet, so very peaceful, that I pluck up some of the chocolate tasting seeds and close my eyes as I lean back. The sublime taste bursts in my mouth. It's definitely a mouthgasm, and I can't keep the groan of pure pleasure in. I don't know how long I was out there, but I come to when angry voices reach me.

"How can she possibly be your mate, when I've heard that you've not even fucked her?" a male voice, full of menace, asks. "It's just like you royals to try and cover this shit up! My father was right about you! The news is spreading throughout the Districts, and I will help it reach everyone's ears. Even the palace won't be able to keep it quiet. You fucking greedy assholes want all the females to yourselves. Well, you won't be able to cover this up. I will make sure this is spread far and wide!" The voice has a touch of madness to it, and I shiver as I continue to listen.

"How the fuck did you get in here?" I hear Ta lose his cool and growl at whoever is here, but his question is ignored.

"She's not your fucking mate, Prince Brennen. You should do the right thing and put her up for bidding so ordinary males can stand a chance to win her. Or perhaps I should take her to the Outsiders." It's only when I hear 'Outsiders' that I realise who this must be.

Talon.

The shouting is getting closer, and I shrink back against the chair. My stomach drops. Damn, that Simone works fast. She's already run to him and told him everything she found out about me They'll be here at any moment, and I don't want to see this male who took her.

"Do you realise who you're threatening?" Ta demands angrily.

"As if I give a fuck about that, Ta," Talon shouts.

"You will never have a female like our mate, Talon. She is ours. You lost that right years ago when you chose to follow your father. Now go, before I send for the guard. If you'd like to go to war, then please do hang around," I hear Brennen sneer, before Talon rounds the corner. I cover my mouth in fear.

He's a huge brute of a man with a heavily scared face, but even that can't detract from how gorgeous he is. His fury-filled eyes lock with mine before they sweep over my body. I cringe back before Ta and Brennen quickly stand in front of me, blocking his view. So, everyone isn't happy about the system they have here, and if I'm put into the bidding, I could end up with four men this man?

"After all I've done for this world, for the fucking royals, you should bow before me," Talon says, then spits at their feet before stalking away.

After a few seconds of stunned silence, Ta pulls me into his arms. "I'm sorry you had to witness that, Araline."

Brennen is talking into their communication device "When was Talon freed?" he demands to know from whomever is on the other end. That's all I hear before he moves out of hearing range. I'm shocked by what's just occurred, but I want to hear more.

"What's going on, Ta?" I ask, as he sits with me on his lap. I try to squirm away but he's not having any of it.

He sighs, and his warm breath floats over my neck. He takes a few seconds before answering. "We have a few, only a few, who seem to think all women who are brought here should go directly into the bidding, so everyone has a fair chance to win her. It's been heating up over time, with more believing that's the proper way." He wraps his arms around me, as if he needs comfort. "They've moved out of our city to live in the wilderness beyond the city's borders. We call them the Outsiders. This is the first time Talon, or anyone, has dared to breach the palace. The royal dragons will want retribution for this threat."

"Yes, Alish did explain a little about them. Is Talon their leader?" I ask, wondering what the hell I've been dragged into.

"Yes, he is, and has only just been released from jail. They didn't think to let us know," Brennen answers as he joins us. Sitting by us, he leans in and kisses my shoulder. I shouldn't like that so much. Really, I shouldn't.

"He probably sneaked in with Simone as one of his men is one of Simone's mates," Ta states.

I gasp. "So let me get this straight; Simone is living beyond the city with a group of outlaws, so to speak? And the ladies wonder why she's like she is?" I shake my head, feeling sorry for her. "She was meant to have been with a dragon, right? Your brother, Brenn? I'm so sorry he's passed, what was his name?"

He grips my hand tightly, "Thank you, his name was Malachite. He was lost during a terrible fight, just before he was due to go and bring back Simone." His voice is low and full of emotion.

I squeeze his hand back, taking a breath I carry on. "But even before she was put into this barbaric bidding system of yours, Talon snatched her and merrily handed her off to five men. Who are all probably like Talon?" I purse my lips, not happy at all with the news. I fully understand why she's like she is now. That Talon looked like he could be a mean son of a bitch, never mind how stunning he was… I can't suppress the shudder.

"We were hoping that by not going to war with the Outsiders when they took her, she would tame them, and they would come back into the Districts. But unfortunately, it's incited them to want more and more," Brennen says sadly, looking off into the distance, worry etched on his face.

I pull away and glare at them both. "So, not only do you have people not on this world that come here regularly to attack you, but you also have a select few living in a kind of wilderness that are angry and want all the women for themselves? Fuck me, thanks for dragging me out here, Brennen." I sneer his name, totally fed up. "You know that everyone knows we've not fucked yet, right? Like it's okay to talk about my sex life in public. I didn't ask for any of this shit!" I struggle until Ta lets me go.

I walk away, though it's more of an unladylike stomp, and head upstairs to the bedroom, where I fling myself, childlike, onto the bed. Closing my eyes, I sigh.

It's not long before the bed dips as their huge bodies join me.

"Can't you leave me alone for, like, five minutes?" I mumble into the pillow, not wanting to even look at them.

"What did Simone say to you?" Brennen asks, running a hand up and down my back, the dress offering no barrier from the heat radiating from his touch.

I huff. "It doesn't matter. I told her to piss off and she left. She's not happy with me. But finding out more about her, I can kind of see why. Did you know that since she couldn't have your brother and one other mate, she's now stuck with five men and has tried to commit suicide multiple times? Can't you see..." I passionately inform them, sitting up. "This way of bringing up women from Earth and them not getting a choice in how they live, is wrong."

"Little Flower, it's the way it's always been done," Brennen says, a frown firmly in place. "Give us and this world a chance. I promise you; you'll fall in love with it."

"That doesn't make it right!" I cry out. "I can't do this. You have to find a way to get me home!" I stumble out of the bed and run for my life out of the palace.

I can hear heavy footsteps following me. I'm not exactly the fittest of people, and they catch me before I leave the palace's grounds. A scream leaves my throat as I'm scooped up effortlessly into Brennen's arms as if I weigh far less than I actually do. These dragons are damn strong. I start to cry; not delicate, girly tears but great, heart-wracking sobs. Ugly tears.

Brennen's body is hot; not in the gorgeous way— don't get me wrong, it is *stunning*— but I keep forgetting their body temperature is far higher than I'm used to. It actually feels heated to the touch. *It must be the fire breathing dragon inside him?* They make it back to the bedroom, where I'm placed in the middle of the bed. They quickly join me.

I'm exhausted. All these spikes and crashes of emotions are taking a toll. I'm too tired to care that I'm in bed with two men. I sniff and wipe my face. Sighing, I close my eyes, praying sleep finds me. I just can't deal with them at the moment.

~

I'm dreaming.

The man I met earlier in the garden, with the scarred face, has kidnapped me, and I'm living with his group of men. There are five of them in total, and they pass me between them like a plaything. They aren't gentle. They don't care if I'm enjoying what they're doing or not. They keep shouting at me to just take it; it's their right to mate with me. I feel their hands, mouths and other parts of them all over my body as they violently take what they want. I'm crying and begging them to stop, but they don't listen. My body is hurting in places that should never feel pain.

They are so excited to finally have a female that they don't care if my body isn't used to being fucked the way they are doing it.

They are all dirty, smelly, and I gag when a cock is shoved down my throat. I contemplate biting it, when the man who took me fists my hair and whispers, "If you bite him, or try to hurt any of us, you think this is bad? It'll go downhill pretty fast. Don't be a stupid bitch. Just take us."

Oh fuck, I can't breathe. He's too big. I'm going to be sick. If my hands were free, I'd try to punch him, but someone is holding them behind my back. They are going to kill me. There are catcalls and shouts of encouragement from men all around me. I'm surrounded by them, all waiting a turn. I want to die. Please let me die.

"Wake up, Little Flower!"

I hear a distant voice calling to me and feel my shoulders being shaken. I know that voice. Brennen. I come to slowly and scream out the pain and terror of my dream. I punch away the arms surrounding me, frantic to not be touched. For fuck's sake, the men... they were hurting me— they were raping me. I sob, my mind confusing Brennen and Ta for those other men.

"What the hell?" Ta looks horrified, and Brennen, using considerable strength, but gently pins my arms so he can pull me in tightly against his chest.

"She's had a nightmare. I'm not surprised really. Are you?" Brennen asks, then makes soothing noises and strokes my back. All I can do is whimper against his chest.

Ta moves in closer and wipes away my tears. "Araline... please, honey, you're breaking my heart here." He presses his lips against my neck.

My body slowly stops trembling, and when the overwhelming panic has subsided, I pull back and look first at Brennen, then at Ta. The acute fear I felt in the dream is still very real, but I'm slowly coming back.

"Do you want to tell us what that was about?" Brennen asks softly, wiping more tears away as they track down my cheeks.

I shudder and pull away, breaking contact with them both. I sit up and bring my knees to my chest, resting my chin on them. Taking a few deep breaths, I try to slow my galloping heart.

"The man with the scarred face, who we saw within the grounds earlier— Talon? He came back and kidnapped me. He brought me to a place where five of them took turns in raping me. It was rough..." I falter as a tear runs down my cheek. "They enjoyed hurting me." I bow my head as emotions swamp me.

I don't see the look of horror in both men's eyes as they hold me between their bodies.

CHAPTER TWENTY-FOUR

*T*a and Brennen scoot up the bed, and their arms engulf me in a hug that warms me from the inside out. Resting his chin on the top of my head, Brennen says softly, "We'd never allow anyone to hurt you, Little Flower. Even if…" He pauses, and I hear him try to clear his throat, as if whatever he was going to say is difficult for him. I hold my breath, wondering what he's going to say. "Even if you decide you can't or won't stay with us, we will still watch over you. You have my word. My dragon would demand that of me, even if I couldn't bear to see you with anyone else. He has feelings for you also, Araline."

My eyes slowly lift to meet his, and I can sense the sincerity of what he just said. A tear slips free, and he gently brushes my cheek to wipe it away.

"Even if you don't feel anything for us yet, no matter what happens, Araline, I will always be here for you," Ta tells me. He brushes his knuckles against my other cheek, and I sniff, rubbing my eyes. He hands me a glass of the refreshing water and I gulp it down. It goes a long way to help calm me.

"I have a suggestion: let's go and relax in the bath for a while. I know you might not be up for it now— fully understandable— but we've been invited to my parent's for a banquet. To welcome our mate to Mertier," Brennen says, his breath hot against my skin.

I take a deep breath. "I'm not sure I want to meet your dad again, Brenn. He's fierce. I don't think he likes me." I pull back until I could look into his eyes. That's a mistake, as they hold me in a stare that's filled with passion. I lean back, which only makes my body hit the hard wall of Ta's muscles.

"Once he has the chance to get to know you, I know he'll love you. Alish will be there, and some of the women you met yesterday. In fact, you'll get the chance to meet everyone. But it's your decision. We'll do whatever you want." Brennen gives me a gentle smile, and I notice he has a dimple just to the right side of his mouth. It's cute, and it makes me want to kiss it.

It sounds like he has a big family. It was only ever me and my parents. I'm not sure I'll be able to handle them all en masse.

"My father, Azure, will be there as well. He's dying to meet you, Araline. But as Brenn said, after that dream, we will totally understand if you want to stay home tonight." Ta kisses my neck, and I can't suppress the shiver of need.

It's not my fault. These men are simply too sexy for their own good. Before I do something I might regret, I nod. "A long soak sounds good. I'll think about the banquet later."

The dream is slowly dissolving, and I feel less scared.

They pull back, allowing me space to get off the bed, and walk with me to the room that has the stunning bath. As soon as we enter, the heat from the silver water hits me. It reminds me of a sauna I visited once, long ago. Ta pulls me to him, and we step to the side as Brennen shifts into his dragon form. I freeze, holding my breath. No matter that I know he's a bloody dragon, actually seeing it leaves me breathless. I guess that will never change.

"Breathe, Araline," Ta whispers in my ear, holding me close as we watch the dragon sink into that strange silver water. He comes up for air, shaking his long mane of inky black hair, and I hear him making a strange noise. I realise he's laughing. The damn dragon is playing in the water. I smile as I watch his antics, my heart slowing as he ducks and comes up over and over. As he rises once more, he sucks in a load of water.

"Don't you dare, Brenn!" Ta is laughing, even though he barks out the order. Before I can ask what's going on, the dragon lets loose a deluge of water.

It hits us, and if Ta weren't holding onto me, I'd have been flung across the room, it's that powerful. As it is, I'm left looking like a drowned rat. The silk dress is stuck to my curves like an obscene wet T-shirt contest, and my hair is plastered to my head. I lean over, resting my hands on my knees as I cough, trying to get the water out of my lungs.

"Bloody hell!" I moan between gasps. Ta pats my back before removing his soaked clothes. As I glance up, still bent over, my eyes are level with his cock, and I start choking all over again. My eyes are streaming. Damn, get a load of that thing. His cock is a thing of beauty. He doesn't have the extra bit like Brennen has and I wonder if it's a dragon thing. He steps back, and I stand, my eyes not quite meeting his. He laughs. Somehow the git knows I was checking out his cock. Well, he did put it right there! I huff. At least my breathing is back to normal, but now my heart is racing at the sight of him naked again.

I avert my eyes and pull off the sodden dress. It lands at my feet with a squishy *thud*. I'm left in those miniscule panties, and they offer little coverage. I blush; it's a bodily reaction I can't seem to control as Ta reaches for my hand and leads me to the water.

Standing at the edge, the silver water gently laps at my feet. I nervously watch the dragon, who is curled up, sitting on the floor in the deep end of the pool.

"Can he breathe underwater, or does he hold his breath for a really long time?" I ask Ta. I watch as he sinks under the water before answering me. When he stands up, I have to make sure my mouth is closed as my jaw wants to drop. I swallow hard, watching the water sluice down his body.

Thoughts— delicious, sexy, scandalous thoughts of what I'd love to do with him— flash before my eyes. I feel my nipples bead and quickly cross my arms, shaking my head, thankful he seems oblivious to my reaction.

"He can hold his breath a long time, and in this water, as it revives dragons, maybe even longer? We've not timed him though." He shrugs and dives back in.

I follow him in and notice the water once again gives my skin an iridescent shine. Floating on my back, I try not to worry that there's a huge black dragon under me, complete with razor sharp fangs and spikes on its tail. The water rolls, and I know he's on the move. I close my eyes until I feel a warm breath blow across my face. When I open them, I see two huge black eyes. He pulls his lips back in what I can only presume is a smile, but all I can see is wicked sharp fangs. *All the better to eat you with.*

I try not to panic, though can't help but back pedal a bit. He follows and nudges my arm.

"You want me to pet you?" I ask with a nervous laugh. His head bobs up and down rather enthusiastically. "Okay then." Lifting my hand up, I gently stroke down his face, over his muzzle, and down the side of his jaw. I swim around him and stroke as much of his mammoth body as I can reach.

Lost in my own little world, I don't feel Ta approach until he's lifting me out of the water. I let out an unladylike squeal, and then I'm sitting with my legs spread as far as they go on the dragon's back. He's sunk back down, so his nostrils are just out of the water, but my feet are still dangling nowhere near it. God, he's bloody huge!

Ta hefts himself up and wraps his arms around my waist. He grips the dragon's mane, keeping me upright as he starts a lazy swim around the pool. It's surreal. I wonder if I've been in a car accident or something, and this is my head injury coming to life. But I'd never in a million years have thought my life would end up on a strange planet with two mates. One a fire-breathing dragon and the other with magical, healing hands. Unknowingly, my hand pets the dragon. I love how he feels to touch.

"Hold your breath, Araline," Ta shouts, just before the dragon ducks and swims under water. I manage to suck in a breath before we are under. He moves with such grace for something so large. We aren't under for long, but I'm still gasping when we resurface.

Ta lets me go, sliding off the dragon's back, splashing me as he plops into the water.

I follow and slide as ladylike as I can off the dragon's back. It was a good idea to use the bath. I must admit, the water has made me calmer after that horrific dream. I swim to the edge, where there are sunken lounge seats set up, and lay down in one. The headrest allows a perfect view of the pool, and I can't help but admire Ta's body once more.

He's not doing anything provocative; it's just the way his body moves in the silver water. He is utterly mouth-watering. I want to take a chunk out of him. My lady parts heat up like it's Christmas or something.

Closing my eyes, my thoughts turn serious. I can either accept that this is my life, or keep fighting. I'm here with two of the most gorgeous men I've ever seen, and they seem to want to be with me. I could live a far better life here than I could have dreamed of on Earth. I bite the inside of my cheek and ponder whether to jump whole heartedly into this new life or keep trying to escape. Bloody hell, when did life become so damn complicated?

Opening my eyes, I watch the dragon amble to the shallow end and shift, and there's Brennen, all naked. I let out a soft gasp. Have I ever seen such a fine example of manliness? Nope, I don't think I have. He turns to face me and gives me a wicked grin. He is seriously sex on legs. I want to lick him all over like a lollipop. And now I'm blushing like mad!

"I'd love to know what is going on in that mind of yours." The low, sexy timbre of his voice sends my lower bits into a flurry of need. *Hush now!* He walks into the water and swims over to me. I can actually see his powerful muscles flexing as he moves gracefully under the water. He comes up and rests his elbows on my lounger. He's very close, and his body heat blankets me. My nipples harden again, and his eyes zoom in as a sexy grin raises his lips.

"You like watching mine and Ta's bodies, don't you, Little Flower?" he states. I can't really refute it, not with my nipples silently screaming for him to take one in his mouth and suck it.

I nod, not trusting my voice.

Ta swims up and joins Brennen on the other side of me. I'm in trouble now.

"I like her watching us. It's good to know she finds our bodies pleasing," Ta says, before his lips press against mine in such a sweet, gentle kiss, it has me sighing into his mouth. His kiss is confident and lazy, not rushing me, giving me time to pull away if I want to.

I don't want to.

While I'm kissing Ta, Brennen leans in and takes a nipple into his mouth. The heat from it makes me cry out. My back arches, silently demanding more, and Brennen listens. Using his fingers, he teases the other nipple while using powerful suctions to bring the other to an almost painful peak.

My tongue slides against Ta's as they tangle in our mouths. Fuck, he can bloody kiss. His hand is in my hair, which is quite short, but he fists it and keeps my head immobile, and I love the domination. He's taking what he wants now, not asking permission. It's a devastating kiss that leaves me panting and making all sorts of noises I think a porn star would find hard to beat. I'm sure I should be embarrassed by them, but I don't care.

Brennen's fingers explore my body, heading downwards, until they find my clit. He teases and circles it before rubbing with powerful strokes.

"Oh, oh!" I have to pull away from the kiss as my body bows off the seat, my eyes close, and I lose myself in sensations.

CHAPTER TWENTY-FIVE

With my eyes tightly closed, I allow my body to feel what these men are awakening. I so desperately need to come; the noises that leave my mouth, I should be shocked, should be. Raising my hips, I grind them into Brennen's hand, demanding more. I'm practically rubbing myself off on his fingers.

"That's it, Little Flower, show me how you like it," Brennen commands, his fingers taking me higher and higher as Ta leans over me to suckle on a nipple. It's peaked and utterly sensitive as his mouth makes love to it.

"Please..." I moan loudly, then shriek as Brennen's fingers enter me, roughly fucking me in time with his thumb brushing over my clit. My body tightens as I'm thrown headfirst into the most blistering release ever. It takes my breath away and leaves me panting against the lounger. I hardly feel it when Ta takes his mouth away and Brennen removes his fingers. My eyes flutter open and I watch as Brennen licks his fingers clean. Why is that so damn hot?

"I am addicted to how you taste, Araline. I could eat you all day long," he growls. I'm enthralled as his dragon scales shimmer just under his skin.

Reaching up, my fingers trace them, and I watch as he shudders from my touch. It's fascinating to see and to know that this man can change into a hulking black beast at any time he sees fit.

"You are beautiful to watch when you come, Araline. I want to do that again and again," Ta informs me. He's staring at my nipple as if he's starving and it's his favourite treat. Glancing down, I see it's still rock hard, perky, and glistening from his attention.

I don't really know what to say to all that. My body is blushing all shades of red as I lower my eyes. Do I thank them for the orgasm? Do they want to fuck now? My eyes ping open at the thought.

They chuckle, obviously guessing where my thoughts have taken me.

"Don't worry, Little Flower, we won't ravish you any more tonight. Besides, we have to get ready for the banquet— if you'd like to go?" Brennen asks, as they help me out of the lounger. We swim over to the shallow end. My limbs are quite uncoordinated as I'm still feeling delicious aftershocks from my release.

Once I can stand, I walk out of the bath with them on either side. Glancing surreptitiously down their bodies, I see they are both rock hard. Now I feel selfish. It can't be comfortable to be that hard and get nothing in return for what they both so generously gave me. I slow my walk and they turn to face me. Taking a deep breath, I blush again. Really, this blushing malarkey must stop. I'm a grown woman, not a blushing virgin!

"Do you two need any help with, um, those?" My hands wave in the general direction of their cocks. Just what the hell I'm going to do with them if they say yes, I've no idea. I gulp at the possibilities.

They both chuckle again and take my hand, leading us to where all the clothes are. I look around for towels but remember we don't need them as the silver water dries off naturally.

"There's not enough time for what we want to do with you when you finally get your hands on our bodies, Little Flower," Brennen says softly, and Ta nods in agreement.

I can't tell them, but my body aches for them now. To do what with it exactly, I've no idea, but I have a vivid imagination as to what they have in mind. *I don't want that. I do want that... No, I don't.* I roll my eyes, take a steadying breath, and turn to look at the gorgeous clothes I now own.

"Okay, let's do this, but what do you wear to a royal banquet?" I ask, biting my lip. My nerves are beginning to creep in. My first introduction to Brennen's mother and father, the queen and bloody king, didn't go too well and I'm worry how other members of the family will react to me. Plus, there are bound to be members of the public there. I step away from them. I'm heading towards an anxiety attack if I don't stop panicking.

Brennen wraps his arms around me. "Breathe, Little Flower. No one will hurt you. I promise you. Once they get to know you, they will come to love you. Breathe for me." He correctly guesses where my wayward thoughts have drifted off to, while Ta runs his hand down my spine, trying to soothe me.

"Let us introduce you to our families, correctly. My father is just going to love you. Wait and see." Ta smiles as I turn in Brennen's arms to face him.

Taking a deep, steadying breath, I nod. If I don't want to be put into that damn bidding draw this planet does, I have to at least try to accept and make a go of this life I'm now living.

"Let us dress you." After a few moments of hesitation, I nod. Ta leans in for a quick kiss, before walking over to a rack of the dresses they seem to love me in so much.

They're all in vivid jewel colours and not the plain black I usually choose to wear. They are all beautiful and I had always wished I'd been able to wear such clothes on Earth. Even though I've worn their choice in clothing since being here, they are still way out of my comfort zone. It screams *look at me, look at my body*. I get that it's hotter here than on Earth, and less clothing probably makes complete sense. I watch as Ta brings me the dress that he seems to like best.

It's a gorgeous ruby red and the softest silk I've ever touched— not that I've touched much silk. It's a wrap over design, with a plunging neckline and a split up the legs to almost indecency. My hands are reaching for it before I realise what I'm doing.

"Go and try it on, Little Flower," Brennen encourages me, gently pushing me away from him. It's then I remember I'm naked, so I quickly undo the only button, keeping it together, and slip it on. It flows like water over my skin and feels utterly divine. Short, floaty sleeves cover my upper arms, which I'm self-conscious about, and there's a hidden built-in bra.

I look questioningly at them, raising my eyebrow. "Um, panties please. I'm not going out in public without any, especially to meet your families." I watch as Brennen walks away and presses a sealed part of the wardrobes. They slide open, revealing panties, rows and rows of panties in a rainbow of colours, and I breathe a sigh of relief. I really don't want to go commando tonight but will still have to move carefully, if I don't, I could unintentionally flash them to everyone. Christ, how embarrassing would that be if I flash my panties to the king and queen? I gulp.

"Fuck, Araline, you look ravishing! I want to peel it off you and fuck you senseless," Brennen growls, his eyes taking a slow appraisal of me. His facial expression shows raw need and makes me step back.

"He's right, Araline, that red with your black hair and pale skin is pretty amazing. I love that it's shorter than other women's here. It shows off your graceful neck, so I can just lean in like this..." I feel his mouth on my neck, and goose bumps erupt as his lips glide over my skin.

"Yes, your hair is very individual to you. I bet others will copy it soon," Brennen says. Mirroring Ta, he kisses my neck.

There's a discreet cough from the doorway, and the young male who did my make-up for the meeting yesterday is here, holding his box of wonders again.

Ta leads me over to the make-up station and I sit in the white leather swivel chair, smiling at him. "Are you going to work your miracle again? I'm Araline, by the way."

He blushes as he sets up. "It's nice to meet you, Araline."

He bows his head to me. "I am Landon, and it's my honour to work with you."

"We will leave you in Landon's capable hands, Araline, and come back in half an hour." Brennen kisses my lips, and Ta follows the sentiment soon after. They are still naked, and I can't help but to admire the view of their bums as they head off to where their clothes are hanging.

While Landon works, he gently hums to himself. I do as I'm told and pull the different faces as he requires, but most of the time I'm watching Brennen and Ta in the mirror. Their bodies make my insides clench as they pull on their clothes. I've only really seen them in what I consider combat clothes. These are vastly different.

Once dressed, Brennen looks every inch a regal royal. He's wearing what I'd call ceremonial robes with tapestry-like, detailed pictures of his dragon during battle. The precious gems, that I am told are in abundance on this planet, are stitched in delicate patterns around the neckline and sleeves. On top of the robe is a long cloak that drapes across his body until it reaches the floor. It's edged with a wide cuff of intricate tapestry that's covered in more gems. It makes his shoulders look impossibly wide. On an Earth man, it might look a bit... well, effeminate, but on Brennen, it takes my breath away at how masculine he looks.

He's downright gorgeous. He turns to face me, giving me his 'making-my-panties-wet' smile. Landon helps me off the seat. I've not looked at his work yet. My eyes are still locked on Brennen. While I'm eye-fucking a dragon, Landon slips my feet into gem encrusted shoes. I glance back at the full-length mirror and a small gasp leaves my throat.

"Damn, Landon, what have you done to me?" I get closer to examine myself. Is that me? The make-up is amazing, a lot more than I would normally wear, more vivid, but damn! I'm loving the vermillion glossy lips. I almost look pretty. I have fake eyelashes on for the first time, and I flutter them. They have tiny black feathers attached to them. They look as if they'd be annoying, but I can hardly feel them. My hands gently touch my hair. He's placed rubies amongst my short lengths, and I sparkle as I turn my head.

Ta and Brennen walk towards me. Ta is wearing a white suit. The jacket is a much longer length than you'd find on Earth, almost reaching his knees. Travelling up one sleeve is Brennen's dragon, embroidered in all its glory and shooting fire, with gems that seem to make it dance. All along the hem of the jacket is the same pattern as on Brennen's robe. Again, it's nothing like I'm used to, but he makes it so sexy. I lick my lips, forgetting the lipstick that's been painted on them. I quickly glance at the mirror, worried I've ruined the look, but it's still there.

"Don't worry; the makeup will stay in place until you remove it when you've finished with it. No matter if you rub it or go swimming in it," Landon informs me while he places a small bottle and pads on the table for me. I nod. Okay, that's good. He bows to Brennen and then to me and Ta before leaving.

"Thank you, Landon," I call out to him, just before he's out of hearing range.

Both men have wide grins on their faces as their eyes track up and down my body. I look down, tugging at the gorgeous dress, feeling self-conscious. This get up is nothing like I usually wear. My clothes were all dark as I didn't like bringing attention to myself. I've never been a sexy, confident girl. Gym classes at school were hell! The other girls, over the years, chipped away at any self-confidence I had until I was left wanting to blend into the shadows.

"You look ravishing, Little Flower," Brennen whispers. He takes my hand and slowly twirls me.

Ta whistles. "Brenn, I don't know if I want any other males seeing our mate looking this good."

I stand still, warily watching them, seeing if this is just one huge cosmic joke. But they look like they're entranced. I've seen a few of my friends' boyfriends looking at them like this, but I've never experienced anyone looking at me with such longing. I have to admit, it's a heady feeling. I smile shyly at them both.

"I know how you feel, Ta." Brennen sighs. "Let's hope no one steps over the mark with her tonight, otherwise my dragon will make an appearance. He's very territorial about her already." He shakes his head and rolls his shoulders, as if the dragon is trying to come out now.

"Let's go. Once tonight is over and everyone's met her, we might be left in peace." Ta grips my hand as we follow Brennen out of the palace.

CHAPTER TWENTY-SIX

We head outside and find the sleek, silver flying vehicle is waiting for us. My stomach flutters, and not in a good way. I'm really not good at flying. I'm not sure of the time; it's obviously night-time as there are no suns shining, and I love the soft pink glow that the two moons give off. It's far warmer than the days back home in England that I'm used to. I look up and stare at the millions of stars that pattern the sky. It's so pretty. I shiver as I think of the people who live so far away but keep coming to this planet and attacking it.

I follow them into the cool interior, which is welcome after the heat of the night. They strap me in and sit on either side of me, each taking a hand. I grip them more tightly than I should. But I'm nervous, I'm about to meet the royal family again, their friends and Ta's father. I take a deep breath, I can do this! But I'd still prefer to arrive by a good old-fashioned car any day.

"If you're ready, My Lord?" The pilot swivels to look at Brennen, waiting for his orders.

"Yes, thank you," Brennen replies, and through the front screen I see the flag fluttering with its dragons proudly depicted.

I take a few steadying breaths and close my eyes as we start to move. My heart beats wildly. I can feel it pounding. I put their hands to good use by squeezing them.

Ta's fingers gently stroke my face. "It'll be fine, Araline." He leans close and places whisper-soft kisses to my neck. With my eyes still closed, I concentrate on what he's doing, which feels pretty good, by the way.

Brennen joins Ta. I feel their velvet soft lips and heated breath, and my head falls back, resting on the window behind us. I forget there's someone else with us until my stomach lurches and I feel us drop to the ground. I won't mind traveling this way if the men come up with inventive ways to keep my mind occupied and by looking at the desire on their faces, I know they are up to the task.

Brennen takes my hand, which, embarrassingly, is still clutching his in a deadlock grip, and places it on his straining cock. He kisses his way up my neck and whispers, "This is what you do to me, Little Flower."

I stare into his eyes like a rabbit caught in the headlights. A cough brings me back, and I blush as the driver opens the door and the steps appear. It's then I remember my hand is still on Brennen's cock. I whip it away, and Ta chuckles as he stands. His hand is still gripping mine, so I have no choice but to also stand. My legs feel a bit wobbly because of what these two were doing to my neck. I rub it, hoping there's no marks. It would be rather embarrassing if I had love bites when we are here for me to meet the important people of Mertier.

The driver winks at me as the men help me down the steps, and I get my first glimpse of the royal palace. Wow, just wow.

Now this is more like what I envisaged a royal palace should look like.

This place makes Brennen's and Ta's place looks squalid. It's a gorgeous, shimmering palace made with the same white marble-like stone they favour here. It has more guards than I can count, patrolling the grounds. It's so high, I have to crane my neck to see the top. On multi-levels the walls seem to be missing entirely, and I can just make out glamorous gardens dotted between floors. How it stays standing is beyond me. There are no walls running around the property to keep people out. None that I can see anyways. But as I squint, I can see some sort of iridescent force field surrounding the palace. I guess whatever it is, it would hurt you, if you were foolish enough to try and walk through it uninvited.

Brennen lifts me down the last step, what sounds similar to a trumpet heralds our approach and the huge, intricately carved doors of the palace slide open. The guards form a walkway for us to pass before I spot Brennen's father and mother, Kyanite and Sha. A man who I presume is Ta's father stands with them. The elder people of this planet scare me. They are so regal. I slow my walk and both men slow with me. Glancing down at me, they smile encouragingly.

I grip their hands tightly. "Don't leave me alone at any time tonight," I order them under my breath. They nod as I plaster on a smile. I have a feeling it looks more like a grimace.

"Brennen, Ta." Kyanite's deep voice greets them both. He grips each of their forearms with firm shakes. They bow their heads and step back. He scrutinises me. "Araline, it's lovely to see you again," he tells me. Before I have a chance to answer, Sha pulls me into a hug, and I can feel my body trembling.

"It's good to see you again. Just breathe. I promise you, no one will hurt you here." She pulls back and her face crinkles into a smile.

"Araline, can I introduce my father, Azure." Ta takes my hand and leads me until I'm standing in front of a man who's the spitting image of Ta. When he smiles at me, I see he's got a few crow's feet around his eyes and specks of grey in his hair. But otherwise, he doesn't look much older than his son. I blush as he takes my hand and rests his forehead against it.

"Welcome, Araline." He releases my hand, and I'm all a flutter. His eyes glitter, and I can tell he's a lot of fun. "It's about time these young whippersnappers had someone to keep them in line." He winks at me as he takes a step back, and I'm back in front of Kyanite and Sha.

They certainly are a formidable couple. It's then I look at what they are wearing. Their outfits scream royalty, wealth, and utter confidence. Kyanite's wearing an outfit not too dissimilar to Brennen's. A long cloak covers a suit that is intricately embroidered with his dragon. Strapped across his chest is an old-looking sword, the handle covered in gemstones. God, these dragons are huge men. I can feel he's trying hard not to be so intimidating, but he's not really pulling it off.

Sha is stunning in all her royal glory. Her spiky crown matches the metal and stones of Kyanite's sword. She has matching stones dripping along her low neckline, around her tiny waist, and covering her shoes. Her gown is a vibrant blue that matches her twinkling eyes. It would look like overkill on anyone else, but on Sha, it just adds to her beauty.

I try and shrink back into Brennen and Ta. I feel like a dumpy carthorse suddenly let loose in a paddock of thoroughbreds. Twinkling music starts just as Sha says, "That's our cue. I think people are becoming impatient to meet you and we are hogging you to ourselves." She grips my hands, smiling. "Again, welcome to Mertier. I am so glad my son finally has his mate." Giving my hands a last squeeze, she turns and takes the arm of Kyanite and they start walking into the imposing building.

I look into Brennen's eyes. The dark navy colour seems to swirl before he blinks, and I see his dragon's eyes staring at me. He glances down my body in a slow perusal and gives me a slow, appreciative grin. Another blink and Brennen nods to me encouragingly.

"You can do this, Little Flower," he tells me softly, as we start to walk.

With both men holding my hands, we enter. I'm so utterly thankful they are here as we walk over what appears to be thousands of red flower petals in intricate patterns covering the floor. We are soon in a room that is just enormous, with hundreds of tables where people stand as soon as they see us. The trumpet instrument announces us again.

We make a slow procession as we are stopped by people wanting to be introduced. My hand is pressed into many male foreheads and the women bow respectively. Their clothes are all brightly coloured and gemstones are sparkling in abundance. I don't remember any of their names. There's far too many to recall. As we head towards a long table that faces the room, I spot Brennen's brothers, all looking rather different now they are dressed in all their finery. They make a stunning group of men.

At one of the tables nearest to our long one, Alish gives me a wave. Smiling and pointing down her body, she indicates she loves my dress and nods encouragingly. She's with her mates, Hunter and Brogan. This is the first time I've seen Brogan, and I have to wonder if there's something in the strange silver water that makes all the men of this world mouth-wateringly gorgeous.

Also sat at their table are the two other ladies she brought to meet me. Zara, who will always remind me of a glamorous tribal princess, is sat with Ryth and her second mate Larz. Her glistening black skin is a stark contrast to Ryth's as he moves in close to take her mouth in a blistering kiss that makes me want to fan myself.

I divert my gaze to Petra before I start blushing, who is with Jovian and her second mate, Logan. She looks even smaller surrounded by such large males. Her mates dwarf her. I study both women, as I sip from my goblet. They look incredibly well satisfied. Their males, apart from Logan, who looks more reserved as he leans back in his chair and taps his fingers on the table as though bored by the banquet, are very touchy feely with them. I'm slightly envious but squash the feelings. I don't need to show just how unsure I am of what Brennen and Ta really feel for me, seeing as I wasn't the one meant to be sitting here.

There's an awful lot of other close family sitting near to

us. I'm never going to get their names straight. Brennen directs me into a chair that's cut out of the marble. All the six chairs where we are sat are the same throne shape with brightly coloured cushions for our comfort on them.

The tables groan under the weight of food and drink. Floating above each table are hundreds of twinkling lights. I've no idea what keeps them up or what's powering them. The food all looks strange to me, but I do notice the chocolate seeds I like so much, so that's good.

Kyanite stands and the room instantly becomes quiet. "Sha and I would like to welcome family and friends to this celebration, and ask that you join us in welcoming our son Brennen, and Ta's mate, Araline, to our home and our hearts." He turns, raising a sparkling goblet towards me. "To Araline, may your life with your mates be blessed with many dragons to carry on the way of life here on Mertier." He bows to me, and takes a sip.

I smile and listen to the loud, "To Araline," before everyone drinks.

Young males walk around waiting on everyone. I don't even know what I'm eating. I just pick at things and try to listen to what Ta and Brennen are saying. Brennen's family is huge; with his father's two brothers, Onix and Jet, and so many first cousins I lose count. I think it might be a good idea to get a book and write it all down.

I can't fault the food. Whatever it is, it's delicious, fresh and bursting with flavours. The wine is heady, and I'm soon losing some of my inhibitions and start to enjoy myself.

After everyone has finished eating, I grab some of the chocolate seeds and follow Brennen and Ta's lead so our table can be moved. I watch in fascination as all the tables sink into the floor. One moment they are there, the next they literally melt into the floor with all the plates, uneaten food and cutlery. I shake my head. *This is different world*, I have to keep reminding myself.

Once the room is cleared, the floor becomes a large dance floor. Oh fuck it; please don't tell me I have to dance. I hate dancing. I always tread on people's feet. I've all the grace of a baby elephant.

CHAPTER TWENTY-SEVEN

Alish, Petra, Zara, and their males join us at the edge of the floor. All three women are utterly jaw dropping beautiful. Again I'm reminded of the old English proverb: you can't make a silk purse out of a sow's ear and the only sow's ear here, is me.

Brennen and Ta, as promised, don't leave me. They stand behind me with hands resting on my shoulders, so we ladies can chat. I remember that Hunter, Jovian and Ryth are Brennen's personal guards and cousins.

"Well, lass, that went very well, and you look beautiful in that dress." Alish smiles at me and Petra nods in agreement.

"I'm loving your hair. It's so different. The rubies in it should become a permanent thing, like your signature look, and red is definitely your colour," Petra tells me as she leans against Jovian.

Zara smiles. "I agree with them both. You've made an impact here. You might not know it, but it's done you a world of good attending with your males." She nods regally at me and I'm reminded that people seem to know we've not mated, as they call it, yet.

Alish pulls my attention back to her. "Araline, you already know Hunter, Brennen's cousin." He nods his hello with a grin. "Now let me introduce Brogan." Alish introduces me to her second mate.

He bows his head and picks my hand up, kissing the knuckles. Tall and blonde, with startling blue eyes, he smiles at me. "It's good to meet you. I'm interested in watching those males of yours become tamed. They were pretty wild growing up." He chuckles when Alish elbows him in his ribs. She glares at him, shaking her head slightly. Hunter rolls his eyes, but he's silently laughing. "What? They have been." Brogan laughs before looking at Brennen and Ta and holding his hands up in defeat. "Hey now, no glaring. This is a family banquet." He laughs, and I feel them both stiffen.

I laugh too, as Brogan winks at me. Oh, he's trouble, all right. I'd love to hear more stories about them growing up. I can well imagine them running riot and getting away with it. I need to find Brogan at a later date and talk to him some more. I have a feeling he'd get a kick out of dropping them in trouble.

"It's nice to meet you, Brogan. We need to chat later." I lean towards him in a conspiratorial manner, and he chuckles.

"Are you trying to get my head taken off?" he asks, before bowing and stepping away. "Soon, Araline." He chuckles.

"I don't think so, Brog," Brennen informs him sternly. But turning to him, I can see they are great friends and he's trying hard to look all threatening.

Brogan moves to where Hunter is holding Alish's hand and stands behind her, resting his hands on her shoulders. Zara steps up with her males.

Ryth brushes his knuckles gently down her cheek, while Larz leans down and kisses her neck.

"Araline, this is Ryth, another cousin of Brennen's, who you met in the grounds of your home." He bows formally and stands straight. He is a huge man, standing head and shoulders even over Brennen. "And this is Larz."

Oh my, he's a beauty, even with a vicious scar running from his right eyebrow and into his hairline. He looks Italian with his darkish, sun-kissed skin and melting chocolate brown eyes that seem to undress Zara without laying a hand on her. Damn, he's smoking hot. He holds my shoulders and kisses my cheeks, both sides. I would swoon, but with Brennen and Ta, I have my hands full of my own sexy males.

"It's an honour to meet the future queen of Mertier," he tells me, before stepping back and taking Zara's hand in his.

I take a breath. Being so close to such men has me all a flutter. I'm unused to being in close proximity to such beauty, and I feel a little off kilter.

Petra is laughing with her males. "Araline, this is Jovian, another cousin. I know, they have a large family." She laughs, as I must have a look of panic on my face. Jovian chuckles and bows to me. He's stocky, shorter than Brennen but wider, with a mane of ink black hair that flows down his back.

"It's good to meet you. Don't take any notice of the gossip mongers here. Take your time and enjoy this process of getting used to a new world." He looks over my shoulder to Brennen and Ta, and leans in towards me. "They are good males, Araline. I can see they are already in love with you."

Again, I'm reminded that my sex life, or lack thereof, is being discussed by people I don't even know. I try to smile but feel tears prick the back of my eyes. I sniff and lean back against Ta. His arms automatically circle my waist. I pull myself together. I will not cry with this new world watching my every move. I cock my head— fake it until you make it, right?

Smiling at him, I reply, "I will try that advice. Thank you, Jovian." He scrutinises me but says nothing as he nods and backs away.

"This is my second mate, Logan." Petra introduces the last of this group of men, and thank God for that. So many damn names!

You know when you meet someone that you take an immediate dislike to? They've done nothing wrong, but they turn your stomach or raise the hair of your arms up in warning? Yeah, this man does all that to me. He has this... I'm not sure what the fuck it is, but I take an involuntary step back. His face is devoid of all emotion. He stares blankly at me before bowing. He's shorter than the other males; thin, with a pointed beak-like nose and bushy eyebrows. His hair is messy, unkempt, and his clothes rumpled, as if he's just gotten out of bed and couldn't care less about what he looks like. He doesn't say a word as he turns his back, stalks to a table and sits down. He ignores Petra and Jovian, and there's a deathly, uncomfortable silence.

"He doesn't say much." Petra laughs but it sounds forced.

Watching her, she seems tense, and Jovian is scowling at Logan.

"He has no fucking manners, that's his problem," Brennen says harshly.

The atmosphere has chilled somewhat after Logan's rudeness. Petra and Jovian join Logan at the table, where he pulls Petra into his lap, kissing the hell out of her. Jovian's hand is resting on her shoulder, and he's talking to them both while they kiss. Petra pulls away from Logan and nods. They stand and Jovian bows his head to Brennen, before they all walk out. Petra sends me a small smile. I've no idea what to make of what happened. I look at Alish and Zara, who are still with us, and their males look uncomfortable.

"Is he always like that? Did I do something wrong?" I frown at Brennen, feeling as if I've just made another mistake. My stomach sinks, and I feel anxious. Ta, as if sensing how I'm feeling, gives my shoulder a squeeze.

Brennen pulls me into his arms. "It wasn't anything you did, Little Flower. He's always been uncomfortable at these large events. He prefers to be in his labs. He's Mertier's number one scientist. A brilliant mind but awfully shy," he informs me.

"He's got a lot better since he and Jovian became mated to Petra. She seems to have brought him out of himself a bit," Alish says, just as the music starts. "Oh, the entertainment is about to start. Let's find some seats."

I have a feeling Alish likes to try and see the good in everyone, as she did with Simone. I'm led to a mound of cushions, like the ones Brennen has in his house. They are large and intricately embroidered. I try and sit on them as ladylike as I can in this dress. I'm really not made to sit on the floor. I'm handed another goblet full of their potent wine and take a sip as the ceiling opens and smaller dragons come flying in. They have to be the cutest things I've ever seen. About the size of baby elephants, they fly around in formation. When some bump into others, it reminds me of an infant school play. So cute.

They fly around and have us all laughing and clapping to their 'show'.

"There's Steel," Alish points out, her eyes tracking her son.

It's still mindboggling that's a boy, now in the body of a dragon, flying around.

Zara points out another young dragon, a bit bigger than Steel, but it looks like they are firm friends. "That's my son, Ligure. He's coming up to his seventh year."

He looks very powerful already. It's astonishing to watch.

Brennen leans in and whispers, "This is how we learn to fly in formation. We are taught from a very young age to control our dragons and be part of a larger team. These are all the children from Earth women and the Royal males here. There's about twelve of them at the moment." He is beaming as he watches the young dragons be put through their paces by an adult dragon that is flying with them. "We all train with the younger ones, help them gain confidence and restraint."

"Restraint?" I question, laughing as one adorable dragon forgets to flap his wings. He plummets to the ground, but the older one snaps his snout with those razor-sharp fangs and grips his tail, before flinging him up into the air. I can hear the giggles from the smaller one.

"Yes, the royal dragons are a hell of a lot stronger than the other males of this planet. We have to be, for we are the protectors of everyone. It's a huge responsibility on our shoulders that we take very seriously."

I nod, totally captivated by the young dragons.

They land just by our feet. I get to mine and walk over to them, with Brennen and Ta behind me. The older dragon bows low and the younger ones nudge each other. Finally they are all bowed. I don't really know what I want to do. Would it be wrong to pet them like large dogs? But before I can do anything, a smaller one breaks ranks and walks over to me. He nudges my hand and then I'm petting a small dragon. I go to my knees, so we are about the same height.

"Well done. That was a pretty good show you all did," I tell him. I'm nudged until I fall over, laughing.

"Careful," Brennen orders, and they quickly step away.

"It's fine. They are just excitable." I'm still laughing as they all come back and demand the petting to resume.

CHAPTER TWENTY-EIGHT

The king and queen walk over to join us; I watch their approach. They mingle with the people and seem far more approachable than the royals I was use to on the TV back on Earth.

I clumsily stand; Ta helps me up in the end as it's not easy getting up off the floor in a dress. My body simply wasn't made for it. God, I'm mortified, my dress is a bit rumpled and I hastily pull at it as I'm flashing a little more skin than they need to see. I watch as the other ladies stand, graceful and ladylike. Something I'll never be, shaking my head I watch the adorable child dragons bow again to their King and Queen.

"Well done. That was a very good show." Sha says, smiling kindly, before going along the line. The young dragons, shift back to boys, all naked and not giving a crap that they are. They must become used to shifting from dragon to boys and being naked around everyone. No one seems bothered. They all seem in awe of the Queen and chat nineteen to the dozen. She takes whatever they are saying very seriously and hands each one a gift.

After she has seen each one, their trainer nods and they shift to dragons once more before flying out of the building.

"Oh my god, they are so sweet and cheeky." I beam at Brennen and he smiles back "It's hard to believe you were ever that small." I laugh, trying to imagine this hulking man in front of me as a small child.

"Oh, I have lots of stories I could tell you, if you want, Araline?" Sha tells me with a wink.

"I have a feeling I need to hear those." I smile and take a breath realising, I'm having fun. I'm on a strange planet, mixing with royalty and have two men, one of which is a dragon. My mind is slightly blown by these facts.

"Mother, I don't think you need to be filling Araline's head with tales of my childhood." Brennen sternly tells his mother but I can see by the crinkle of his eyes and his dimple that he loves this woman greatly.

"And anyway, I was usually with him when he did whatever you're thinking of telling our mate, so that also incriminates me too." Ta joins in, just before his father slaps his hand on his shoulder.

"Indeed you were, Ta. Oh, the things these two got up to, Araline." He shakes his head in mock agitation. "We worried they would become too wild for any respectful mate to want them. But I think you're more than enough to handle these two." His grin was infectious and I was laughing as a loud gong sounded.

Excitement seems to spread through the banquet attendees like a wildfire. Everyone rushes back to their seats and Sha and Kyanite nod to us before leaving to retake their seats. Why do they get proper seats and the rest of us have to lounge on the floor?

Kyanite presses something on his chair and a large square shape appears, painted on the floor.

I watch as six men enter the room, all huge with rippling muscles. Two I recognise as Brennen's brothers, Ragan and Ace, but I have no idea who the rest are. I wonder idly if the food here makes them this big. They are wearing what I'd call black, work-out jogging trousers, no shoes, and nothing covering their chests. And oh, what chests they have. I can't help but to admire such well-formed pecs. I cough, covering the fact that I'm slobbering over a few naked torsos. *Get a damn grip*, I tell myself sternly.

Each man carries a different weapon, like a sword or knife or a wooden staff. They march in and stand in a straight line within the square, in front of the king and queen. They bow as one and stand, as if awaiting orders.

"You may begin. The winner will get this pot of gems," Kyanite states, as he lifts a large silver, urn-like pot that's overflowing with bright, different-shaped gems. It looks like it weighs a ton, but he lifts it effortlessly.

There's a blur of movement as they move with breathtaking skill, precision and deadly speed.

"What are they doing?" I ask fearfully, but it becomes blatantly clear as the sounds of clashing metal against metal resound in the large room.

Fighting!

"It's all part of our training but tonight is just a bit of fun. A chance to show off their skills," Brennen answers as his eyes track his brothers. One of whom is being fought by a massive male with a deadly-looking serrated machete kind of thing. It appears brutal and it doesn't look like they're just having fun. "There are six dragons and six normal males. They are all trained in the same way but the dragons have a huge advantage. We are stronger, faster, and more adept to healing after a fight."

"So why are they fighting normal males then? Surely that's an unfair fight?" I watch as two men are thrown out of the square, seemingly unconscious. They are quickly dragged away by the servers.

"Not really. In a battle we have to be prepared for any sort of fight. If they have trained with dragons, they are used to fighting someone much stronger. It gives them an edge."

I watch as they continue to fight. I'm awed by their skills.

The fighting is vicious, with all combatants getting bloody. But somehow it's beautiful to watch. I've never been big on watching boxing matches on Earth. Not a great lover of any kind of sports really, but even I can acknowledge the grace and beauty of the fighter's movements. I wince when a howl leaves a man's mouth as he's brutally kicked from the square. He lands at my feet, unconscious.

I look at Brennen as I realise it's Ace. He leans in as if to examine him. I quickly look at Sha, wondering how she can stand it. I'd hate it if one of my sons was in a fight and was unconscious. She looks worried until Kyanite leans into her and whispers in her ear. She nods and looks a little more settled.

"He'll be fine, Araline." Brennen shakes his head. "He should have known they would double up to take him." He kisses my lips tenderly. He's not overly concerned about him, and we watch as he's carried away and we are left with only two in the square.

"That's my brother Ragen and the other is Cain. Cain is not a dragon but is a ferocious warrior. I'd think twice about fighting him. He doesn't take any prisoners alive. But as this is only a demonstration, no deaths are allowed, he and Ragen are very close. I think if and when Ragen is ready for his own mate, Cain will be the second mate he chooses to complete them" he tells me as the two men stare at each other.

Watching them, I can hardly believe they are friends, never mind close friends. The animosity is almost palatable.

"Come on then little dragon, let's see what you have." Cain shouts to Ragen, the unimpressed smirk on his lips make him look bored. His finger beckons him forward.

I understand the "little" was meant as a slur as Ragen is anything but small.

"He's trying to bait him." Ta whispers, my hand is gripping his tightly as I can see this fight will end up bloody.

"Cain, always loves to fights the dragons, he says it's because he can inflict the most harm and we will still live. He says it's the best training he can get." Brennen informs me giving my other hand a squeeze.

Okay then...

I don't realise I'm holding my breath; the fight is set at a crazy pace. Punches are jabbed, grunts are heard and I'm shouting with the rest of the people for who they want to win. Cain is a fantastic fighter, dodging Ragen's fists as fast as he can, ducking and weaving he manages to get behind Ragen and wrap his muscled arms around his middle and lifts him off his feet. The strength that alone must demand is incredible. He squeezes until Ragen goes limp and I think it's all over. But just as Cain relaxes his grip, thinking he's won, Ragen viciously throws his head backwards and I wince as I hear the crunch of bone as his head makes contact with Cain's nose.

Cain howls with pain and releases him, throwing him across the square. He shakes it off, wiping the blood dripping from his nose and charges for Ragen. Ragen is ready and ducks low, sweeping his leg out and Cain is caught and falls to the floor.

Ragen immediately jumps onto his back and with both hands clamped on his head he twists. Even me, being totally untrained in any sort of fighting technique knows if he twists much more, Cain will die. Cain visible stills, he's panting as his right arm reaches out and he makes a fist.

An almighty cheer rises up as Kyanite nods.

"We have a winner. Congratulations, Ragen," the King says as he stands and waits until Ragen helps Cain up from the floor. The two nod to each other and then hug, manly slaps to the back. They seem to be best buddies again.

"I almost had you, Ragen." Cain jabs him playfully in the ribs.

"*Almost* won't win those gems!" Ragen jabs him back, laughing.

"I just don't understand how you can punch three bales of shit out of someone, then turn around and be friends." I shake my head, and everyone stands and claps as Ragen is handed his winnings.

Ragen puts the urn on the floor and scoops a couple of handfuls of the precious gems and hands them to Cain.

"Oh, that's a nice thing to do." I smile. One thing I do like is good sportsmanship.

"Told you they were good friends," Brennen repeats. He pulls me into his chest, wrapping his arms around me as his lips feasts on mine.

God, this man— dragon— can kiss. I wrap my arms around his neck and cling to him. Honestly, if I could, I'd climb up his body until it was hard to distinguish who was kissing who. I think the wine from the meal has made me a little tipsy.

Our tongues duel while my hands move up his neck, and his silky hair flows through my fingers. I'm lost, so completely and utterly lost in the kiss, that I forget we are in a room full of hundreds of people. I'm unaware that talking has ceased and all heads are turned in our direction. I'm panting, my nipples are hard, and I can feel my body becoming needy, and still he carries on his devastating kiss.

"Get a room!" someone shouts out, and soft laughter fills my ears.

The spell is broken, and I pull away, blushing. I hide my face in his chest, where I can feel a rumble of laughter erupt.

"I'm sure you have much more interesting things to be doing, rather than watching me kiss my mate." Brennen laughs, and Ta stands behind me, shielding me, until I'm ready to turn and face everyone.

The first person who catches my eye is Sha. *OMG*, I've just eaten her son's face. What must she think of me? But she winks with a smile. Then I see Ta's father, and he's grinning at us all.

I'm so embarrassed, but I'm also incredibly horny. Dare I

take the next step and let these two men have their wicked way with me? The images floating around in my mind of what the pair of them could do has me salivating. Pulling up my big girl's panties, I pull Brennen down so I can whisper in his ear.

"I need you, Brenn." My voice is a little breathless. Ta leans down as well. I look at them both, my cheeks heated, but I repeat my wishes. "I need you both. Now."

Huge grins break out on their faces, and they turn and bow to the king and queen. I follow and bow my head. They each take a hand and we walk out of the room. I turn and look at the ladies I know, and they are both smiling encouragingly. Their males have a knowing glint to their eyes. I'm not going to think about the fact that everyone knows exactly what we are leaving for.

The flying vehicle is hovering, waiting for us to board. Do they keep it on permanent standby? They strap me in quickly, and Ta gently turns my head. His eyes flash with silver as he stares into mine, and then his lips descend. He kisses me so sweetly that I sigh into his mouth. Brennen talks quietly to the driver, who silently leaves. Brennen presses buttons, and the windows around us become blacked out— for privacy, I guess. We are moving, flying smoothly, but my mind is on Ta. He deepens the kiss while his hands cup my breasts and his fingers tease my hard nipples through the silk material.

I squeeze my thighs together, trying desperately to add pressure to my clit. It's actually throbbing with need. I've never felt this clawing need, this desire flooding my senses. Oh bloody hell, these men. I have a feeling they have the ability to destroy me. But I want more. I want everything they have to give me.

CHAPTER TWENTY-NINE

"Little Flower," is breathed against my neck, which sends goose bumps over my flesh.

"Brenn, Ta." I sigh, feeling Ta's lips brush softly down my neck and into my cleavage. The dress that they chose offers no protection from a determined male. He nudges the material over, and my breast is bared. I flush when his lips suck a nipple into his mouth. I should be embarrassed. Really, I should. The soft suction of Ta's lips makes my nipple painfully hard, and the noise of satisfaction he makes has me blushing anew.

"Someone could see!" I gasp. I know the windows are black now, but could someone see as we flew past? I'm not into being watched.

"No one would dare to watch us, I promise you," Brennen murmurs against my lips, before taking them in a blistering, overpowering kiss. His tongue slides into my mouth and the moan that erupts from me has one of my hands trailing up his arms until it rests on his shoulder.

While Ta's lips make love to my breast, his hand brushes the dress aside, so my other breast is free. His fingers dance around the nipple until I am arching into his touch. My body is aflame with potent desire, such that I'd never felt before. To be honest, if my brain could function I'd be overwhelmed and a little scared at how much I crave their touch in just a short space of time.

These men know how to inflame me like no one has ever bothered to try before. Especially not the pig spawned from hell, Giles. After just a few soft touches and kisses, they have me writhing and needing so much more. Brennen's kiss is devastating, and I'm moaning into his mouth as his tongue twirls against mine while Ta's fingers trace around my nipples. He makes them feel so tight and hard as my arching back offers them to him.

"More, please..." I whisper, gasping for breath. I'm not entirely sure what I'm begging for. I've never been in a situation like this. *Am I really about to do this?*

I've never felt anything this intense. I never came during sex. I don't think my body works the same as other women's as I've always been left hanging, as it were, but I know without a shadow of a doubt that Brennen and Ta wouldn't stop until I was a mindless, boneless pool of sated languidness.

The flying vehicle slows and lowers to the ground. Ta makes quick work of the buckle, and before I can catch my breath, I'm lifted effortlessly. Brennen stalks down the steps and heads towards the palace, and Ta holds my hand as he follows. My legs wrap themselves around Brennen's middle, and I find myself grinding against his hard, covered cock. I can't believe how I'm acting. I'm like this wanton slut. I must be drugged, as I've never felt this overwhelming need before.

I should be shocked, but I'm not.

Ta drops my hand and walks in front. I presume he's opening doors as my mouth is back to devouring Brenn's. I can feel we are walking up the grand staircase. Once we are in the bedroom, Ta steps in close behind me and lifts the dress over my head. I moan in frustration as I have to stop kissing to take my arms out. I fling it to the floor before turning so Ta can take me into his arms while Brennen undresses. I feel Brennen's fingers on the thong before it's ripped from my body.

Ta is already gloriously naked. My hands run over his chiselled chest until they grip his shoulders tightly.

"Ta," I moan, just before his mouth takes mine viciously, not seeking permission but diving straight in.

I'm mindless when I feel Brennen step in close behind me, running his hands down my back until he dips a finger between my ass cheeks and rims the tight, puckered hole.

I whimper.

"Lay her down, Ta. I want to taste her," Brennen demands.

My back hits the silk, and before I can catch my breath, his mouth is on my sex.

"Oh my God," I moan, as his tongue circles my clit. I close my eyes and lose myself to the sensual assault he's inflicting. "Ta," I cry out in wonder, as his tongue joins the mêlée. Two tongues probing into me, two tongues licking my clit. I can't catch my breath. I'm going to die here!

Tongues and fingers enter me, and my legs are spread wide and my feet are placed on the bed so they can gain better access. A rich scent fills the air, and I feel one of their fingers breach my tight asshole. Oil— they've covered their fingers in a scented oil to ease any discomfort I may have felt.

I shudder; sensations have my body shaking with the need for release. "I need... oh God, don't stop. Don't stop!" I hiss between clenched teeth. Oh fuck, I need to come.

Brennen's fingers are in my ass, slowly fucking me. I feel an almost scorching, white heat hit my clit, and I get up onto my elbows, panting. I watch Ta's glowing, healing hand pinch my clit between two fingers, and I'm flying.

I come with an almighty scream. The heat to my clit from Ta's fingers sent me over and over with waves of pleasure. My whole body is shaking as I slowly open my eyes. Never in my life have I felt anything close to that. My own hand and the few toys I own does nothing to compare.

I stare at them in wonder. "How the hell did you learn to do that?" I gasp.

They grin at me, full of cocky awareness of what they just produced from my body. *Bloody hell their beautiful.* I stare at them in wonder.

"We are nowhere near finished with you, Little Flower." Brennen licks his lips, and I blush when I realise he's enjoying my flavour. I glance at Ta and find him busy licking me off his fingers. *Bloody hell.* I'm beginning to realise just how damn sexy it is watching that.

"Come here," Brennen growls. I find myself hoisted into the air as he swaps places with me. Before I can register what's happening, I'm straddling his wide body while he lies on his back. I feel his hand take his cock, and Ta raises me until I'm on my knees. I feel the blunt head of Brennen's cock starting to fill me, and I wonder what his extra bit will feel like when it's rubbing against my clit.

"She's wet and hot, Ta, but we need her more so. Stroke her. I want to watch as she comes again," he orders, and Ta moves to the front of me, circling my clit with his fingers.

I stare into Brennen's eyes. He seems mesmerised by me, by my reactions. He lowers his lashes and focuses on Ta's fingers stroking me, dipping into me, making my body feel as if it belongs to someone else, I love how it reacts to their touch. My eyes flutter closed, and my hips take on a life of their own as they ride Ta's fingers. I turn my head, bringing Ta's head down to mine. I need to taste him. I want more from these men than I've ever wanted before.

"Please, Ta," I whisper against his lips. "Please, I need you. I need you both."

He pinches my clit, my back bows, and I feel my release flood from my body. In the next instant, I'm crying out as Brennen thrusts his cock upwards and fills me.

"Fuck, Brenn. You're too big," I cry out hoarsely. My body stills, even while the delicious feelings are still making me clench around him. *He's too big. Fuck! He's too big!"*

I'm panting as my hands rest on his shoulders. His face is full of wonder. Almost euphoric. I watch as his dragon scales shimmer just under his skin. It's a wondrous sight.

"How does she feel, Brenn?" Ta asks, his hooded eyes staring where Brennen's cock has opened me wide. I was right, his extra smaller cock rubs me in just the right place. "She looks beautiful, stuffed full with your cock. Just like we knew she would." Ta stands on the plinth that surrounds the bed, and his cock is within reach.

I take him in my hand— though he's more than a handful — and stroke him. I want him in my mouth, in my body— fucking me somewhere. Ta closes his eyes but soon snaps them open, as if he can't bear to stop staring at where Brennen enters my body.

"She feels so tight, deliciously wet and— fuck, I need to move!" Brennen groans. He grips my hips, then begins to move me up and down. The strength that must take is mind boggling, and I remind myself these aren't human men. Brenn is a fucking dragon.

"I want her to come again before you fuck her," Brennen says through gritted teeth. "I'm not sure I'll last that long, but we can try."

CHAPTER THIRTY

I no longer pay any attention because my body is crying out for more. Who knew it could feel like this? I certainly didn't. I try and keep up a rhythm on Ta's cock but it's becoming difficult to concentrate on anything. My hands fall to my side and I shudder. I'm not actually doing anything. Brennen is lifting me up and down, fucking me with forceful thrusts, and his extra appendage rubs my clit on every downward stroke. He grinds into me, filling me to such a point it'd be painful if my clit wasn't being stimulated constantly.

Ta drops his head and nips my nipple, sucking it into his mouth before biting on the hard tip, while his fingers stroke down my spine until he rims my asshole.

"Yes! Don't stop. Don't stop!" I yell, my eyes tightly closed. It all comes to a point and I come splendidly, falling ungracefully onto Brennen's chest as I twitch from the release.

"I have to be in her, Brenn. Now!" I hear Ta before he

moves up onto the bed. He presses kisses into my spine and keeps me pressed against Brenn's chest.

I can't think. I can't do anything but try to catch my breath. Brennen's extra smaller cock is twitching against my clit, and it keeps me inflamed. I've never in my life been this wet and turned on. My heart is hammering in my chest and I'm panting as I feel Ta's fingers slip into my asshole again. I can do nothing but mewl. I start to shake as I comprehend what he's about to do.

I've never had anal before. Some of my girlfriends love it, some hate it, but as his fingers slip past the tight ring of muscle, I feel Brennen growl. He can obviously feel Ta's fingers against his cock through the thin membrane.

"Fuck me, Brenn, she's so fucking tight." Ta bites out as he pulls free his fingers and smothers his cock in the fragrant oil.

"Slowly, Ta. I don't think our Little Flower has ever been taken like this by one man, never mind two. Take it easy," Brennen orders his voice full of emotion as he tries to keep a firm hold on his emotions.

"Wait!" Through the haze of my last release and lust, I cry out as I feel the blunt head of Ta's cock start to penetrate me. Both men freeze.

"Am I hurting you?" Ta murmurs, running his fingers down my spine, making me arch towards his touch.

I stare into Brennen's eyes, but I can't articulate what is going on.

"No, you're not," I whisper. "Um... I've never been touched there." Heat flames my face, and I feel inexperienced and not sure how to continue.

"It's okay, Little Flower, we won't hurt you. Let us show you how good it can be," Brennen promises, as his fingers dip between our bodies, moving his extra smaller cock, stroking it against my clit.

The fire is soon building, making me shake with need, and still Ta hasn't moved. I twist my head, and he winks at me.

"I could never hurt you, Araline. You're my mate. I have waited so fucking long for you to be under me, for my cock to be in you. I want nothing more than for you to enjoy your first time with us," he informs me. His large body is held still with supreme strength, and I see his muscles bunch with the effort.

As Brennen's finger strokes me, I can feel my body hurtle towards another release. I've never come so much in my life. I didn't know my body was capable. I nod, close my eyes, and give myself up to enjoying all the sensations they are forcing me to feel.

How the hell will I survive this?

"I can't come again," I moan, but knowing they won't allow me not to.

"Oh, but you will." Ta's confidence has me trembling.

Ta's cock is oiled and slips through the strong ring of muscle. They are both in me. My eyes flash open when I realise I have two cocks in me. I'm panting, and my hands grasp Brennen's shoulders in a death grip.

"Oh fuck. Oh my…" I stare into Brennen's. Instead of his gorgeous midnight blue eyes, they're black. I realise it's his dragon who is staring back at me.

"You have no idea how beautiful you look right now. Nestled between your mates. Being fucked by your mates until you forget to breathe. But we will breathe for you, Little

Flower," he tells me. His voice sounds different, thicker and lower.

Is his dragon talking to me? I wonder, before his lips take mine in a blistering kiss. Just as Ta pulls out a little and starts a slow ride.

"Make me come, please!" I beg, my voice full of emotions as they move. Even though I only just told them I couldn't come again, my body is betraying me.

They move like a well-oiled machine. If I could form coherent thoughts, I'd wonder where in the hell they learned this technique. One thrusts in while the other pulls back. One in, one out, over and over. All the while, Brennen's extra cock is caressing my clit. Ta's hands are gripping my hips in such a tight hold I know there'll be bruises come tomorrow. But I don't give a flying fuck!

"Fuck, Brenn, I won't last long. Make her come," Ta moans. "Now, Brenn!" His agonised cry is mirrored by the way he loses control of his hips.

"Come on, Little Flower, we need to feel your body quiver around ours," Brennen breathes into my ear, sending the order straight to my bits below. They obey him immediately.

"Brenn, Ta!" I scream as my body bows— as much as it can when I'm hemmed in by two sex gods. They join me with their own releases, and their roars of passion cascade down my spine. This release is shattering. My eyes flutter closed, and I rush headlong into oblivion. These two males have fucked me into near unconsciousness.

"Well, that was…" Ta groans as his cock pulls free from its new favourite place to be.

"Fucking amazing," Brennen finishes for him with a grin,

as he too slips free, his extra appendage laying shrunken atop his larger cock.

Rolling onto his back, Ta strokes his fingers down my now unconscious body, his face full of awe. I'm still on top of Brennen as he kisses my shoulder and hops off the bed. Going to the bathroom, he brings back a few warm, wet flannels, just as Brennen gently manoeuvres me off his body and onto the bed.

"I never dreamed it would be that good with our mate," Brennen states, as he grabs one and gently cleans my body. They wouldn't allow their mate to sleep with their releases and cooling sweat marring me. After he is satisfied, he cleans himself and throws it uncaringly to the floor.

Ta quickly follows and gets back into bed, pulling the cover over us all. "Should we wake her up?" he wonders aloud, bringing my fingers to his lips to place gentle kisses on the tips.

"No, let her sleep. Her body needs to rest after what we did to it," Brennen says, leaning down and kissing a nipple. He has to pull himself away before he loses control and takes me again. He was right; my body will need to rest in between their lovemaking.

CHAPTER THIRTY-ONE

I come to with a snap. Eyes open wide, I bolt upright in bed, gripping the thin sheet around my nakedness. Flashes of what I did with Brennen and Ta whizz around my mind. *OMG!* They didn't? But by the way my body aches deliciously in all the right places, they most certainly had. I close my eyes and groan when I remember what I did and how I acted. Ground just swallow me up whole now!

"Good morn, Little Flower." Brennen sits up and kisses my shoulder, while I feel Ta's fingers stroking up my spine. I'm not sure I can ever look them in the eyes again. Good girls simply don't act the way I'd acted with them. *TWO MEN!* My brain screams at me.

Brennen gently turns my face so I have no choice but to stare into his midnight navy blue eyes. My skin blushes heatedly and I drop my eyes. "It wasn't a dream?" I mumble hopefully.

"If it were, we all dreamt it, Araline." Ta nips my earlobe as he sits up.

"Oh, dear." I groan and bury my head into my knees as I bring them up and wrap my arms around them. "What you did to me." I whisper into my arms.

Brennen sits up straighter, pulling me along with him until the three off us are sat resting our heads on the beds headboard. "Did you not enjoy it, Little Flower?" They both wait, I huff, they aren't going to allow me to wallow in my embarrassment are they?

"I loved it. I've never had sex that made me feel like that before." I'm blushing so much I can feel the heat my skin is giving off. "It was a little overwhelming." Inside I was thinking, it was the kind of sex that made you want to call your girlfriends and dissect it, it was so good. But I had no one I could call here. Well I could call Alish? But this kind of sex is the norm here, it wouldn't be exciting to her.

"But you've had sex before right? Maybe not the anal and two men together, as we are told that's not all that common on Earth." Ta asks, he's watching my reactions to them.

I take a breath, "No, most men won't share their girlfriends or wives. I know it happens, of course, but I've never done anything like we did." *Please don't ask me anymore personal questions,* I silently beg.

"Are you sore, did we hurt you at any time?" Brennen asks, his concern is easy to see.

I place my hand on his cheek, smiling, "No, you didn't hurt me. It was," I raise my eyes to the ceiling, trying to think of a word that will do what we did justice. "Bloody fab." Their grins in return are worth all the embarrassing questions.

"Now, can we please go for a bath, I need to soak some muscles that aren't used to being so well used." And again I'm blushing.

Ta flings back the covers enthusiastically which end up in a rumpled heap at the end of the bed, before stepping out and holding out a hand to me. I take his hand and move gingerly to the edge of the bed. Okay I feel sore and well and truly used. I stand slowly. Brennen walks around the bed and we make our way to their special bath, but first I need the loo.

I meet them both, after I've done what I needed to do, they are already in the water and I lean against the door, watching them. They are sex personified. How the hell did I end up here? Mated, I roll that word around, such a different way to think about being with someone, or someone's. What will happen to me if they get bored of me? Or they find another who will fit them better? I'm not trained to be a queen, for fucks sake!

I start to panic, but Brennen says, "come on in, Little Flower."

"Yes, come join us." Ta beckons and dives under the water. I'm treated to flashes of his biteable ass, which heats my blood. Down girl…

I walk into the shimmering, silver, water and submerge myself. While under the water I spy Brennen swimming over to me. His hard body making the water ripple as he powers towards me. Not wasting any time, he pulls me into his arms, kissing me with such tenderness; I'm left breathless as my breasts squash against his chest. I'm becoming more than a little achy down below. I've never been one to crave a man's touch; most men on Earth have little to offer in the way of satisfying sex as they are too selfish and only care about their needs. Well, I can't cast aspersions and say they are all like that, but the ones I'd had sex with certainly were.

I now know Brennen and Ta both have so much to offer. I have been put first on a few occasions now and I have a feeling they have ruined me for anyone else. It's a good job my feelings towards them are growing. Maybe I could fall in love with them, given time? I freeze mid kiss, how rude! But love them? *no... no... no...* my mind yells at me. I'm not allowed to fall in love, I have to escape somehow and go home.

Home, my shoulders slump as I remember, I don't have a bloody home. Brennen pulls back, "Where has your mind gone to, Little Flower?" he brings my chin up with a finger and I have no option but to look him in the eyes.

He is so beautiful, I know beautiful is usually used to describe women, but this man truly is. He smiles at me and his dimple shows, very cute. "So much has happened, Brenn, it's a little unsettling. My life has changed beyond any imaginings I had." My hands stroke his powerful shoulders; this need to touch him is an unconscious thing that is growing.

"I know, Araline, I can only promise that we will both cherish you for however long we live."

My heart stutters, he can be awfully charming. Without thinking, I lift my head and my lips glide across his. I brush my nose against his a couple of times and lean my forehead to his. "All this frightens me a little, Brenn." I admit to him in a whisper.

He holds me tightly against his body; he's hard but makes no demands. "I wish I had behaved better when I came to get you." His warm breath tickles my ear as he whispers back. "I will endeavour to make it up to you every single day."

I pull back and he looks so sad. Ta presses kisses across my shoulders when he joins us.

"We will love you, Araline; you will never be left wondering who comes first in our lives. It'll always be you." Ta says softly.

Well, okay then. I squirm until Brennen releases me and I back away from them both. I have a couple of questions, "So, what's the rules? In the bedroom I mean. Do I have to be with both of you every time? Can I be with one without the other or will feelings get hurt? I need to know what's what. As unlike the other ladies I've not been schooled in your ways." I can feel my skin heating, but I wait for their answers.

Ta is grinning and Brennen's dimple is there as he's smiling wide.

"You can ask us anything, we will always answer you. Nothing if off limits or a stupid question. We want to make this as easy a transition for you as possible." Ta tells me.

"Whatever comes natural at that time is fine, Little Flower. Say if you're in the grounds and Ta finds you and you both want to fuck, then its fine. No hearts will be broken, the same if I wake you up and we fuck and Ta's working, nothing is wrong with what goes on within the three of us."

"You only have to touch me and I'll be ready for you, whether Brenn is there or not." Ta waggles his eyebrows at me suggestively and I can't stop the giggle erupting. "Has that answered your worries?" he reaches for me pulling me through the water until he can kiss me. He takes his time, slowly exploring my mouth as I wind my legs around his waist.

His cock is mere centimetres away from me and I find myself rubbing my pussy along the length. I'm a hussy and there's no way I'm stopping now, my body is ready for him and he takes my queue and enters me in a forceful thrust.

Opening my eyes I stare behind Ta to where Brennen is stood in the water watching us, his eyelids are half closed, full of lust as he slowly strokes himself. Now that's hot to watch and only fuels my desire. His hand is full with his cock as he pumps his hips into his hand. I lift myself up and down Ta's length and he is stretching me.

"Fuck, Araline! You feel so damn tight. I love how my cock feels surrounded by your heat!" Ta moans against my neck.

His erotic words only add to the way my body reacts to him and my breasts sway gently in time with his thrusts. The water also adds to the moment as it feels divine splashing me as I ride Ta's cock. His eyes devour how they move and I bring one up, offering it to him. I'm rewarded with a low sexy growl, taking the tip into his mouth, sucking loudly on the nipple.

"Oh god, I love how you feel. Fuck me, Ta, please!" My head falls back and I lose myself to the moment. I'm breathing heavy and can hear Brenn panting as he wanks in time with Ta's cock fucking me.

My nipple pops free, they've never been this hard or

sensitive. I kiss him and he devours me, his hips thrust harder and faster as his cock rubs a spot hidden deep inside me.

"Oh my god! I'm coming, Ta! Fuck!" I cry as my body tightens and I buck as I shatter on his cock. I slump, resting my head on his shoulder as he comes hard, I can actually feel his seed pumping deep inside me. I've never felt that before, my eyes open and I watch as Brenn joins us and comes spectacularly. His head back and legs braced as his body spasms he roars out his release.

His eyes stare into mine and it's an intimacy I've never experienced, I have to admit it made me feel kind of powerful, that this great male was overcome with urges and just had to come while watching me fuck. It's heady.

Ta presses kisses to my neck and covers my cheeks, making me giggle. He's grinning as he slips free from my intimate embrace and we both groan.

"Thank you, Araline that was beautiful, you were beautiful." He tells me, before lowering me into the water. We swim over to Brennen who kisses me softly.

"You looked so sexy while Ta fucked you. I could watch you two all day. It's hot." He grins while running a hand through his hair.

"It was hot watching you, Brenn and I have to admit I liked being watched." I blush, I've never had sex while someone watched, I wasn't an exhibitionist on Earth. I like how I am with these two, I feel sexy and body confident for the first time ever.

He kisses the tip of my nose, "You affect me greatly, I had to touch myself, but it didn't feel as good as when I was in you. My hand lacks your heat." He laughs softly as I duck my head and I know I'm blushing again.

"Come on, we need to get out. I'm afraid I have some training to do." Brennon informs us. "I've got tactics to go over with my brothers and I know my cousins will be there as well. I'll only be gone a few hours, I'm sure you two will find something to occupy yourselves with while I'm away." He winks at us and we walk out of the water.

I have to get used to the fact that I'm dry as soon as I'm out of the water. It's strange. One minute you're wet, the next you're dry.

"Actually, I need to catch up on some royal correspondence, if Araline doesn't mind being alone for a couple of hours?" They both look at me, I can see worry etched on their faces. "But I don't have to if you're not ready to be alone?" he brings up my hand and kisses the inside of my palm.

Well *thud*! There goes my heart. Some kisses are so sweet and personal that they make my knees go weak. "I'm sure I'll be fine. I might go outside and take a look around the grounds?" They nod encouragingly. We walk to the clothes and I pull on something for comfort. I find a matching bra and pantie set in the same colour as Brennen's eyes, a pair of loose-fitting black trousers and a soft as baby's skin, silk floaty top in a sapphire blue.

Once they are dressed, we head downstairs, I'm between them both and their body heat, keeps me reminded that they aren't quite human. At the bottom they each take a turn and kiss me goodbye, wow, they really know how to kiss. I'm a horny mess by the time they leave. Just before they do Brennen leans in and whispers, "Don't touch yourself, little flower." I gasp as I cotton on to what he means. "I want to give you your next orgasm."

I know I'm blushing again. I can feel the heat rising until my whole face is burning. He chuckles and Ta joins in. Incorrigible males. I watch as they leave. Brennen has his personal guards with him, and then I'm alone.

CHAPTER THIRTY-TWO

I turn and realise how quiet it is, I'm alone. Okay, I can do this.

I head to the room that Sha and I left the men talking when they came to visit. I know that leads to the gardens. There's a guard following me a few hundred yards away, but I try to ignore him. I don't know much about gardens, I've only ever lived in flats, but even to my untrained eye, these grounds are beautifully cultivated. The myriad of colours pop brightly and the scents from the overly large flowers fill the air. I find a private nook and sit on a white marble seat that is carved in the shape of a throne, with purple, velvet, cushions and lean back. There's a pretty stream of their pale silver water, with fish like creatures jumping and splashing as it meanders its way through the grounds and the tinkling sound of it flowing over the white stones is relaxing.

Leaning back, I sink into the deep cushions, tucking my legs under me and close my eyes, it's so peaceful. I'm still trying to get used to this planet. The way of life here is different to anything I'm used to on Earth and the fact that one of the two men that are mine, is a bloody dragon. *A dragon*, my mind shouts at me.

My eyes are still closed; I'm drifting off to sleep when an urgent, angry shout rings out. I jump and my eyes snap open, I scream as I feel strong, male arms wrap around me, lifting me effortlessly out of the seat. A black hood is hastily plonked over my head rendering me blind and I'm thrown unceremoniously over someone's shoulders. Whoever it is, is moving incredibly fast.

I'm screaming and kicking out for all I'm worth. What is it about this place that the males think it's okay to treat me like this! I can't see jack shit! But I can hear shouts and orders being given. They must know someone is kidnapping me.

"Who are you?" I cry out, "What the fuck are you doing to me?" I kick him as hard as I can, but he only grunts. "Brennen, Ta." I scream loudly, raining punches on his back but all I'm doing it hurting my hands. I'm terrified, with the hood blocking out all light I'm beginning to feel claustrophobic. Dread fills my stomach as I have an awful suspicion of who this is. "Ta!" I scream over and over, my throat becoming hoarse until I feel weightless as whoever is holding me throws me into the air. "Fuck!" I'm screaming when another set of arms grab me and I'm thrown onto a solid floor. I stay as still as I can, trying to catch my breath. We are moving so I guess we are in one of those flying vehicle things.

"You will pay for this." I screech, sitting up as the hood is snatched from my head. I stare into the eyes of Talon, his heavily scared face full of fury. My stomach drops. Closing my eyes, I try to halt the hysteria from bubbling free.

My nightmare is becoming a reality.

"I'm sure I will, Araline. But it'll be worth it." He tells me, crossing his arms across his wide chest. He's leaning against the side of the blacked-out windows. We are travelling fast, not that I can see anything of where we are, but I can hear the wind hurtling over the vehicle.

"You can't do this. I'm mated now. I belong to Brennen and Ta. Take me back!" I demand, glaring at him. I shuffle backwards, keeping my eyes on him, in case he tries anything, until I can pull myself up into the seat.

"I know. I can smell their stench on you. We aimed to have you out of there yesterday, but we couldn't. We have you now, though."

"Why are you doing this? I heard you only just got released from prison. You know when they catch you and they will catch you! I don't think you'll be given that chance again." I watch him, praying that Brennen and Ta are coming for me. He has a tick of annoyance going in his neck as he glares at me.

"It's nothing personal; you are just a means to an end. We need those bastards who decide the rules for the rest of us to know that we no longer live by their rules. After you, every female brought through the vortex will be taken and distributed in a fair way," he tells me, his huge body seems relaxed, as he leans against one of the blacked out windows.

"You doing this, taking the women now, makes you no better than the Rumos that Ta were telling me about," I hiss, how the hell do I end up in these positions? Just lucky, I guess.

His face mottles with red. Oh boy, I have pushed his buttons and he's seething. "You do not understand what you say. I don't want to go through the vortex again. The people on your planet Earth are little more than children. I have little interest in them, apart from the females, now they hold my interest tightly."

I don't really know what to say to that, but I realise I'm in deep shit. "What do you want of me? Are you going to hurt me? Rape me?" I whisper, feeling as if my life could very easily be coming to an end as I'd kill myself rather than live like that.

"No." He looks disgusted that I'd think of that; let's hope he's a man of his word. "We do not harm females, no matter what you've heard. But you will be given to whoever wins the bidding. Everyone who decides to live as we do, their names will go into the bidding and five will be pulled out."

I stare at him in horror. *Five?* I close my eyes but can't stop the wave of revulsion that starts in my stomach and rolls until I lean over and vomit. I'm gasping for air as I continue throwing up. After a few dry heaves he wipes my mouth with a cold cloth and hands me a glass of water.

He opens a hatch and throws a bag and a wooden trowel at me. "You made that mess, clean it up. I'm afraid you won't get waited on hand and foot where we are going, princess." he stares at me and waits. I stare back, refusing to move. "Now. Do not make the mistake of ignoring me!" he growls menacingly, his fists clench and I move before he has to repeat himself.

I hurriedly clean the floor the as best I can, retching the whole time. I'm useless around bodily fluids and my stomach wants to empty its contents again. I breathe through my mouth, so I don't have to smell it. I stand, handing the bag to him and he shoves it back into the hatch.

"Pour this over it." He hands me a small bag and I pour it over the wet patch. Its white crystals that soak it up and the smell is alleviated, a bit. I go and sit over the other side just as the driver presses a button and a whoosh of cold fresh air pumped throughout the car, flushing the smell out.

"You will get used to your new way of life. We don't have the riches that the royal dragons have, but we can keep you sufficiently," he tells me.

Suddenly, the flying car is hit with something and we careen to the left. I scream and hold on for dear life.

"Talon, they've caught up with us," the driver shouts over his shoulder.

Talon curses, stalks to the driver and takes the controls. "Of course they have. You keep them busy, and I'll get us home." He orders and I watch as the other man withdraws, what I presume is a weapon. He grabs some cord that is in the hatch and ties it around his waist; he attaches it to a silver ring by the door and looks at me.

"You might want to hold on." He observes and opens the door.

I grip the seat arms and hastily pull on the harness straps. Once I'm clipped in place he leans out and starts firing at whoever is behind us.

"How much further?" The man shouts at Talon as he continues firing at whoever is following us. His shots, which remind me of lightning, brightly light up the sky.

"Almost there! Hang on! I'm taking us in," Talon shouts back, as his hands fly over the buttons in the cockpit space.

The man immediately swings himself back into the car and slams the door shut. He hurriedly straps himself in just before the vehicle plummets down.

"Oh fuck!" I scream as I'm weightless for a few seconds at the sudden drop, the only thing keeping against the seat and not splatting against the window above me are the straps.

"We're in." Talon grins back to the other man. "They won't be able to follow us. We are safe, for now." The other man smirks at me and I shrink back against the chair.

"What do you mean, they can't follow?" I ask, fearful of the answer but needing to know what's happening.

"You'll soon see." The man sat opposite replies. His eyes are roaming all over my body and I feel dirty as he continues to openly leer at me. We land with a thump and my body is jarred so much that my teeth rattle.

"Sorry, princess, I know it's not your usual landing. But get up," he tells me, while he quickly undoes his straps and stands waiting for me to do the same.

I stare at him, mutinously. "No," I tell him, folding my arms across my chest.

Talon doesn't even think about it. He removes a long knife from his boot and stalks towards me. I shrink back as he makes quick work of cutting me free. Before I can even shout out, I'm hoisted over his shoulders and he's out of the car with a jump.

I am so fed up with being tossed around by these oversized males. I boot him in the chest, and grin with satisfaction when I hear him grunt. I give myself a mental high five. I look up, the best I can being over his shoulder at where I am. There are wall scones lit by flame as we head deeper into the darkness. It's a cave and its then that I realise we are underground. It's probably not a good time to inform them that I'm petrified of being underground. I hated cave exploring when I was younger and went away with my parents to Cornwall. They tried to get me into the caves. I hated it then and I have a feeling I'm going to hate it now.

Talon turns a sharp left and we suddenly enter a cavernous room. I put my hands on his shoulders so I can lift myself up and see more. There are rows and rows of what look like, old fashioned wooden beach huts with a small wrap around porch. That's what they look like and I realise they are what they live in here. There's a hole in the centre of the ceiling of the cave, which must go straight to the surface, as it floods the area with a lot of light. Could it be my way out, somehow? There are men standing on their little porches, talking, but that all stops as we walk past.

CHAPTER THIRTY-THREE

*T*he silence is deafening as we pass by the little wooden houses, until we walk into the large beam of light that the hole in the middle of the room provides. Talon steps onto a platform and lifts me off his shoulders. I watch as the men amble over, there are no other women until I spot Simone staring at me. I swear her face flashes with regret briefly until it's quickly replaced with her usual haughty expression. She heads my way and I notice she is guarded. Two men walk by her side, one with his hand on her shoulder. How the hell had she gotten out the other day to the palace to meet with me and why would she willingly return?

"We hit the palace today; this is Prince Brennen's and Ta's mate, Araline." That is met with cheers and cat calls to me.

I stare at them, trying to mask my fear. I know I'm in a far worse predicament here than I ever was at the palace, and its only now that I'm realising how restrained my two mates have been with me.

"When will the bidding start, Talon? I fancy myself a bit of that!" Was shouted out from someone at the back. I couldn't see who, but it was met with more jeers.

Talon laughs roughly, "I know how you feel. I just might put myself in for this one. She's a little hell cat, let me tell you." He pulls me closer to show me off, and I stomp on his foot as hard as I can, but it barely registers.

"See what I mean?"

"We can cure her of her more wayward tendencies!" Was called out from someone. That was met with manly laughter. I was not happy with the way it was going. I can only pray that Brennen and Ta will rescue me soon.

"If she's already mated to them, then we need to do this fast. You know they'll be coming for her." Another man calls out. There are rumblings of agreement.

"We will do it first thing in the morning. Everyone who is interested in entering the bidding, form a line and come and have a look at your new mate!" Talon calls out, while gripping my wrist, making escape impossible.

My stomach drops as nearly every damn man quickly jostles for a place in the line.

"I will not do this! You can't make me! I'm already mated to the next king of this fucking planet! He will kill you all!" I yell at Talon, pulling at his hand, which is shackled around my wrist. "Let me go!"

He leans in close and growls in my ear, "If I let you go, who will protect you until you are mated to the chosen men tomorrow? Do you really think the men will not want to try out the newest female?" he glares at me, "Until you are mated here, you are a temptation. They won't be able to stop themselves from taking. Now, do you still want me to release you?"

The words sink in, and I almost need to vomit again. "No." I whisper, "Don't let them touch me." I can feel tears start but I will be fucked before I let them see me cry.

I stand still while each man in the line, states his interest and hands over a jewel. Some hand over more, some less. Each one takes his moment to size me up. I feel dirty, I'm a slab of meat as I'm told to turn this way, then that. By the time the last man has entered his intentions I'm shattered. All I want to do is crawl into a bed and sleep. At least in sleep I can escape this madness.

"Okay, you know the rules gentlemen. Go to your shelters and stay there until the morn. We will come back here, and the bidding will start. Lance has got the job of now writing the names of who wants in the bidding. So, we will see you all in the morn." Talon informs them all, they do as he says good naturedly and I'm left with Talon and Simone with her two guards.

I really don't know what to say to her, she's looking at me in pity now.

"I'm so sorry, Araline." She lowers her head. "I wouldn't wish this life on anyone."

"Simone!" one of her guards, who I presume must be one of her mates, bit out.

"Take her home." Talon orders gruffly and she is dragged away, her head turns towards me, silently begging for help.

What the ever-loving fuck can I do? I'm stuck here as much as she is!

"How can you treat women like this? She isn't a

possession to be dragged anywhere you demand! You should be ashamed. You're a bunch of disgusting cunts, kidnapping women so you can fuck." I spit at his foot, I can't think of a more profound way to show how disgusted I am with him and the other men here. I don't like using the C-word, but sometimes it just fits.

I'm fuming and if looks could kill, well, Talon would be a shrivelled-up corpse. But he just glares at me, while the cavernous place clears and the excited men leave to stand on their decked front porch of those little wooden houses, chatting. Talon takes my hand and leads me around the vast underground space. No matter that they are nowhere near me now; I feel their lustful gazes tracking us as we walk.

I'm guessing if Talon didn't have such a tight control over them, my being here would create mayhem and a free for all, I shiver with fear.

There are unlit tunnels which are impressively large, leading off to God knows where, sunk into the surrounding walls. So many that I soon cotton on as to why he's showing me them and my heart sinks. I can't remember where the one we entered was. I am lost. There would be no fleeing; I am utterly stuck with them.

We stop outside one of the huts and Talon holds the door open for me to enter. I cross my arms over my chest and stare mutinously at him.

"We can do this the easy way, or the hard way?" he glares at me.

"Why the fuck would I make anything easy for you? You kidnapped me, and tomorrow you're going to force me into a mating with five other men. Fuck you!" I scream at him, my eyes burning with tears. "Put it this way, if you force me to do this, and Brenn and Ta can't rescue me for whatever reason, I will kill myself the first opportunity I get. *Do you understand me?* Even if I have to sharpen a stone from the floor, I will keep trying until I die." I turn away, the sight of him making me want to vomit again.

I hear him sigh and his voice lowers so none of the other males can hear him and he looks around to make sure we are quite alone. "No one is here to hurt you, Araline. There are strict rules in place. No women are to be harmed. Period. If anyone should try to hurt you, come to me. I'll kill them myself." He promises quietly. "Now please come inside, I've had some food and drink brought in. There's a bed to sleep, you must be exhausted." He walks towards me and steers me inside, what else can I do at this point?

CHAPTER THIRTY-FOUR

Brennen

"What do you mean they flew into a fucking mountain?" I roar, thumping a fist on the table, which gives an ominous creak under the force. Jovian wisely takes a step back and watches wearily as I pace around the large marble table.

The table is the royal dragon's special Districts defence tool. The top is a water like liquid that shows pictures of the area we think Araline is now being held. It only works for the reigning family and all we have to do is talk to it and what we want to see will appear. It's kept in the war room of the main palace where we have strategized many battles in the past.

I rub a hand frustratedly over my face; never in my worst nightmares did I think I'd be here, planning the rescue of my mate. I huff and black tendrils of smoke filter from my nose. My dragon is exceedingly pissed off and wants to find Talon and his band of merry men and shred them, while they are still breathing. He craves to hear their screams as their blood flows down the streets.

"Exactly that, one minute they were in front of us, we were blasting them, and then they weren't." Jovian ran a hand through his hair, while he eyes me wearily. "We almost hit the fucking sheer wall. There must be a way in that we don't know about."

My parents, King Kyanite and Queen Sha, stand off to the side, talking low to Ta and his father, Azure. Every dragon is present, waiting for their orders as are the civilian army. All in black, battle ready, it's an impressive sight as they stand, backs straight arms held loosely to their sides with legs braced apart.

"I will rein hellfire down on those bastards." I growl, trying valiantly to pull back from anger. I was taught better than this! I'm a royal dragon for fucks sake, but it's my mate that's been taken from me. I feel powerless for the first time in my life, and I don't like it, not one fucking bit. Taking a few, deep, steadying breathes I roll my shoulders; I can feel my dragon pacing inside me, wanting to extract his own justice to Talon and his friends. They didn't know it yet, but they are dead men walking.

They had best enjoy their last few moments of life, I think darkly.

Father calls out to the General of the non-dragon army ranks. "We know roughly where they escaped to, take your men and we will meet you there. Set up camp and wait for us. We know they must have other exits but it's the only place we can start from." The General nods and barks out his orders to his men, who quickly file out of the war room, leaving only the dragons behind.

"We need the surrounding Districts on lock down; just in case they have any sympathisers who might think now's the time to attack if all the army is at the mountain. Azure, will you and Ta please liaise with the Council members and make sure our people are safe from any splinter cells, they might have." Kyanite gives Ta and his father their orders, knowing they will be affective at carrying them out.

Resting his hand on my shoulder, his voice full of emotion, Ta tells me, "Bring her back. Brenn for fucks sake I need her. We need her." I nod, fearing what would become of us if she were lost to them.

CHAPTER THIRTY-FIVE

I enter the small wooden houses, it's bigger on the inside than I'd imagined, just like the Tardis. Think basic, rustic wood log cabin. The main room has a couple of sofas decorated with brightly coloured cushions. Off to one side is a few cupboards, no kitchen that I can spy. I walk around and spot a bathroom with a hole in the roof. *What the hell is that for?* I look questioningly at Talon as he follows me around.

"Watch." He orders, pressing a button I'd missed by the entry to the bathroom. I watch as water gushes through the hole in the room. "It's a natural waterfall we have tapped into. I'm afraid it's not heated, princess." He shrugs and I grimace at the thought of standing under the cold water. But I suppose it's better than nothing. Not that I'll be here long, Brennen and Ta will come for me. I cross my fingers praying I'm right. Walking into the other room, it's a bedroom that has a bed, more cupboards and that's it. It's not exactly homely.

BRENNEN

There's a knock on the door and I follow Talon back into the main room. He pulls it open and takes a silver platter covered in food from whoever is there, kicks the door shut and places it on one of the cupboards and starts dishing it out onto two smaller plates. He hands me one as he sits, beckoning me to join him. I stay standing, taking the plate I shovel the food in. Not caring what the hell it is, if Brennen or Ta can't reach me, I need my strength to escape. Talon raises an eyebrow at my lack of manners but I'm past caring whether he approves of me in any way.

"Let me explain a bit of what happened here?" he asks while I'm shovelling in the food. He waits until I nod. "My brothers and I were brought up slightly different to other males but once my father was put to death we decided to band together with a few likeminded males. We feel that the way the royals and the Council use the vortex isn't fair. We want a system where the normal males of Mertier are granted a female as often as the royals are." I place my food on the plate and pay attention. "Yes I snatched Simone, but I can promise you she's not been harmed."

"Oh, I'm sure in your warped mind she's not been harmed but using her body as a fuck toy, well, I assure you, have fucking harmed her!" I shout, my heart hurting on Simone's behalf.

"No male has touched her when she's has refused. I made sure the males that won the bidding were good males. She's unhappy at not living at court; she wanted all the rich trappings that would give her."

I'm not sure whether to believe him or not but before I can reply when there's a harsh bang on the door, and I jump, my heart racing. *Can my anxiety get any worse?* It's flung open and the man standing there has me shrinking back, trying to hide in the shadows. He's large and scary looking, with a probing, dark gaze that lingers over my body, tracing my curves with envious eyes.

Talon snaps his fingers, abruptly bringing the strangers attention back to him. "Why have you broken the rules, Fyn? You know you're not permitted to be here or see her till tomorrow morning like all the rest when the bidding starts." He stands, glaring at the intruder. His stance is one of aggression, but I notice he tries to angle his body to defend me, his hands closing to fists, hanging at his side while his legs are braced, he's ready to pounce.

"The royal army have begun to surround the mountain. Thought you'd like to know." Fyn answered sarcastically, his eyes swivelling to me once more; he's almost drooling, like a dog. It disgusts me and I stand more closely behind Talon. Out of the two of them I'll take my chances with him over this Fyn.

"Fuck. But it was to be expected." He stares at Fyn, "How many roughly?" he shifts his body so more of me is protected by his and the other man's agitation is almost palpable. I'm sure if Talon wasn't here, I'd be in dead trouble.

"The whole fucking army." Fyn growled, "They are surveying the area, getting ready for when the fucking dragons arrive. "Let's hope the woman is worth all this aggravation!" Fyn glared at Talon. "We should have just snatched a normal woman. But no, the great Talon has to go a step further and put the rest us in jeopardy!" he sneers.

I wonder what he means, but I dare not say anything as anger permeates the air.

"I only took what I was owed— what was promised to me years ago!" Talon shouts back.

If they didn't cool it, I can see it all kicking off. The idea of them fighting gives me an idea, keep them at, fan the flames and sneak out.

"Perhaps you, Fyn, should be in charge." I murmur, but just loud enough for them both to swivel in my direction. Talon's face is filled with an incredulous look, while Fyn smirks.

"You've no idea what you are saying." Talon tells me, while Fyn steps closer.

Here we go!

"Well it seems to me you've gone and gotten all your men killed. You know they won't allow any of you to live now, and for what? A fuck?" I slowly edge away from Talon, moving along the wall slowly.

"She's right, you fuck." Fyn roared just before he dives for Talon and that's my cue.

They are rolling on the floor, exchanging brutal punch after punch. What little furniture there is in the room is soon smashed to pieces, and I have to duck a couple of times so I don't get hit by flying debris.

I bolt. I fling open the door and head around to the back of the house, no one is around. It seems all the other men are doing as Talon instructed and staying inside. I run hell for leather into the nearest pitch-black tunnel. I've never known anywhere as dark. I literally can't see my hand when I wave it in front of my face.

I slow, putting my hands out trying to feel my way. I walk to the left until my hands touch a solid wall. Okay, I feel a bit better at being able to touch something even if I can't see anything. With my hand grazing the wall I walk forward, knowing at any time the men will realise I'm not there and come looking.

I'm breathing heavy; I'm petrified that my fate will be the same as Simone's. I sniff but pull myself quickly together; I've not got time for hysterics just yet. Later when Brennen and Ta rescue me, then I can fall apart, but not yet.

I have no idea how long I've been walking for. It seems miles and miles, but I suspect it's only a few hundred yards. I jump when the wall curves around a sharp bend and I enter another cavernous room. It sparkles; I smile at how pretty it looks. Covering the walls and ceiling are thousands of beautiful white flowers that glow and pulse. They are alive, and as I walk further into the room, I can feel the beat that whatever they are, are pulsing to. Kneeling, I bury my hands in the red like earth, I'm stunned. I can feel the beat. It's coming from deep underground. It's eerie. I don't know what to make of it. Pulling my hands free I hurry to my feet. I'm sure I just heard angry voices. I run as fast as I can to where I've spotted another tunnel and enter it quickly.

"Agh!" I scream as I fall feet first into a hole. I scramble to find my footing, but land hard on my ass and the breath is knocked out of me. I can't move, as I can't breathe, I panic trying to look around. I'm now in a smaller tunnel, I'm going to have to crawl, it's way too small for me to stand. I hate tight spaces, it's one of my nightmares and I'm living it right now.

Once I can breathe, I inch forward on all fours; it's still

pitch-black and using my hands I feel the ground before I move. I don't want to fall down another hole. Alice in Wonderland, I don't want to be! Bloody hell, I've seen horror films based pretty much on what I'm doing. Poor girl, in a cave. What could possibly go wrong? I feel tears on my cheeks and angrily wipe them away.

If I could get back to Earth, I think I'd kill Macie for not warning me what could happen if I took her shifts cleaning the church. Thinking back, I stop crawling. She only cleaned the church. It was a very part time job. But she had everything she could ever dream of. The best of everything. She couldn't have afforded that on part-time wages. Whoever she was or was joined to, obviously kept her in a manner she would expect to enjoy here. Trying to think back as to how we met, I remember bumping into her at a pub. She was gorgeous. If I fancied girls, then there she was. We kind of fell into a friendship at my local pub. I tripped, and my pint spilled all over her expensive blouse. She hadn't even batted an eyelid. No bloody wonder, when I moved in with her, her house was pretty spectacular to say the least. I wasn't used to such wealth.

Pulling my mind back to the here and now, I have to escape! Inching forward I finally spot a pinprick of light in the distance and head towards it. It's slow going as I'm still nervous about falling again. I feel my way towards it, my heart still pounding and I'm sweating. My bodies not built for this sort of thing!

The closer I get to the light the louder I can hear something, a low whoosh, whoosh. I stop to catch my breath and listen, trying to work out just what it can be. But let's face it, on a strange planet it could be anything. I need to get out and that's my only way, I crawl towards it, almost there, I lay flat on my belly and sort of shuffle forward. I peer out into the light and see a forest. I have to squint as the suns are bright and I've been in darkness for a while now. I must have come out on the other side of the mountain. There's a ledge I could hang down and drop onto, that's not too far off the ground. It's the only way out so, I squeeze through the hole and walk out onto the ledge.

I hear shouting and I quickly flatten against the rock face.

"Fucking find her!" I bite my knuckles in fear as Talons voice rings out clearly. "She can't have got far!"

The *whoosh, whoosh* is back, and I hear the screech of a dragon, then fire and screams. The heat hits me and I have to launch myself back into the hole. The bloody thing zinged my hair! *Think, Araline, think.* How to let the nice friendly dragon know I'm here.

CHAPTER THIRTY-SIX

After some time, when I've finished biting my nails, I lay flat on the ledge and crawl on my belly as if I'm a bloody commando, to the edge and peer over to see what's happening. Well, well done dragon, a few men are on the floor, their bodies still twitching, having been barbequed by its flame. Strike one for the dragon. But some of the forest is now on fire also, making my getaway a tad precarious.

Talon is nowhere to be seen, thank fuck, and I can't hear anyone else down there so if I'm going to make a run for it, the times now. OMG! My body isn't made for this. I heft myself over the edge and now I'm dangling there, my legs hanging in mid-air. I don't like this; I've never in my life had a go at rock climbing. My hands begin to slip. Here goes nothing. I let myself free-fall, biting my tongue until I can taste blood, so I don't scream. The last thing I need is to alert Talon where I am.

I hear the great whoosh, whoosh of dragon wings and

before I can comprehend what the fuck is going on, I'm in its claws. I'm saved! Hurrah!

"I don't know who you are but thank you!" I shout over the flapping of wings. I relax back, but then I realise I'm up in the air, flying again. My stomach rolls but my mind is taking off that as there are shouts coming from the ground. Damn it, we've been spotted!

The dragon heads higher and higher and we are soon soaring through the air. The land and people are far away, there's no way they can possibly catch up. Pulling my knees up, I wrap my arms around them, I'm really not a good flyer.

"Where are we going?" I shout, as I don't recognise anywhere below us. We seem to be heading away from the mountain but not in the direction of the city. "Hey!" I scream as the dragon dips fast. We're plummeting towards the ground in an alarming rate.

I shut my eyes and wonder if the damn dragon is on a suicide mission and has decided to take me along for the ride. But we land gracefully and opening his claw I tumble onto the dry dusty ground. I lay there for a moment, thanking god I'm still alive. Still on the floor I watch as the dragon shimmers and turns back into a man.

"Holy fuck!" I shout, standing quickly I back away. "But... But..." I repeat, stupidly I stare at Talon. "You're a royal?" I don't get it; I was told only royals could turn into dragons? Have I fallen asleep and dreaming? Or hallucinating?

"Yes, Araline. I am a royal fucking dragon. I bet Brennen forgot to mention that." He sneers, walking towards me. "My father was the second brother of the King. But revolted against him because they had a difference of opinion. When he was put to death, his sons were banished and banned from ever having an Earth woman."

I don't know what to say to that, I stare at him stupidly, my mouth opening and closing like a damn fish gasping for breath.

"Let me get this straight. You and your brothers are royal dragons, which have been kicked out of the family because your father had a case of different opinions with the King?" I step away from him, scanning the area in case I can make a run for it, but who am I kidding? If he's a bloody dragon he'll have no problems in catching me. "Why wasn't I told any of this?" I am going to batter Brennen and Ta when I see them again. My legs give way and I sag onto the floor. It's dry like a desert; I've no idea where the hell we are. My eyes are stinging due to both of the suns being high in the sky and not having any of those protective visors.

"You must see that the royal way of doing things when it comes to human females, is wrong?" he grates, coming to stand where I'm sat.

"Yes, totally. It's barbaric to expect women to just accept that they will be handed to men to enjoy and reproduce. Women are nothing more than walking wombs here." I state, feeling lost and frightened, all I want to do is go home. I was just beginning to feel like Brennen's palace was my home and now, not so much. Will I always be in danger here? Will the males that don't agree with the King always seek me out and use me as a pawn to their cause.

"Are the men of Earth so perfect?" Talon interrupts my thoughts. He sits so close I can feel his body heat. "Are they so worthy of your love? I have walked on your Earth many a time, where did you think our males learn about what females enjoy in bed?" He glances at me with a wry grin. "I have seen what is happening there, how some men treat women they profess to love? It's sickening," he spat out.

They learn about sex on earth? Well I suppose they have to learn somewhere and I have to give him credit for his argument. The men, certainly some of the ones I've come into contact with, aren't worthy of love. I shake my head, "No, some of them aren't." I whisper.

"Every single woman we bring here is loved." He stated, as if that made it any better.

"Simone isn't. She's damaged. I heard you handed her off to your right hand man, along with four other men. That's not right. That's slavery, Talon, surely you can see that?" I look him in the eye and see the look of pain briefly that flashes across his face.

"What happened to Simone isn't usual. We've already had this conversation." He rubs a hand over his face, in frustration. "We aren't the monsters you want to believe we are. We are a dying race and would have perished hundreds of years ago if we didn't have the Earth women join us. We want to love and cherish you all. Until we find out the reason why we can't have females, until then, the only way is to bring them here."

I sigh, "Again, I get the reason why, I do, and I suppose the women who come here have known all their life what awaits them. I just find it all rather mind boggling." I tell him, and I do understand the why. If Earth could only produce males and were offered a way to breed then, yes, I expect they would grab it with both hands. Does it make it right? I don't have the answer for that right now.

"We just want a fairer system, where every male has an opportunity to be entered into the bidding. At the moment it's only who the Council deems worthy enough. Of course, the dragons are our priority, we understand that they are our defence and as such deserve to be."

"I get that. Can't you arrange a meeting with Kyanite? I'm sure if you put your ideas to him, he'd listen. It only seems fair that he does." I ask, hoping he'll see sense and fly me back as well. I stare at him; he doesn't resemble the frightening male that crashed Brennen's palace. Oh, he's still scary; the scar on his face doesn't allow you to forget that. But he's only carrying out what his father believed. There are a quite a few that follow what their fathers believe in without question.

"Believe me, we have tried. There was such bad blood between our father and the King that I don't think he can bear to even look at us." He stands hands loosely by his side. He's looking into the distance and I stand with him.

"What is it?" I ask, peering into the never-ending dessert. "I can't see anything."

"You will, your human eyes aren't as powerful as dragons." He closes his eyes and seems resigned to whatever is heading our way.

I hear it. The *whoosh, whoosh* of wings, many wings. I hold my breath, yes, there are dragons coming! I can see the sand their wings are kicking up into a sandstorm. It's a spectacular sight. "Are they your brothers, or the other royals?" I wonder out loud.

"These are yours." He tells me.

I watch as the magnificent dragon's land a few feet from us, whipping up the sand until I have to cover my eyes.

CHAPTER THIRTY-SEVEN

There are a lot of dragons, but I don't care, I'm saved! Hurrah!

A dragon shimmers and my Brennen stands there, naked and proud. He looks positively furious; the anger aimed at Talon is almost palpable. I turn, facing my abductor, I feel pity for him. Where had that come from? He's lost his family, his whole world because he's stood by his beliefs.

No, I don't agree with his methods, but I have to admire that he is willing to lose everything to stand by what he believes is right. I hear more *whoosh, whoosh,* and look behind me, his four brother's land, taking position behind Talon. This could get ugly, real fast.

"Talon!" I hear Brennen roar, "I am going to kill you!"

I watch in horror as he charges towards Talon, his face a picture of utter rage. He's like a raging bull after the elusive red flag. A few other dragons hurry to follow, not wanting

Brennen to face a foe without them. He skids to a stop in front of me and grabs me until I'm squished against his chest.

"Are you unharmed, Little Flower?" his hands run over my body as if to check that I am okay. I notice they shake a little, ahh he really does care. He brings his face down and kisses me. Oh, what a kiss! Everything is forgotten for a few blissful seconds before he's pulling back.

"Yes, Brenn. I'm fine." I smile reassuringly up at him as he leans in, pressing his lips against mine. I wrap my arms around him, home. He is my home and I finally acknowledge that.

Pulling away he points towards the rest of his dragons, "Go to them, Araline. They will see you safely back to the palace. Ta is impatiently waiting for your return." I walk away, towards the waiting dragons. Turning, I face where Brennen and Talon glare at one another.

With speed I can't track with my poor human eyes, Brennen's fist smashes into Talon's nose. The audible crack as the bone shatters is loud enough that even I can hear it. Blood spurts from it, which he wipes angrily away.

"You really fucked up when you took my mate." Brennen yells at him.

Talon retaliates with a lethal punch to Brennen's chin. The crunch makes me cringe and I start to run back to them, only to be pulled back by a dragon.

"Brennen," I scream, and watch as he turns to face me, only to have one of Talons brothers kick him in his back, sending him sprawling to the ground. What a coward's way to fight. Fuck, I caused that. I scream as Brennen shouts in frustration and hauls himself up. All the dragons, apart from the one I'm with quickly join him and it's on now.

I instinctively fall to my hands and knees, rolling into a ball as the men shift to dragons. All I can do is, stay still and pray I don't get flambéed as I feel the heat from the flames. I'm lifted from the floor, the dragon I was stood by has me in its claw and I'm placed away from the line of fire.

The noise of the dragons screaming has me putting my hands over my ears before they start bleeding. The fighting is horrific to be this close. I watch as they literally tear each other apart. I have to stop this; I have to find a way to get their attention before they all end up fried or worse.

Come on Araline, think! I stand, brushing off the sand. I can whistle, loudly. Putting my fingers in my mouth I whistle, it's like a fog horn going off; I learnt to do it from my dad when I was young and I used to love doing it, people found it incredulous a noise like that could come from a little girl, it used to make us laugh. It really is loud. I do it a few times until they all turn in my direction.

"That's enough!" I scream. "Talon, your men must have known the consequences and what would happen to them, when you kidnapped me! You are flouting the laws of this planet. Whether you agree with them or not, you are in the wrong! Now stop being wankers and go with Brennen and sort this shit out! I'm hot, dirty and fed up with being a bloody pawn. Grow a pair of balls, sort it out or piss off for good." I'm shaking with anger. I'm covered in sand, I feel sweaty, dirty and desperately tired. I'm running purely on adrenaline and I'm about to crash.

They stare at me. I giggle, acknowledging it's a hysterical

giggle out of being so scared at the sight of huge ass dragons frozen in place staring at me as if I've grown two heads. "Now!" I shout.

They shift back to males and Talon says softly, "She's feisty, cousin. I like her."

Brennen shakes his head, staring at me. "I'm beginning to realise that."

"Talon, tell Brennen what's going on. Why you do what you do, explain to him why families should stand together and not hurt one another just because you believe in different methods." My hands are on my hips as I try and get them to talk.

Talon rubs a frustrated hand over his scarred face. "We didn't have the upbringing you had, Brenn." He says softly.

"We know." Brennen interrupts him, his stance is still one of anger but at least he's willing to listen.

"As much as I hate saying it, we are a product of that upbringing." Talon sighs heavily, and his brothers shift uneasily behind him.

"And we feel nothing but guilt that we didn't get to you all in time." Brennen says. I walk back over and stand by his side. He picks up my hand he kisses the palm gently. "You can come back with me, and we can talk to the King. Or you can go into hiding and I guarantee you, you will be hunted and executed without a hearing in front of the Council. You kidnapped the future Queen!" He looked at them; I see sadness in his eyes. It's then I realise this won't have a happy ending. This family is ruptured; I can only pray they find a way to mend it.

"We can try, but you know what your fathers like, Brenn." Talon says sadly as if he knows his fate.

"Your brothers can stay here." Brennen instructs, already turning away from him.

"No, we all come back. I think that would show we are all in agreement. If I come alone, what guarantee do I have that he won't just kill me? No, my brothers join me." Talon stood his ground, and I knew he wouldn't be moved on this.

A few strained minutes pass before Brennen gives a curt nod and I breathe a sigh of relief. I really wasn't in the mood to witness a blood bath.

"Talon, I'm going to stay behind and let our men know what's happening." One of Talons brothers says he had shifted back to human, god; these dragon men aren't shy of being naked.

"Good idea, let's hope we can tell you what's happening." Talon replied dryly.

Brennen coughs, shaking his head. "You have no men to inform. Our troupes have taken them all into custody by now." Brennen drops the bombshell and I see the fury that ignites in Talon's eyes.

"What about Simone, Brenn? She was there as well?" I ask, my hand grabbing his. "She is innocent in all this!"

"She's going to be staying in a place that's safe for her; I give you my word Little Flower. No harm will come to her." Brennen tells me, the truth is evident in his eyes and I nod.

There's nothing else for Talon and his brothers to do, either run and be in hiding for the rest of their lives or follow Brennen back to the city.

After a few minutes of thinking, Talon nods, and his brothers fall in behind him, waiting for orders.

"Follow us." Brennen orders and puts me down. "I will carry you, Araline. Are you ready?"

I don't really have a damn choice, do I? I nod, too tired now to really care. Fuck it, I just want to sleep and have a bath.

He shifts into his dragon and holds open his razor-sharp claws for me to step into. I do and sit down; he closes it around me until I'm enclosed within them. They feel as strong as any steel prison would. Leaning against them, I close my eyes as he unfurls his wings and we are airborne again. If you had told me last year I'd be involved with dragons, I'd have died laughing. But here we are.

I try desperately not to react as the floor disappears from us, but I can't stop the whimper as he climbs higher and higher. I can move my body as he's not holding me too tightly and I spy Talon and his brothers flying tightly behind us, with Brennen's dragons behind them. It's a pretty awesome sight, I've seen them all before, but to be up close and personal it's pretty impressive.

I'm glad to say the flight home isn't as eventful as it was to get to the mountains, and we soon land in front of the King and Queens's palace. I'm released from Brennen's claws and walk a tad unsteadily towards the steps, where Ta is waiting for me. He pulls me against his chest, lifting my face he covers it in soft kisses before taking my lips in a blistering kiss.

"I thought I had lost you." He whispers against my lips. "I don't think I'd have survived if anything had happened to you." He lifts me up, effortlessly and I wrap my legs around his waist. I'm oblivious to where I am as his kiss heats my blood. Pulling back, I realise I'm really safe and burst into tears. I sob into his shoulder as Brennen walks up and wraps his arms around me, kissing my neck.

"You're safe, Araline." He whispers. "Take her home, Ta. Love her. I will join you both once I've sorted the mess with Talon."

I twist in Ta's arms and face Brennen, sniffing I get my crying under control. "Listen to them, Brenn. Try to work out a solution without banishing your family. I'm sure you can do this."

He stares at me, "I will try, but it's up to the King." He wipes away my tears and nods his goodbye. I watch Brennen walk away, and part of me wants to run after him. He has such a strong walk, like the predator that he is. Talon and his brothers are surrounded by the dragon guards, they aren't giving them space to shift and fly away. I know they've done wrong, but they are Brennen's family and as I've never had one really, I want him to make whatever's going on between his father and cousin's, right.

After Ta places me on my own feet, he takes my hand, places a pair of visors over my eyes and leads me towards another flying vehicle, I wonder if I will ever get used to flying so much? But I somehow doubt it. Once we are seated and I'm strapped in, it takes off and Ta turns to me, "Are you sure they didn't hurt you?"

I can see his eyes are full of worry as they glance over my body as if I'm hiding some bruises. "No, they really didn't hurt me. But I'm glad I was rescued when I was. If I hadn't managed to get away, I don't think I'd have wanted to live if I'd been handed off to five of the men." I sigh, close my eyes and lean my head against the headrest, god I'm tired. I realise I've not slept all night and I'm exhausted. My body has been pumping adrenaline into my system to aid me in escaping but now I feel myself crashing.

Ta tenderly brushes his hand over my cheek, "Sleep, Araline. You are perfectly safe now." His lips gently kiss mine and I'm asleep before I can kiss him back.

CHAPTER THIRTY-EIGHT

I'm overheating; I fling the silk covers off me restlessly. Coming awake more fully, I realise I'm naked and in bed, turning I look at Ta. He is truly beautiful and looks completely at peace as he sleeps on his side facing me. I love his silver hair, so completely different to any man's hair I've ever known. One of his hands cups my breast and my nipples harden as I feel a wave of erotic longing flood my system.

Without a thought I stroke his chiselled jaw, then lean in to kiss his velvet soft lips. God help me, I need him. I can't wait for Brennen to come home to have the pair of them again, but I need Ta now. This lifestyle is confusing. I start to pull away as I don't want to hurt Brennen by fucking Ta while he isn't here. *When did life become so god damn confusing?* I know he explained that it was perfectly all right to be with one while the other isn't around. But I'm still too new to this.

"Come back here." Ta pulls me closer, obviously awake

now and his kiss, oh my, its heated passion. As our tongues duel his hand skims down my body until he's stroking my clit with such carnal knowledge it has me trembling in his arms.

Ta pulls back from the kiss, his eyes flashing silver to match his hair, which I'm beginning to realise they do when he's highly aroused or angry. "Fuck you're so wet and ready for me, but I have to taste you!" he pushes me onto my back and I watch him through hooded eyes as his lips leave a trail of devastation. He presses kisses on his journey to my straining clit.

"Ta..." I moan when his lips fully suck my clit into his mouth. "That feels so good! Don't stop!" I beg. My hips thrust upwards and one of his hands pins me back to the bed. I can't move and for whatever reason I find that just sexy!

So intense are the feelings they have me screaming, not that I'm aware of what I'm doing. I'm lost in the maelstrom of peaks that rush me head long into the most glorious orgasm! My body arches, but Ta keeps me pinned to the bed. He's not content to the one release he wants more.

"Give me everything!" He demands as his warm breath tickles me before he dives back in and sucks my now tender clit into his mouth.

"I can't!" I shriek as I feel his fingers slip into me with ease; they rub a certain place, deep inside that has my eyes popping wide. Stroking me, demanding silently that I will give him what he wants. The heat that mended my ankle, is now stroking me on the inside! I don't think I can handle it. It's scorching me, but at the same time it throws me straight into another orgasm. "Fuck! Oh fuck, Ta!" I feel my whole body shaking as he keeps me flying higher and higher.

Before I can catch my breath, I'm flipped onto my stomach and as my cunt is still clenching with the release, he thrusts into me. I groan at the invasion, as we move up the bed with his powerful thrusts, until my hands grip the headboard.

"Araline, you feel fucking perfect. Squeezing my cock so hard! I won't last!" Ta cries as his hips pound into me, it's almost brutal but damn it, I love it.

He brings my body upright, until my back is snug against his chest. My head falls back and rests on his chest; I briefly close my eyes as I feel his fingers travel down my body until he parts my lower lips and strokes my clit. His other hand grips my hip in a vice like hold, which I just know will leave bruises, he ploughs into me. I can't catch my breath as he shows no mercy, not that I need any. Varying the speed, he slows his hips and draws my leg up so he can get in even deeper! God, he rubs my clit and I'm bucking into him chasing my orgasm. My knuckles are white from gripping the headboard as I feel it growing, almost there, almost there!

With a well-timed pinch to my clit, I'm thrown into another release.

"Fuck, Ta! Fuck, fuck, fuck, yes!" I scream incoherently. I've lost control of my body as my head slumps forward and rests on the headboard. He lowers my leg but continues to fuck me.

"Fuck, Araline, you grip my cock so hard. I can't..." he moans as he reaches his own release, but I'm too lost in the fog of my post orgasm to take much notice.

He collapses on top of my back, biting my neck and making me yelp, before rolling us until we are side by side. Our bodies are slick with sweat but I'm past caring. My heart is beating wildly, and my body feels like a pool of mellow jelly.

"OMG! I needed that." I moan as he pulls his cock free from my body.

He turns me and kisses me with such passion, I'm lost once more. But too quickly he pulls away and sits up, "Come on, we need to wash the other men's scents off you. If I can smell them, then Brenn's dragon will for sure." He leaves the bed and walks to my side. Leaning down he effortless pulls me into his arms and picks me up. Damn this man is strong. I snuggle into his warm body and close my eyes as he walks towards the bath. I've fantasised many a time about being in a man's arms, just like this.

My eyes open once the water is lapping at us. I love how this water feels on my nakedness. Unlike Earth, we don't use any kind of soaps to get clean, the water does it all. After dunking my head a few times even my hair feels refreshed. I stop to admire Ta's body again as he swims a few lengths, I still can't believe that he is mine. He's leaner than Brennen but he has sporty muscles that show he must do some sort of physical recreation. But I have no idea what. To be honest I've not really wanted to know much about either Ta or Brennen as I've only wanted to leave, now I want to stay, it's about time I learnt more about them both.

"Ta, I'm hungry." I tell him, just before my stomach growls angrily making me blush as we walk to the edge of the bath, he follows me, giving my ass a slight tap, but hard enough to make me squeal.

"I should have fed you sooner. I'm sorry Araline." He looks ashamed as if it's his job to make sure I eat.

"Hey," I pull him down and kiss him, whispering against his lips, "Its fine, I'm not going to die if I miss a few meals." As always as soon as we are out of the water then we are dry. It's pretty amazing, one minute your wet, the next your dry.

Ta reaches for a button on the side of the wall and talks into it as I get dressed. The underwear fits like perfection and a floaty silk skirt flows around my ankles. A soft T-shirt clings to my curves a little more than I like, but by the way Ta's heated gaze travels up and down my body makes me feel more confident in it. I spy some flat shoes and slip them on my feet. I have to admit, I'm getting used to the luxurious clothes here. They are utterly feminine and make me feel all girly as I swish the skirt around. While I'm twirling around Ta is getting dressed, once he's ready he laughs at my antics and nods towards the doorway.

"Come on, let's get you fed." Taking my hand we walk down the magnificent staircase until we are seated on the multi coloured cushions with a mountain of food in front of us.

"How many did they think they were feeding?" I look in astonishment at all the verity and amount that was on the glass server plates. "Are we expecting company?"

Ta laughs, "No just us, Brenn will eat at the palace." As he explains, he picks up my plate and heaps it with a bit of each, placing it in front of me. I'm not used to being waited on, it's kind of nice. I wait until he has his own plate filled, then picking up the weird fork I take a cautious nibble.

OMG! The pure, clean taste bursts on my palate. This food, whatever it is the most delicious I've ever had. It's so much better than the cheap food I could afford on Earth. I try to slow myself as I'm shovelling it in like a right uncouth pig. I wipe my mouth with the back of my hand, to make sure I'm not dribbling, but seriously this food. I shake my head and close my eyes as I enjoy it. Opening them I look at Ta, he's not eaten anything yet, but watching me with pride shining out of his eyes.

"I am so happy you enjoy our food." He joins me and starts to eat. I try to imitate his impeccable table manners. If it's true and I'm meant to be a queen one day here, then I need to start behaving like one, and not shovelling the food into my gob. It might be a good idea to get hold of Alish and get some etiquette lessons in.

"Tell me, Ta, what started the argument between the king and his brother and why was it so bad that he put his own brother to death?" I chew my food, looking at him expectantly.

He swallows and looks thoughtful before answering. "They had always had a tenuous relationship. Rhodium was a malicious male. He was vicious to all his sons. He believed their dragons needed to be beaten into submission. He wanted his own mini army that he could control and that would answer only to him. Brenn's father didn't agree with him on a lot of points. Rhodium also wanted to bring as many women as he could through the vortex. He wanted to have women in positions of servitude to our people. Make them into slaves to be used in any way we saw fit." He put his knife and fork by his plate as if he found the idea of eating while telling me this distasteful.

"Rhodium, before he was put to death, had brainwashed his sons into agreeing with his wishes. I fear that the council will end up putting all five brothers to death." He looks sad, reaching over I give his hand a squeeze. He looks at me and smiles. "Those boys used to be little hell raisers. Always in trouble and acting out. We didn't catch onto what their father was doing to them until it was too late. We suspect he beat their mother to death, but we had no proof and by the time that happened the boys were young males. After their father was put to death, they went into hiding before we could bring them in for help."

"But in the gardens, I heard Talon say, "You should bow down to me for what I've done for Mertier." What did he do?" He was silent for a while as our plates and untouched food is cleared away. I smile at the server, a young boy who grins happily back at me. I pop some of the chocolate seeds into my mouth and have a mouthgasm at how delicious they are.

Ta waits until they've left. "Many years ago, Brenn's mother was taken by the Rumos, the ones that attacked just after you arrived and taken off world. Her second mate was also murdered by them and she was missing for a long time. But Talon and two of his brothers went up there and retrieved her. As soon as they were back here, they were put in jail. It was thought if they were in jail, they could be un-conditioned to what their father had beaten into them. But it didn't happen. I know it sounds barbaric, but we want them to be able to live in our society. Not be outcasts, but at present they are just too dangerous to the women to be allowed that. They have been in and out of jail over the years many times but eventually we let them go. Is a sad situation." His voice is full of emotion. "I used to play with them all as a young male. We learnt to fight together. I had no clue as to what their sadistic father was doing to them all. They brushed off the bruises as ones they got while training." He looks away, I sigh, it's obvious he feels a bit to blame for not reaching out to his friends.

"People suffering from abuse often hide what they are going through. It's no one's fault but Rhodium's. I'm glad he was put to death, but I don't want Talon and his brothers to have the same fate. That's not fair." I say wishing I could come up with a solution for them all.

"I hope Brennen can reach a happy conclusion. I'd hate any more deaths as a result of a mad man." Ta says softly, bringing his goblet of their potent wine he takes a loud gulp.

I haven't touched a drop since the party at the palace, so I tentatively take a sip. OMG! It's strong. I place it back quickly, knowing only a few sips will have me drunk again. "I do to, how do you kill a dragon anyway? I don't expect it's an easy thing to do?" I ponder, how on earth, or I should say, on Mertier do they could kill something so powerful.

Ta shudders, "We have a certain metal which renders the dragon dormant in a body. Once a male is bound in it, they cut the head off. Beheading is the only thing that will kill a dragon host and once the dragon has no host it turns to vapour and dissipates."

"That's so sad." I whisper, thinking of how awe-inspiring the dragons are and not wanting to see a single one put to death. "I really hope it doesn't come to that." I pop a couple of the sweet things into my mouth that I seem to have become addictive to hoping they can lift my spirits, but no. I slump into the cushions but jump as the door slides open and Brennen is stood there.

CHAPTER THIRTY-NINE

*H*is eyes flitter over me then goes to Ta, he rubs a hand over his face before he stalks towards us.

"How did it go?" I stand; with about as much grace as a baby hippo, really I'm not used to all this sitting on cushions malarkey. His arms surround me and pulls me into his chest. He's warm and I eagerly hug him back.

He pulls back before saying, "They've been locked up at present. Until we and the Council can come to some sort of agreement as to what to do with them."

"Ta has been explaining about their father. He sounds a right wanker!" I look up into his deep navy eyes, they look troubled and I just want to ease him a little, but I have no clue as to what I can do for him.

"He and his brothers are all kind of fucked up and it kills us that we didn't find out until it was too late. They were already too far gone under his control. But sometimes there is no easy way out, if they are considered too dangerous to live with us, then we don't have a lot of options." He picks me up; I quickly wrap my legs around his waist.

"Enough of talking, we can't do anything at the present. But I need you, Little Flower." His voice drops to a sexy, husky whisper as his head lowers to nuzzle my neck. His velvet soft lips graze a sensitive spot that has me arching into his body.

"I have to talk to my father, see if we can come up with a solution." Ta tells us, as he steps in and presses kisses to the back of my neck. "Take Araline and forget for a few hours. I will probably be back later tonight." He lavishes me with a kiss when I turn to look at him. His tongue slips into my mouth and I can't keep the sigh from slipping free. Bloody hell, these men!

"I know now's not the time, and I know you've explained it before, but I don't understand this lifestyle. Are you sure it's okay for me to, um..."? I can feel my face blushing, ducking my head I mumble. "Be fucked by you both separately? Are you sure it doesn't hurt anyone's feelings?" I'm now wondering if maybe I should have questioned Alish? I don't want to offend either male.

Ta brings my head back up they are both grinning.

"Little Flower, we know your new to this, you can ask as many questions as you need, as many times as you need. We only want to help you become accustomed to your new life. It's always your choice. If you want sex, it doesn't matter who you go to. We are both your mates. If only one of us is around and you get horny," Brennen wiggles his eyebrows playfully, "then he will do whatever you wish."

Ta leans in and whispers, "I had the pleasure of your body

earlier. It was one of the best moments of my life." He kisses me, and oh my, my blood sings in my veins. He pulls away far too quickly for my liking. "Now Brenn, will have the pleasure of hearing you cry out in passion."

Well I guess that explains it. I have to remember it's a completely different culture to what I'm used to. I nod, "Thank you, I didn't want to hurt anyone's feelings."

"You couldn't if you tried, Little Flower." He kisses my forehead, and I melt. I love those kisses. "Ta, we'll see you later." Brennen tells him, before marching away, with me still in his arms.

"Bye, Ta." I call out, blowing him a kiss.

We spend the next few hours, blissfully learning each other's bodies. It's tender and romantic and he has me crying out in ecstatic release several times. But I'm still not used to seeing his dragon scales shimmer just under his skin and his eyes turning into dragon eyes when he wants me to know that he's present with us. His two cocks that protrude when he's hard is an added excitement for me to learn about. I take extra time to see what makes him cry out with pleasure when I touch them both. When he takes me doggy style his extra, smaller cock, that is still quite impressive, fucks my ass, so even though I'm not, at present with two males it feels like I am. Utterly mind blowing!

I don't know, between Brennen, Ta and the dragon, they are going to keep me in a permanent state of arousal.

We finally pass out with me sprawled on his chest and his cock still buried inside me. We are a sweaty mess, and my heart is trying desperately to slow, I'm panting, and I glance up into Brennen's eyes.

"Oh, Little Flower, you do please us." He runs his fingertips down my spine, causing me to shiver.

I've never had sex as much as I have the last few days and certainly never with two men! The women on this planet who have five men have my upmost respect, how do you keep up with that amount of men? It baffles me.

"You are amazing, Brenn. I never knew sex could be like this. You both best keep your stamina up as I've lots of time to make up for the shitty sex I had before." I smile and close my eyes, but I feel his rumble of laughter and he hugs me tighter.

"Whatever you want, Little Flower, it's yours. Anytime. Just come to us and we will do our very best to keep you satisfied." He tells me, flexing his cock inside me, I moan.

"I'm tired, let me sleep." I whine, what does he do? He laughs as he pulls his cock free and we both moan at the loss. He rolls us, so my back is pressed against his chest and pulls the silk covers over us.

"Sleep. You are safe and loved." His hand cups my breast possessively and I do as he says, I fall asleep with a happy smile on my face.

At some point later, half asleep I feel the bed dip and another warm body slips under the light cover. "Ta?" I murmur, before I snuggle into him. Their bodies are far warmer and feel like my own personal hot water bottles. His arms go around me, and he kisses me sweetly.

"Sleep, Araline. We are here." His hands caress down my body and I do as he says and fall into a deep sleep.

The next morning, I wake startled and sit up quickly.

"What is it, little flower?" Brennen asks me, sitting up he

manoeuvres me until I'm sitting between his legs, with my back against his chest.

Ta comes to and also sits up, rubbing the sleep from his eyes. "You okay, Araline?" he asks, looking concerned.

Now I feel silly, I was having a dream and these two males took front and centre stage. A very erotic dream. I blush and duck my head, "Sorry, was having a vivid dream." I mumble.

"Oh, tell us." Ta insists, by the wicked gleam in his eye I know he's noticed me blushing and probably has a pretty good idea what the dream was about. My hormones are raging today. Being in such close proximity to them would have that effect on anyone, I reason with myself.

"Was it something like this?" Ta moves with speed, and before I can cry out, he's lying on his front, my legs have been parted and his mouth is on my clit.

Brennen's hands are on my breasts, pinching my hard nipples. While his mouth nips at the sensitive bit on my neck. He's holding me in place as Ta does naughty things with his tongue.

"Does that feel good, Araline?" he whispers in my ear. He hooks his feet under my legs and spreads them further apart, allowing Ta more access to my body.

Fuck, I'm lost as my eyes flutter closed and my body demands more. "More, Ta, please." I gasp as he slips a finger inside me.

"Fuck, the view from here is enough to make me come." Brennen growls as he rests his chin on my shoulder, looking down my body to where Ta is feasting on it. I can feel his hard cocks in my back as I sink deeper into the fantasy that has become my life. I don't recognise myself, who is this girl being ravaged by not one but two men. I'm lost, if they stopped now, I know I'd be the one to demand they continue.

I'm imprisoned within a cage that Brennen's legs and arms have formed around me, which keep me from moving too much. I can feel his heated skin as his mouth nips my neck. It's so much pleasure, almost too much as I chase my orgasm.

"Please, please." I moan just as Ta uses his fingers and rubs my clit. I feel the blinding heat that I'm becoming used to surround my clit and I'm flying. My eyes are screwed shut as my body bucks under the onslaught of wave after wave of unadulterated pleasure which floods my system.

Before I can comprehend what's happening, I'm flipped onto my stomach and Ta's cock is buried in me, in one, hard thrust. I'm face to face with Brennen's cocks. I enthusiastically suck on the main one and tease the smaller one, well, it would be rude not to, as I'm here and all.

"Fuck, yes, suck me Little Flower." Brennen roars as my eyes skim up his body and I watch with fascination as his dragon scales shimmer just under his skin. I stroke my hands up his chiselled abs and the scales follow my hands. As if the dragon is seeking my touch. I look into his eyes they flash to his dragon and I know he's here with us. All the while my mouth is using his cock as if it's my favourite flavoured lollipop, I suck and slurp, loving that I can get this powerful being all hot and bothered.

Ta runs his fingertips down my spine and dips around me. He grips my breasts roughly and I revel in it. I arch my back, pushing my body against his harder, silently demanding more.

"Fuck, you feel so tight wrapped around my cock. So wet and hot. I can feel your pleasure coating my balls. Fuck your dripping for us!" I can't answer; all I can do is moan around Brennen's cock again as Ta's white-hot fingers pinch my nipples.

I'm being used and used hard. I wish I could say I hated it. But fuck, I so don't! I want them both again. I remember how it had felt to have both cocks in me. I pop Brennen's cock out of my mouth, and he groans. I'm not sure Ta will be able to stop as he's thrusting into me for all he's worth.

"I need you both," I pant, "Please, both of you. I need to feel you both, in me!" I cry as my nipples are pinched, which sends blinding need straight to my clit. "Please, both of you fuck me!"

Brennen pulls me off Ta's cock, and he grunts. I feel my cunt ripple with the need to be filled.

"On your back, Ta!" Brennen orders, and as Ta moves into position; Brennen lifts me and impales me once again on Ta's cock.

"Fuck!" Ta shouts and pulls me in close to kiss me, his tongue thrusting into my mouth just as his cock is doing to my body. Brennen moves in tightly behind me and I can hear the noise of lube being stroked onto his cocks and fingers stroking it into me. I whimper into Ta's kiss and grip his shoulders tightly.

"Hurry up, Brenn, I don't think I can last much longer! I want her to come again before we do!" Ta barks out.

My whole body is shaking as Brennen starts pushing his cock into the extra tight hole. I hold my breath until he breaches the firm ring of muscle. Once full in I moan and my mouth clamps onto Ta's shoulder. I bite him so hard that I can taste his blood.

"I'm sorry. Oh, fuck Ta. He's in me!" I groan.

"Does it feel good?" he asks as he slips a finger between us and begins to stroke my clit, it feels overly sensitive, but I can't stop rubbing myself on his finger. "You feel fucking amazing, so tight. My balls need to empty into you."

"I'm going to come, oh fuck. It feels... it feels so good." I pant. The feeling of being full, with two cocks, is indescribable. A breathy sigh leaves me when they start to move in perfect synchronisation. One in, one out, over and over until I don't know whose body belongs to who.

I'm squashed between them and I realise I don't want to be anywhere but with them. They've opened my eyes to what my body is capable of and I never want them to stop.

"Come, Little Flower!" Brennen orders as he loses control and their soon both thrusting without coordination.

It's too much, too much pleasure, too much eroticism for me to handle.

"Fuck me. Fuck me hard!" I scream just before I'm hit with an orgasm that has my body bowing and my pleasure gushing from me. I swear, I'm seeing flashing orbs of lights behind my tightly closed eyes.

"Fuck, Brenn, I'm coming." Ta shouts as he thrusts into me one last time. His face is one of pure masculine pride as he lifts his fingers and sucks off my juices. "You taste so good. I could live of your releases." He whispers as Brennen joins him, he comes and roars out his release.

Brennen is panting as he rests his head on my shoulder,

presses light kisses onto my heat flushed skin. "Little flower," he pants, "let's do that again?"

"Again?" I ask incredulously, he's got to be joking! "Let me sleep first, then a bath then we might... might do it again. You've both worn me out!" I mumble and I'm unconscious before he can form an answer.

CHAPTER FORTY

Six months later

The past six months have been a revelation, and I haven't stopped smiling, I even wake up with a beaming smile on my face most days especially when I think of the delicious things that they do to me almost nightly or daily, or just whenever the mood dictates. Holy hell, I wish I had a phone; I really need a girly chat. Okay, I'll ring Alish when I can and see if I can go over for a visit.

With that decision made I fling off the silk sheet and pad into the bathroom. After taking care of business I wade into the silver water and sink into its warm embrace. I let my body fully submerge and look at my skin. It gently glows the silver that I now associate with this planet and the dragons.

I'm suddenly thrown as Brennen jumps in, his dragon's body making a small tidal wave that has me tumbling under the water. I feel its claws around me as he lifts me free. I'm coughing and spluttering as I try and catch my breath.

I smack its claws without thinking. "Did you have to do that?" I glare into its eye as he brings me up for a better look. His great body is shaking with laughter. "Oh, you're so damn funny." I growl at him, "Let me down, you overgrown lizard."

Ta walks in and barks out a laugh, "An overgrown lizard!" he doubles up with laughter.

Brennen places me gently back into the water and before Ta realises what he's up to, he uses his vicious tail and smacks it into the water. Ta is forced onto his knees from the sheer weight of water that is cascaded over him.

He takes a moment to catch his breath, "Very funny." He grumbles before diving into the water. He swims over to me. After tenderly kissing me he asks, "How are you feeling, Araline? If you had any soreness from us last night, the healing water should be taking care of that right now."

I nod, "Yep, felt better straight away from getting into it. I was a little tender. But not too bad." I smile at him as Brennen circles us under the water. I watch him take a turn around the pool, for something so large, he is certainly agile. He surfaces right in front of me, his face mere inches away, I have to force myself not to run screaming from the bath. He huffs through his nose, black tendrils of smoke floats to the ceiling and I realise he wants petting.

"Such a needy dragon." I laugh as I stroke his muzzle. He stays still as I work my way around him, stroking and kissing his soft scales. He glistens with the sliver from the water and he starts this purr. Like the noise a kitten would make. I glance at Ta, "He purrs?" I ask as Brennen brings up his tail, curling the razor-sharp barbs around me he lifts me onto his back.

"Evidently he does, for you." Ta answers with a grin.

Smiling, I relax on Brennen's back and think about my life now. I've no idea what the day is, or how long I've been here. It feels ages but it can only be a week at the most. All my ideas of escape have melted away. I really didn't have anything waiting for me back on Earth. Twisting, I straddle the wide back of the dragon, "I want to call Alish. I'd like to visit her if that's possible?" I ask.

"I think that's a great idea. Both Brennen and I are required at the Council today to finalise about Talon and his brothers." Ta tells me, he stepping out of the water he goes to the panel of buttons on the side of the wall and talks into it, after he's finished he tells me, "We will drop you off on the way to the Council. You'll be safe at Alish's, as Hunter and Brogan, they have their own guards."

I nod, and roll off Brennen's back, swimming to the shallow end I walk out and I still find it incredible that I'm immediately dry and refreshed. I quickly dress and the males follow me as we all head outside to the awaiting flying vehicle, with its proud flag depicting the dragons. Brennen plonks a darkened visor over my eyes, I glance up at both of the suns, which are high in the sky and I have to admit I'm glad he remembered them, it's the one thing I keep forgetting to bring with me. They are shining brightly today.

Ace, one of Brennen's brothers pokes his head out of it and grins. "I heard you requested transport, so I hoped on one." He gives me a wink, cheekily. I roll my eyes. "Everyone who's needed is heading to the Council." He said sombrely as we boarded, and I am strapped in.

"Yes, that's where we are headed; we first need to drop off Araline. She's going to spend the day with Alish." Brennen informed his brother.

"Okay, let's get going." Ace sits at the controls, programming in his course.

My stomach rolls a little as we lift off, but other than that it's a smooth flight and we are soon landing in the gardens of another beautiful mansion. I smile and wave to Alish as she's waiting by the open doors with her mates by her side.

The door opens and I'm helped out. Honestly, I've no idea how I managed before these two males came into my life, insert eye roll. It's lovely to have such attention, but sometimes it's a bit overwhelming. I not used to such full-on attention from anyone, let alone hunks of males.

"Welcome, Araline." Alish beams at me. Hunter and Brogan bend down to kiss her, each taking his turn to kiss her thoroughly. By the time they leave us, I'm blushing on their behalf!

"It's beautiful here, Alish." I tell her as I look around. It's smaller than Brennen's— um... my place, but stunning in details. The strange, bright flowers that are banked on either side of the drive release puffs of scent that is gorgeous, so fragrant it has me closing my eyes in pleasure.

Ta and Brennen surround me and kiss me goodbye. "We are always within reach, little flower. Use Alish's comm if you need us for anything." Brennen informs me with a smile.

"Have fun." Ta whispers in my ear before they head with

Hunter and Brogan to fly to wherever the council is. I wave them off, turning back to face Alish.

"Those males!" I use my hand to fan myself.

CHAPTER FORTY-ONE

"*I* agree, lass." Alish laughs, linking her arm through mine. "I've had food prepared; we can eat while we chat and Steel is at school, so we won't get interrupted."

I nod, following her; I'm a bit disappointed that Steel won't be here, I was looking forward to seeing more of the little boy. I wonder wistfully if I will become a mother to a little dragon. I have no idea where that thought came from. I wasn't interested in having children on Earth. But here…

"You only have the one son, Alish?" I wonder about that, she's been with her males a long, long time, do they use birth control? I now realise I've had unprotected sex a few times, will I now be pregnant? My steps falter, and Alish turns to face me.

"Yes, only the one, but we will have more. We've been unlucky that we've lost a couple." She looks sad and I can't help it, I hug her tightly. Wishing I'd not brought the subject up. She pats my back, "It's okay, Araline. Dragons are only fertile every decade, so we have to time it very carefully. We are going to try for a non-dragon baby next. It's a good idea to have dragons grow up with siblings that aren't like them; it gives them a good background of how to use their strength around non dragon Mertier's."

I nod, silently wondering when Brennen will be fertile, but I've had sex with Ta as well, could I be pregnant with his? *OMG!* There's so much to think about. She leads the way through her home and it's gorgeous as every building seems to be here. It's in the white marble with gold thread running through it, which I suspect now, is actual gold. It's large and spacious with natural light flooding it as the back seems completely open. I can't see any windows, there's just no wall.

We head outside, she hands me some visors and I put them on, thankfully. I'd left the ones Brennen gave me on the flying vehicle, she does the same and we sit on some low cushions.

I've no idea why they insist on sitting on the floor, after six months I'm still adjusting to their ways.

I eye the brightly coloured food; I have to admit it's far better than anything I've had on Earth. It makes Earth food seem dull, bland and boring.

"Please, help yourself, Araline." I follow her actions and soon we are eating and I'm loving the heady, fruity wine. It's not as strong as the few I've tried here. I'll have to remember to ask Brennen to get some in, as it's delicious. "Now, are you okay after your abduction by Talon? It sounded horrific. We were all so worried about you." She asks earnestly.

I swallow my food and take a long sip of wine. "It wasn't the best, I was really scared but knew Brennen and Ta would move that damn mountain if needed to get to me. But, I kind of understand where Talon is coming from. His father really did a number on him and his brothers." I shake my head, sadly.

"Yes, Hunter's only just learning how much of a tyrant he was towards his own sons." She shakes her head looking forlorn. "I hope they can come to a resolution that will benefit everyone but I know Kyanite had a deep rooted hatred towards his brother, so it might not end up as we would like it to."

"Yes, I fully understand that, but the sons can't be blamed for what their father forced them to believe. The one good thing is that Simone has been removed from her mates and is being looked after. I just hope she can now look forward to a life she finds a little more tolerable."

"Let's hope so." She smiles and we eat in a companionable silence.

"So, Alish, tell me, how old were you when you knew of this life that was destined to be yours?" I pop a bright purple flower like thing into my mouth. It tastes similar to grapes, sweet and juicy. There's not a lot of meat on the menus, which I don't mind as I was fast becoming a vegetarian on Earth, so this has just pushed me into not eating it. Thinking about it, I've not seen any animals here? I will have to ask about that.

"The small village I grew up in, in the Scottish Highlands were surrounded by a mystical boundary. And I always knew that I was coming." she looks off into the distance, "My mother was the village witch. She wasn't really a witch, more healer. But you know how humans love to give women labels if they don't understand what they do. We were lucky to have had the clan, if she had been labelled a "witch" in a non-magical place, she probably would have been burnt at the stake." She took a bite of her food.

"Was it difficult knowing you'd be leaving everyone behind you? It must have been hard making and keeping friends if everyone knew you'd be leaving them to a much better life?" I ask her, thinking that I wish I had known what was going to happen to me. I'd have prepared myself, somehow.

"No, lass, as everyone knew, I was treated like the chosen one. I had special privileges. I was let off chores. I had a fine time. I was instructed that I would be having only two mates." she winked at me, "I know you; yourself know how wonderful that can be."

I blush, "I have to admit, if I'd known on Earth how good it is being taken by two men. I'd have enjoyed myself way more than I had." I laugh as I pick up my wine and drink some more.

"In case you were wondering, Mertier follow the same calendar as you did on Earth. They found it was far easier to mimic that than try to get the women to get used to another way of doing time, et cetera." Alish smiles and brushes her hair that's fallen across her face away. Is long and wavy and a gorgeous natural red, I'd give my right arm for hair that luscious. "I really do need to get this cut. You have the right idea, being short. Don't know why I didn't think of it before, where it's a lot hotter."

"I was wondering about time and months so that's good to know and hell no, you shouldn't get your hair cut! It's gorgeous." I tell her vehemently. "I'd kill for hair like yours." I grin at her.

"Okay, then lass. But maybe just a few inches off." She pulls it up from her back a few inches, gesturing how much she like off.

"Yes, that would be far better than getting it hacked off. Alish, about…" I hesitate, biting my lip.

"What are you not asking?" she grins; I think she has an idea.

"Well, you came here a couple of hundred years ago, yes?" she nods, eyes sparkling. "Well, the sex education in my time on Earth wasn't brilliant. But back when you were there it wasn't talked about at all, was it? How did you prepare yourself for having two men?" I feel my face heating; I'm blushing for England."

"I did wonder when you would get around to this subject. The chief, of my clan, the leader, was very frank. When I was old enough, it was all explained to me. In very deep detail." She laughs, "I was shocked, I cannae lie, but it was my destiny, I can still remember the smell of the highlands, the heather. But I don't miss the long, dark winters. This weather is much more agreeable."

"Was you homesick at all, after your arrival?" she falls silent, and as we have finished our meal, some young men come to clear it all away and bring out some of the seeds I've fallen in love with.

She waits until they have left, "I was for a while. It would be hard not to be. But it was such an amazing day for me. You wait until you see the celebrations tomorrow. I've been told that it reminds some of birthday parties on earth but on crack, whatever that may be." She smiles and it lights up her whole face.

I laugh, thinking of the comparison between crack cocaine and a party. I had visited New York in America once and had always said it's a bit like London on crack so I can kind of get it. "I'm looking forward to it." I smile, "Do you need any help in preparing for it or anything?" I ask, not sure what to expect.

"Oh no lass, it's all prepared by the mates of the female. We don't have to lift a finger." She beams, and I again think of the difference between some men on Earth and the males of this planet. I was lucky to get a card from some of my ex's, let alone a bash like this 'arrival day' party is beginning to sound like.

"Is it a dress up kind of party? I don't want to underdress or anything." I ask, god can you imagine if I turned up in plain trousers and a tee shirt and everyone is dressed to the nines? How awful!

"Yes, all your finery, Araline." She nods with enthusiasm. "I've had a dress specially made for the occasion."

"Okay, well I hope I don't let you down." I wonder what the hell to wear and decide to go through my wardrobe when I get home. I hope Landon's free to do my makeup again.

She grips my hand tightly. "You only need to be yourself, lass. You could never let me down." She gives it another squeeze before we hear a few voices coming through the house. "Here come the males. Shall we join them?" She stands, and I follow.

CHAPTER FORTY-TWO

We head towards where the rumbustious voices are coming from, and I catch more of a glimpse of Alish and her mates' home. I still find it strange that they are called mates. It's breathtakingly beautiful, with high ceilings and ornate sculptures of dragons dotted around. It's spotlessly clean and tidy, but as with my home with Brennen and Ta, they must have staff that look after it, and them.

I come to a stop as we see them all. I spot Brennen and Ta talking with Alish's males, plus Talon and his brothers. I smile. They must have come to some sort of agreement or I suspect they wouldn't be here. Brennen beckons me to join him.

"So, what happened?" I ask, as his arms wrap around me, pulling me in nice and close.

"What happened? What happened?" Talon grins at me, he

looks totally different. No longer the angry male I first saw in our grounds. "I'll tell you what happened. This male of yours told the King, his father, and the Council members that we should be shown complete leniency and they listened. I'm in awe of this male!" He punches Brennen on the shoulder. "There are a few conditions, of course, which we are more than happy to comply with. Our men, which I was more worried about than us, to be truthful, will be given the chance to join Mertier's army and will be given homes and will be considered in all bidding's that take place from now on. Fairly. I'm happy to say they've all accepted. My brothers and I will become royal guards, just as all dragons are." He lowers his voice, emotion flowing from him. "Our father, may he never rest the asshole. Made us the males we became, but it's our choice to continue his beliefs or to be part of the family we were born into. We never had this chance as young." His brothers nod in agreement.

"We never knew how bad you had it, Talon." Hunter explains, his guilt clear to see and Alish rubs his arm and squeezes his hand. "And you never gave us a chance to help. All we saw were angry males, which hated the royals and didn't want anything to do with their own family."

"We didn't know any different, our mother died suddenly and with that, all love died in that house of horrors." One of Talons brothers informs us. "We were brought up to believe everything our father said was the upmost truth. His word was law and if we dared to question it, we ended up broken."

I shake my head, even on a different planet there are still evil parents, I shudder at what these males have lived through.

"We are on probation. We aren't let off completely. We have to prove ourselves which we fully understand." Talon looks like a different male, and as I study his brothers, they all look like the world has been lifted from their shoulders. They are smiling and relaxed.

"Well, this is happy news." Alish claps her hands together, "And I expect you all to come to my arrival day celebrations tomorrow."

They all bow their head to her, "We've never been to one before, we would be honoured to."

Ta walks up and Brennen hands me over, he hugs me tightly. Talon turns to face me, "This is all down to you, Araline, you made Brennen listen to you and to me. Without that I think the outcome would have been entirely different. So, we are all indebted to you, anything you require we will try our upmost to do." All five of the males turn to me and bow low. Each murmuring their agreement with Talon.

I smile, thanking god I went with my gut and made Brennen talk with them.

"Okay, as much as I love this family reunion, we need to get this place, arrival day party ready. So please fuck off," Brogan laughed, and everyone bid their goodbyes.

"We'll see you tomorrow, Alish. Thank you for today, it was needed." I tell her as we hug.

"You are more than welcome, lass. We will have many more. But I can't wait to see you tomorrow." She excitedly tells me.

"I can't wait to see what it's all about." I say as we head outside with Talon and his brothers.

"Are you going back to the home you shared with your father?" Brennen asks Talon.

"Yes, we will completely obliterate everything 'he' made it into and make it ours. It's large enough to home us all, so it makes sense to use it." Talon answers, they bow to us before shifting into their dragons and flying off.

I look at Brennen and I see he's looking thoughtful, placing my hands on his shoulders and bring him down to kiss him, whispering, "You did a good thing," I'm smiling as I press my lips against his.

After we kiss, Brennen says, "Ta and his father did all the hard work, I just had to make my father see that it made sense."

Ta grins, "I couldn't see five dragons put to death." Shaking his head, sombrely.

"Well then, you did good, Ta." I tell him, bringing his head down for a kiss.

A flying vehicle is waiting for us and I'm quickly strapped in. We don't have a driver, Brennen quickly programs in where we want to go, and we start to move. I'm still not sure how I feel about so much flying and clutch their hands. Now seems a perfect time to talk to them about something that's on my mind, to keep my mind off the fact that we are flying.

"So, I've been talking to Alish." I look at them both, each sat by my side. "She told me dragons only become fertile every ten years?" Brennen nods, "So when will you be fertile, Brenn?"

"In about two years. We will have that long to decide if we want a dragon baby by then. We will be alive for many years; women are of child-bearing years far longer than on Earth. As you must have already figured out as Alish's dragon son is still very young and she's been here for a couple of hundred years." He says, picking up my hand, kissing the knuckles.

Okay, that's one down, now its Ta's turn, "And you, we've not had protected safe sex while I've been here. Could there be a chance I'm pregnant already?"

"No, the Mertieran's, non-dragon males of this planet, have the ability to make their bodies produce sperm or not."

I stare at him dumbfounded. "Wait, what? You can make your body produce sperm at will? How is that even possible?" My mind races with how that could be possible.

"And I have two hearts, as all Mertieran's do. One lasts many, many years, the second one takes over when that one dies and lasts for as long as the first one did. You aren't on Earth, and we are not human men." He quickly reminds me, placing my palm over his chest so I can feel them again. One heart is beating for forcibly than the other. The second heart is like a faint shadow as it beats quietly.

I don't really know what to say to that, I'm rendered speechless.

"After Alish's arrival day celebrations tomorrow, Ta and I would like to take you to the Seven Pools of Serenity." Brennen says softly. "My dragon wants to mate with you fully and mark you as ours." He leans in and nibbles the lobe of my ear. It sends shivers racing down my spine.

"Is that when I will get my own markings like all the women who are with dragons have?" I ask, Ta leans in and his lips caress my pulse point on my neck. *OMG!* These males.

Brennen looks into my eyes and I'm bewitched as a slow,

hot as sin smile appears. "Yes." His face lowers and his lips brush against mine.

I feel my stomach drop and it's not just because we are coming into land at our home. I wonder hazily when I started to think of it as *our* home?

CHAPTER FORTY-THREE

We walk in a companionable silence into the palace, before I turn to them, "So, this arrival party tomorrow, I've been told it's a dressy affair?" I chew my lip, now I'm wondering if I should have gone shopping for something special. It sounded like it was similar to black tie events on Earth. I had hated them. I had always felt uncomfortable, being on the larger size when all the other ladies looked like beautiful, colourful peacocks, strutting their sexy bodies. I couldn't even in my wildest dreams begin to look as good as them.

"The arrival parties are a huge deal, Little Flower." Brennen brings my hand up, brushing my knuckles with his velvet soft lips. That simple gesture has my skin heating with a rush of arousal. "It's our way to celebrate the day our mates come into our lives. We wait many years for you, we want to express how much we love and honour you." His smile makes his dimple appear, it makes me want to kiss him, it's such a sweet sexy smile.

"We can't wait for it to be yours." Ta grins, "It'll be like all your fantasies coming true. Because having you here with us is just that."

Oh, these men!

"Are you hungry? Did you eat at the palace?" I ask, desperately trying to curtail my wayward thoughts. I run my hand over the cool marble, realising that's why they use it to build everything. It stays cool under the harsh double suns this world has. "If not, I'd quite like to figure out what to wear tomorrow."

"We've eaten; let's get your first arrival day clothes ready." Ta takes my hand and Brennen follows as we head up to the huge closet.

I want to look bloody amazing. I have a feeling everyone will be their finest. I walk along the lines of hanging clothes, running my hands over the mixed textures.

The last few months on Earth have been such a struggle. I was living out of a suitcase and on friend's sofas or spare bedrooms. Those suitcases had been filled with second-hand clothes. Not that there is anything wrong with second-hand clothes, but I craved something of my own and here it all was.

I knew I wanted the rubies in my hair again; everyone seemed to love them at the palace party a few months ago. I stop and pull out a black dress that catches my eye. The material is the softest silk and flows beautifully down to where the hem is split in multiple places. It glitters with rubies which are sown onto the silk in intricate patterns. The sleeves are strings of rubies, attached to a wide, ruby encrusted cuff. A deep vee at the back and front will make wearing underwear tricky, without flashing people.

I spin to show them, hoping they like it as much as I do. "This one," I tell them gleefully. I shake it gently to show off how the bottom flutters with all the splits.

"Excellent!" Ta picks up a pair of shoes, "And perhaps these?"

These are a gorgeous pair of stilettos. "OMG! Dorothy shoes!" I hurry over and practically snatch them out of his hands to clutch them to my chest. I can't stop smiling, they are sensational. I kick of the ones I'm wearing, stuff my feet into them and walk up and down. They are incredibly high. I'm used to wearing trainers so know I'll have to keep practising in them.

"Dorothy shoes?" Brennen wonders aloud with a questioning look.

I wave off the question, still enthralled with what's on my feet. "It's from a years old film, it doesn't matter. I love them!"

With a shrug Brennen walks to where his and Ta clothes are. He quickly pulls out a formal suit that compliments my dress and Ta also decides what he's wearing.

I yawn, it feels like it's been an extra-long day and Brennen takes my hand, "You need to rest, Little Flower. You will need all your strength tomorrow. Come let's go to bed."

The three of us get undressed and I can't help but to admire their bodies as they remove their clothes. They are all mine and I stifle a giggle as I get into the mahoosive bed and pull the silk covers over my body.

"What was that giggle about?" I obviously didn't hide it

well enough Ta asks as he slides into the bed and pulls me into his arms. He spoons against my back and I rest my head on his arm, facing Brennen as he joins us.

"Nothing." I mumble and sigh when Brennen strokes a finger down my face. It's an extremely gently touch for someone as large as he. I watch fascinated when his dragon scales shimmer under his skin and I stroke them, enjoying the fact that he moves his body following my touch.

"I love your hands on my body, Little Flower. But tonight, you need to sleep." He leans in and kisses me. Our tongues caress one another's and without thought I'm arching towards him.

Ta kisses my shoulder, "I think she needs more than a kiss, Brenn." He slips a hand between my legs and feels how wet I am already. "Brenn, she needs us, she's utterly drenched."

I sigh again as Ta's fingers slip into me which turns into a pleasure filled moan as he rubs an extra sensitive spot. My eyes roll back, and I give myself up to the erotic feelings that flood my mind.

Brennen kisses his way down my body pressing hot little kisses to my fevered skin. His lips suck my nipple into his mouth, and I cry out at the hard pulls that seem to connect with what Ta is doing.

"Oh, god, yes Ta there just there!" I manage to gasp as the special thing he does with his hands light up and I feel the blinding heat on that spot buried deep inside me. I scream as I erupt, Brennen bites down on my nipple. That combined with the heat has my body spinning out of control and I come gloriously.

I slump into the bed, breathing hard as my heart races.

"That was amazing." I tell them as Ta pulls his fingers free and Brennen moves back up the bed. Ta leans back and grabs something but I'm too relaxed to worry about that.

"Little Flower it was. We love to make you come." Brennen tells me as he lifts my leg up over his thigh, so I'm scissored between them both. My eyes pop open when Ta pulls my ass cheeks apart and his cock slips into my extra tight sheath. Before I can become accustomed to his cock buried deep in me, Brennen positions himself so he can enter me from the front.

I am wedged between them, nice and tight, I can hardly move, but I'm quite happy for them to do all the work. I close my eyes again and relish the feelings as they begin to move in and out of me. I'm panting and moaning loudly when Brennen leans in to take my mouth in a blistering kiss. His kiss kicks up the eroticism a notch while his fingers circle around my nipples, teasing them until they are as tight as they've ever been.

"You feel so good around my cock, Araline. Fuck, so hot and tight I never want this to end!" Ta breathes into my ear.

I have to admit, I'd quite happily for this never to end but my body is rushing me towards another release. "It's too much! I can't, oh fuck!" I wail as I'm forced into another orgasm.

"I have to come!" Ta shouts as his body thrusts almost brutally into mine. He joins me in his release and his powerful body quakes at the force of it.

"Fuck!" is all Brennen manages to growl before also coming. He stares into my dazed eyes and I see his dragon blinking back at me.

"You are mine, Araline." Brennen's voice is lower, more growly as he tells me this and I know it's his dragon talking to me.

"Yes." I say sleepily, "I think I might be." He laughs and we all moan as both men pull free from my body. I can't keep my eyes open. I feel the mattress give and then a cloth is being wiped between my legs. Once they are both happy, they return and this time I kiss them both on the lips and fall into a deep sleep.

CHAPTER FORTY-FOUR

The follow morning, I wake afresh and ready for this arrival party. I hope I'm not disappointed as it's been built up to be this magical, amazing thing. I feel hot and it's no wonder as my mates are wrapped around me. How did I become this bloody lucky?

"Good morning, Araline." A voice has me sitting up in bed; I quickly remember to pull the sheet up with me. Its Landon, he's holding his magic box of makeup. "I need to start to get you ready for Lady Alish's arrival party; you can meet me in the room we used before? I've had food and refreshments brought up also."

I rub my eyes, trying desperately to wake up. "Thank you. I'll be with you in a mo."

"A mo?" he asks, staring at me.

"Um, in a moment." I tell him and comprehension dawns on his face.

"I will see you in a mo, then." He grins and I look around for something to put on.

"Brenn, Ta, wake up." I nudge them awake and its adorable to watch these two huge males struggle waking up.

"I have to go and get ready for the party." I tell them and grab one of their tee shirts as I climb over Ta to get out of the bed.

"Fine, fine," Ta grumbles and lays back down, obviously intending on sleeping some more.

"Go bath and get ready, we will be right behind you." Brennen smiles at me as I pull the soft tee-shirt over my head.

"Good idea." I blow them both a kiss and head towards the massive bath. I use the amenities first and brush my teeth. They don't have toothbrushes or toothpaste but reddish leaves that remind me of fresh herbs. It tastes great and leaves my mouth fresh and clean. I head to the bath and walk into the silver, shimmering water. I dunk myself under a few times and relax for a few minutes, but I know Landon is waiting. After I find my dress and slip it on, sans underwear, I make my way to where he is.

"That dress has to be my favourite I've seen you in yet, Araline. Good choice." He smiles at me and hands me a glass of what looks like orange juice. It may not look like it but damn, it tastes like oranges on steroids. Bursting with flavour and very sweet.

"Wow that's pretty good." I say as I sit on the tall chair ready for him to work his magic on me once again. There's a plate piled high with brightly coloured food. And I pick the whole time he's doing his thing.

He gets me to look this way, then that way. To pull funny

faces and move my eyes, so he can create whatever he's doing. I'm not allowed to look in the mirror, so I have no clue as to what he's doing.

"There," he steps back and look critically at his work. "I believe you're ready." He bows slightly as Brennen and Ta joins us and wow my jaw drops at the sight of them. Utter perfection. The suits are styled as the same as the ones they wore to the palace banquet. Longer line jackets and Brennen has his cape on again, it makes him look so much the prince he is. This time they are in black to match me. Brennen has a dragon in flight, blasting fire in rubies and other stones. Ta is also in black and has rubies dotted along his cuffs.

"You two look fabulous!" I tell them, hoping off the chair. They don't reply, they are staring at me; I turn away, wondering what they are gawping at. Then I spot myself in the mirror.

"Fuck!" I exclaim without thinking. My short hair is spiked, and he's used the rubies in it again. It looks pretty good. I turn my head and watch them sparkle. Then I look at my face, he's stuck gems, a mixture of red and black around my eyes, framing them and the fake eyelashes again with tiny feathers on, I flutter them and giggle. My lips are ruby red and glossy with tiny rubies lining them, which will make kissing interesting. On my hands I've already seen the pointed talons of false nails he's stuck on them. Each one also has rubies on them. I just pray they stay on.

"We look fabulous? You look sensational!" Ta looks at me in shock. "Honestly, Araline, I just want to take you back to bed and fuck you. I don't want other males looking at you as I might have to kill them." he looks troubled at the thought.

"Hey," I say softly, "they can look all they want, I only want you two." Ta looks somewhat relieved.

"He's right, it may be a problem." Brennen walks around me, running his fingers over the silk dress. "You're so beautiful, little flower." He twirls me and the bottom of the dress flutters around my legs, just as I knew it would. Facing me, he slips his hand through the vee at the front and circles my nipple until I moan. They both stare as if fascinated as my nipples peak and you can quite clearly see them both through the material.

"Beautiful Araline." Ta joins us, Brennen hands me off to him. Ta picks me up, effortlessly, twirling me in his arms.

I laugh, having fun with them both. They are so damn gorgeous. Never in my life have I imagined that I would end up with men, as in plural and such fine specimens as these two are.

"Come on, let's go. I want to see what they've arranged for Alish. They do like to try to outdo each year." Brennen says as he takes my hand and I walk between them both, down the stairs and out into the grounds where a flying vehicle is waiting for us.

The journey is uneventful, and we are soon landing in Alish's, Hunters and Brogans home.

My jaw drops. The difference from when I was here yesterday and today is remarkable. The grounds have been turned into a winter wonderland. And for a planet that is circled by two suns that's some feat. Everywhere I look is covered by sparkling white snow, but it isn't cold, how the hell they managed this is mind boggling.

I watch as people, and I have to say I'm pleased I dressed

up as they all look amazing, dressed in all their finery, but in their arms are presents. Boxes small and large are being handed to staff to place on a huge, is that a Santa's sleigh? I giggle it's not just a winter wonderland, its Christmas, or their interpretation of it.

"Christmas!" I grin at Brennen and Ta. Do they even celebrate Christmas here? I wonder.

"Yes, we were told that this was Alish's wish this year as she missed the winter from the Scottish Highlands, where she originally came from. Of course, we adapted Earth's Christmas here. We found we all enjoy celebrating it and as more females joined us, they brought with them, their ideas of what Christmas was all about. So, we mix and choose how we celebrate it. We will want to do whatever you did for Christmas. I'm sure you have some traditions you would like to keep, and we will help you keep it alive." Brennen explains as I try and take in all the decorations.

But then another thought invades my brain, presents! We haven't got Alish anything. My eyes widen as I look at them both. "Oh fuck, Brenn, Ta!" I pull on their hands until they look at me.

"What is it Little Flower?" Brennen looks at me, perplexed. "No one will hurt you here." He and Ta look around as if I had sensed some sort of evil.

"No, no, it's not that. We haven't brought Alish a present." I point to where a few people are passing over their presents to be stacked on top of the sleigh; I begin to panic, biting my lower lip, wondering how we could have made this faux pas?

Ta pulls me into his body, wrapping his arms around me

before I can have a full on melt down. "It's already been delivered." He says softly and I feel my anxiety melt away.

"Oh, what did we get her?" I must admit I feel somewhat miffed that they didn't tell me.

"We gifted her a breeding pair of Lapholfs." Brennen informs me.

"Huh? What the hell are they?" I have no idea what a Lapholf is?

Brennen looks thoughtful, and then explains. "They are similar to your Earth's horses. They are very precious and guarded fiercely as they don't breed until they are over two hundred years old. We know Alish has wanted a pair for a long time. So, I asked the Council if there were any that we could gift her. Luckily for us, a pair had just come into season and could be given to a new home. You can only rehome them in pairs as they mate for life. As do we dragons." He gives me a heated look that makes my insides turn to mush.

I feel my face flush and give my head a slight shake. "Well, that sounds like a fab present, Brenn." I tell him.

"Fab?" he asks, a little bewildered by the expression.

"Fab is short for fabulous, it means something very good." I watch as he nods, understanding what I was trying to say. I'm sure there have been a few things that I've said that has made no sense to them, but they've been too polite to say.

CHAPTER FORTY-FIVE

We continue wandering through the winter wonderland they have created for Alish's arrival day festivities and I have to admit it's hard to take it all in, there's so much to see. It's breathtakingly beautiful.

There are children running around giggling happily and throwing snowballs.

"The children have never seen snow before," Ta tells me, as we watch the boisterous boys play.

There are entertainers strolling through the party goers, doing incredible magic tricks and illusionists; there one second, vanished the next, to the crowd's audible pleasure. Young males are carrying around cut glass servers, overflowing with tasty treats for everyone to try. Glancing up, I notice birds with vivid coloured feathers, putting on a colourful acrobatic display.

It all reminds me of the story, *Charlie and the Chocolate Factory* by my favourite childhood author, Ronald Dahl.

Everything is bright and larger than life. But this is my life now. I take a steadying breath and Brennen signals for some drinks. We each take an impressive crystal engraved goblet that has mist floating on the top. My eyes widen in surprise as each sip tastes different to the last and the liquid changes colours.

"This is incredible!" I shake my head trying to take in all the sights.

"But is it fab?" Brennen grins at me.

I chuckle, "Yes its bloody fab!"

"I heard that Alish misses the snow that she used to play in as a child. So, Hunter and Brogan modified it and well, here we are." Ta gestures with his hand.

"Well, they did good." I laugh as I spot Alish's son jumping into a mound of snow, laughing with his friends.

"Araline!" I turn to see Alish walking towards us, hand in hand with her males. "Well, what do you think, lass?" she asks while hugging me.

"I think its bloody fab, it's amazing, Alish." I smile at her protective males who grin back. They are obviously pleased with themselves and they deserve to be a bit smug.

"Happy arrival day, Alish." Brennen and Ta tell her.

"I remember the day you arrived and how content your males became." Brennen says, pulling me closer. "And I couldn't wait until I was given a mate. You just wait until it's her arrival day. Ta and I will show you all what arrival days are all about. As Araline says, it will be "fab"."

I grin up at him as he presses a kiss against my gem encrusted lips. Pulling back, I tell Alish, "You look gorgeous; everyone has pulled out all the stops."

She smiles back, "Thank you. This is the one day, we go over the top."

We observe everyone, they glitter and sparkle as they move. I wasn't the only one that had gems on my face but happily I didn't see anyone else with them in their hair.

"You look beautiful, Araline." Alish beams. "I'm glad you have your rubies in your hair. It's definitely going to be your signature statement."

"Thank you." I'm still a little uncomfortable with how little clothes they all seem to wear and hope over time I will get used to it. It's all still a little overwhelming at times.

As if picking up my feelings, Ta stands behind me wrapping his arms around me and leans in to nuzzle my neck. Okay, that feels so good.

"Did your presents arrive, Alish?" Brennen asks, giving my hand a gently squeeze.

"Yes, they did. They have been making themselves at home. I love them!" she beams at us.

I pull away from Ta, if he kept that up, I'd demand he takes me somewhere secluded and I'm sure that's not allowed at this kind of party.

Alish laughs softly and gives me a knowing wink, which only succeeds in making me blush.

"She's not stopped petting and making a fuss of them all day." Hunter says as he brings up her hand to kiss her knuckles.

"They are the hit of the day." Brogan agrees.

"You will have to come and see them, Araline and perhaps we can go for a ride?" she smiles, and we hear her name being called by another guest.

"I'd love to. Now I think you need to go. We are monopolising you. Have a wonderful arrival day." I look questioningly at Brennen to check I had said the right thing, he nods.

"I will, lass, and thank you again all for my gifts." Hunter and Brogan nod to us as they go to mingle with their guests. We meander through the throngs of guests, stopping to have chats and introduce me to even more people. I'll have no hope in remembering their names, so I just smile and say hello. Every time a server walks past, I help myself to a little nibble of whatever they are carrying. Each thing tastes divine, the flavours exploding on my tongue, just delicious.

I'm still trying to process everything that's going on around us, when I gasp.

Four hulking, fur covered beasts prowl by, pulling a vehicle, which is hovering over the ground. It reminds me of my old wooden sleigh, but on a much grander scale. Their proud, strong faces with shining silver eyes, take in every little detail of their surroundings. They are overlarge dog like creatures, maybe more like Earths wolves than dogs, I muse. Their jet black, extra thick, soft fur brushes my legs, and I can't stop myself, leaning over I stroke them. I have to wonder how the hell they cope with the heat that the two suns generate, with all that fur. Their tails are held high and straight but are tipped with a lethal looking barb that will inflict a lot of damage if they were to ever use it.

"What are they?" I ask Brennen, fascinated and excited that they have more animals here, as I love all animals.

"They are Dwarlies. Like a version of Earths dogs and wolves." He informs me, stroking one as they carry on walking past. The children in the sleigh are giggling in excitement and thoroughly enjoying themselves. "You won't see them all that often. They live in and around the mountains where it is cooler. They come out in the evenings and winter."

"I've been wondering if you had any animals on this planet. I've only seen your brightly coloured birds and dancing and singing fish. Now I know you have at least two more different breeds." My eyes track them as they move slowly through the party goers.

"We have a few different breeds. They are mostly wild animals." Ta ruffles the fur as the last one walks majestically past us. "These four belong to Brennen's parents who lent them for Alish's arrival day party."

I smile as the children shriek with happiness as the Dwarlies speed up.

"They look ferocious but are gentle souls." Brennen takes my hand in his and Ta joins his actions with my other hand, and we stroll until we find a snowy path. We follow the winding path and come across an ice sculpture in the shape of a wide throne. It has richly coloured pillows and throws, even though it's not cold to the touch. Very strange when you think of ice, you immediately think it's cold. This isn't.

We take a pew, relaxing and watching the wondrous sights. We are brought food and drinks and I have to smile at how different my life is now. Who would have thought? I know I wouldn't have.

"Just think, if I hadn't been working in that church and my friend hadn't been taken into hospital. I wouldn't be here." I shake my head, realising how bloody lucky I am at being able to experience everything this world offers. I have to admit, even if it's only to myself. I had been dreadfully jealous of Macie when I first arrived here. She'd had everything on Earth, riches, a fabulous figure, happiness. Everything I had craved. She had known what was going to happen to me when she was in hospital. I can't even thank her for her selfless gift of these two males. Of this life of wonder I've found myself in.

"I know. I can't believe our luck at that. It was meant to be, Araline. We know you can't love us yet, but we hope you will do at some point." Ta tilts my head upwards so our lips can touch. "You are our blessing, Araline." He whispers before kissing me.

His kisses are sheer bloody magic. His tongue gently slides against mine as I sigh. He cups my face in a tender gesture as my heart speeds up, but he pulls away far too quickly and I'm left clenching my thighs together to try and bring a little relief.

"I love your kisses, Ta." I tell him, my voice is a breathy whisper. Blimey it was only a kiss, but it's left me needing so much more. There are children present, I remind myself, taking a steadying breath.

Brennen whispers, "In a few hours we'll be taking you to the Seven Pools of Serenity, where we will make you ours for all time and for all to see. My dragon can't wait to mark you as his." He leans in to press kisses to my neck.

My body shivers and not because of the ice and snow that surrounds us, but with lust and need for them both.

"Come on, if we stay here, partially hidden I will end up ravishing you." Brennen stood and we follow. He's right, if we stay here, I'd let him.

CHAPTER FORTY-SIX

I'm nervous, anxious and altogether far too hyper to be sitting still. My lip will be red raw if I keep biting it but damn it, I'm nervous. We left the party, bid farewell to Alish and I whispered where we are going. I wish I'd had more time to talk to her about this Seven Pools of whatever. What will happen? Will it hurt getting my markings? She smiled at me and told me to enjoy myself. She had a secret smile and looked wistfully at her males who promised to take her there again soon.

I feel clammy as the flying vehicle whizz's along, its night-time and the two moons are providing the creamy light, so the driver has no problem seeing where he is going.

"What will happen?" I ask, I'm trembling, and Brennen takes hold of my hand.

"We are going to love you until you can't breathe without us." I watch as if caught in a spell as his eyes blink and then they are the blackness of the dragon's eyes staring back at me.

"I need to make you mine, Araline." The dragon growls at me, his hot breath tickles my neck as he leans in close, it stands to reason it's hot as he breathes fire, I reason with myself. It's still Brennen's voice but deeper, thicker. I turn and can do nothing but stare at him.

"Just don't hurt me." I whisper, still staring into the dragon's eyes. Scales shimmer under Brennen's skin as I cup his face. He turns and kisses my palm, such a romantic, tender thing to do.

"We couldn't hurt you. You are more important to us than life itself. You are our mate. Your wellbeing and wishes are ours to cherish and bring into being. Your body is ours to take to heights that will have you screaming our names. We live only to please you." Brennen says as his dragon slips away.

"Araline," Ta gently brings my head around to face him. "Trust is earnt, I understand that, but if you give us your trust tonight, I promise you, you will have whatever your heart desires." His lips brush against mine and I stop thinking and allow myself to just react to the feelings these two males bring into life, like no one has before them.

After some time, I gulp as we drop gently to land. This is it then, time to put on my big girl's panties and see this through to the end.

I unbuckle my harness to stand, Ta and Brennen each take a hand and we walk down the few steps where I take my first look around. Well, this place has either been blown out of all proportion, or the best bits are yet to come.

"Is this it?" Dismay is etched into my voice. I feel a tad let down. After everything I've been told about this supposedly magically place and everything it's been made out to be. It's just another mountain. I feel my shoulders slump in disappointment.

"You will see." Ta grins, walking in front of us as we make our way to an opening in the rock face.

"We have it all to ourselves. For the whole night." Brennen takes my hand and I have no choice but to follow them both.

We enter through a wide crack in the rock. It still looks somewhat boring, but I plaster a smile on my face and pray it gets better. We walk through a smooth walled corridor; the rock feels like warm marble as I brush my fingers over it. It's the white and gold that is used in most of the buildings that I've seen so far and makes it feel less repressive as it's quite a narrow walkway. The twinkling of lights comes from within the walls, but I can't see how it's powered.

When we turn a corner, it opens up into a gigantic underground cavern, at least a few football pitches in size. My mouth gaps open as I take in the view. At the far end a silver waterfall gushes and fills the seven pools, each one different in shape and depth. Now I know where the name came from. It's filled with sweet scented, brightly coloured flowers and indigenous greenery that are growing in abundance and makes it feel like a tropical oasis.

I can't wait to step into one of the pools, they look so inviting. Brennen moves in behind me and I shudder with excitement as I remember just why we are here.

"Are you ready, little flower?" he whispers, his breath tickles my neck.

Ta moves in front of me and goes to his knees, removing my shoes. He massages my instep on each foot, and I can't repress a moan of pleasure.

Brennen unzips my dress, allowing it to pool at me feet. I'm naked beneath it and I feel Ta's eyes gaze up my body. "You are so bloody gorgeous, Araline." He whispers against my body as he kisses his way up until our lips fuse together. While we kiss, I become aware of low, male chanting.

I pull away and concentrate on where it's coming from. "What's that?" I don't understand the language and I don't particularly want an audience.

"It's generations of dragons that have come before us, welcoming you home." Brennen walks a little away from us and plucks a large, bright fuchsia flower and offers it to me.

I smile, taking it from him. "Thank you."

"Smell it, Araline." Ta instructs me.

I take a sniff. "Oh my god!" I moan, taking a deeper inhale.

Ta, hands me a sapphire coloured flower and I eagerly smell it, now knowing what to expect. It will smell of his essence just as Brennen's flower had smelled of his.

"Is this some sort of magic?" I wonder. "How do you do it?" I take great gulps as I smell them both; I could quite easily become addicted to these flower scents.

The light drops until all that's lighting this giant underground room are the twinkling gems in the rock wall.

"Each flower will impersonate the scent of whoever picks it. Why don't you choose one to give to us?" Brennen asks, giving my ass a gentle tap as I walk away from them both.

I'm eager to find the perfect flower to give them. Looking around, there are so many to choose from. I stroke petal after petal until I spot a multi layered flower, in the brightest red. I pick two, walking back towards them, its then I remember I'm stark bollock naked. I falter, chewing my lip as my insecurities flood my mind.

I hear a low growl and stare helplessly into Brennen's deep navy eyes.

"Little Flower, our gift. I wish you could see yourself through our eyes. You are perfection, you are bloody fab." He uses my words, making me smile a bit. "Now, bring us your scent, I need to take it into my soul."

I walk slowly towards them; my hips may have been swaying a little bit more provocatively than usual. But hey, I can work it when I want to. They track me with lust etched into their obscenely handsome faces. I watch their reactions as I hand them each my chosen flower. Both close their eyes and Brennen's dragon scales shimmer under his skin. Ta sighs and shocks me by eating it, then Brennen devours his and by the look on their faces I'd say it tasted pretty good.

Following their lead, I eat the flowers they gave me. Bloody, sodding hell, it's them. The flowers taste of each male.

"OMG!" I swallow and eat the rest as if starved. "I need more." I demand, feeling heat flood my body, sexual need has my eyes devouring them. "You have too much on, get naked. Please." I beg, cupping my breasts, offering them the hardened tips.

They don't need any further instructions and are naked and hard for me in a few seconds. The chanting has increased, and I swear I can feel the beat, thrumming throughout my body. I sway in time with it; I'm not a natural dancer by any means. But I feel empowered as they track my movements. I'm a siren calling for mates to take me, to make me theirs for all time.

Ta and Brennen stalk towards me but I have the need to run and make them catch me. I giggle, feeling drunk; perhaps the flowers have some sort of drugs in them. I don't care; I love how I'm feeling. I take off; I laugh some more as I hear them give chase. I've never been a runner, my boobs just aren't built for it, but luckily they catch me quite quickly and I find myself being rugby tackled from behind.

"I have you now, Little Flower." Brennen whispers just before we fall into the nearest pool.

I can't keep the squeal in as we hit the warm water. I'm released so I can swim to the surface just in time to watch Ta dive in. His arms are soon around my waist pulling me tightly against his chest so he can nuzzle my neck.

Brennen moves us to the edge where there is a ledge so I can stand. At least I won't drown, how thoughtful. He towers over me as he stands on it also. "Tonight, we will make you ours. My dragon will mark you as his. We are as one from this night on." He glances around the vast room and I follow his stare.

The gems that were scattered all over the walls have now joined together to form the shapes of dragons. Some are crouching, some in mid-flight and others breathing their fire, all in glorious technicolour. I'm fascinated by how it feels like their eyes are on us.

"That's our ancestors, here with us, welcoming you home and to celebrate our joining." He says, bringing his attention back to me. His eyes flash black and the dragon scales are just under his skin.

I run my fingertips down his chest, his muscles tense and flex under my touch. Falling to my knees I stare at his cocks, the second smaller one peeps out towards me and I lick my lips, needing to taste him again.

Ta moves in and slips his hands around my body until he palms my breasts, tugging gently at my nipples. My moan echoes around the vast room, as my head falls back onto his chest and I forget about Brennen's cocks as Ta's fingers feel so damn incredible on me.

"God, Ta, I love how you make me feel." I moan, my hands latching onto Brennen's main cock. He growls when I stroke him. I stare into his eyes as they roll back and his hips pump into my hand.

Ta's hands leave my breasts to skim down my body until they delve between my thighs to find me not just wet from the water. I'm aching for them; I need to feel them take me. They've turned me into a woman I hardly recognise, who feels drugged by the mere sight of them both, but I don't give a damn. I need their dark possession.

"I have to taste her Brenn," Ta says roughly, and pulls his hands away.

"No! Don't Ta, I need you." I beg, needing his hands back where they were. Wow, that didn't take long. They've reduced me to begging already.

Brennen leans down and takes my lips in a brutal kiss, its rough and bruising and I know my lips will be swollen come tomorrow, but I give him it back in spades. His hands fist my hair, holding my head in a position he desires. He dominates me at every step as our tongues duel. He lifts me but I'm past caring, the flowers have only heightened my need for them both.

I feel a warm, wet tongue thrust into me and I scream into Brennen's mouth which continues to devour me. Ta's tongue slides between my folds, slips around my clit just before he sucks it into his mouth. My body shakes and I feel my release approaching fast.

"Suck me, Little Flower." I'm ordered and I hungrily suck Brennen's thick cock as if I'm on death row and it's my last meal. I hunger for him; my body aches for them both, I'm lost in a sea of sexual desire that I never want to end.

"Fuck!" Brennen growls as my hands tease his second, smaller cock. "Yes, suck me harder." My eyes drift up his body and he's watching what Ta is doing to me.

Ta, grabs at the nearest flowers and drips the sweet scented, droplets of nectar onto his fingers. He slips them inside my tight asshole and I cry out. I realise that the flowers have produced a lube like substance that eases his entry.

I can't concentrate on Brennen's cock, and it pops free just as Ta goes back to sucking on my clit. Rhythmic pulls that has me grinding my hips and riding his fingers that are buried deep. "Ta, Brennen." I cry, "Please, I need to come. Please!" I beg them; the storm that's rising within me is a raging electrical current that needs to be released.

Brennen cups my face staring deep into my eyes. "Look at me Little Flower." He orders and I strain to open my eyes, I'm standing on the precipice and my body wants to burst. I'm wound so tight my whole body is shaking like a sapling in the wind. "Keep looking at me when you come." He demands.

I have to obey him and when Ta's heated fingers on one

hand pinches my clit, I explode. Screaming I stare into the dragon's black eyes as he blows white flames over my breasts. I can't keep the second orgasm at bay and come again, with Ta's white hot touch and the dragon's flames I don't stand a chance. I've not recovered from my first orgasm, but the second one hits hard, and I almost black out.

Once Ta has eked out every single cry from my body, he slips out from under me. I fall to all fours, a panting, sweaty, sticky mess. I'm gently turned over, onto my back and I feel splashes of refreshing water being splashed over my overheated body.

"I love how you taste, Araline." Ta smiles at me, lying in the shallow water next to me. "And Brenn, those markings on her breasts are exquisite. It'll make her nipples extra sensitive tonight." He grins up at Brennen who runs a propriety hand over my breasts, I yelp as I peer down at them.

CHAPTER FORTY-SEVEN

I have raised lines, quite a few of them which travel from my nipples, outward. On each breast and around my nipples are circles which cover the whole areola area. I stroke them.

"Ouch!" They look like I've sunbathed to long and are rather tender. "You've even managed to get the nipple!" I stare at Brennen in wonder, he looks rather proud of himself.

"They are just the start." He tells me as he lifts my legs up until my feet are resting on his shoulders. He doesn't wait for me to reply, just picks a few of the flowers that Ta used. I watch, mesmerised as he drips the lube like substance onto both of his cocks. The way he strokes himself has me salivating for him.

I know what's coming and I eagerly roll my hips to entice him.

"I need you." I say, then turning to Ta, "Kiss me," I demand.

Ta devours me and catches my cry as Brennen slowly enters my body. His smaller cock rubs deliciously over my sensitive clit. Fuck, he's big, I'm full, stuffed with him and I relish it. I want everything, all they have to give me. Brennen waits until my body softens around him and then squeeze him tightly to continue.

"Fuck me, Brenn. Do it, now!" I beg, needing him to move, to press his body into mine with force, until I'm delirious with the need to come again.

Pulling away from his kiss Ta rises to his knees on my left and holds his cock while he presses it into my mouth. I moan at his taste and take him deep down the back of my throat. I gag but calm myself as he pulls out a little. I use my hands to cup his balls and gently tug them. I love the moan of pleasure that he makes when I do that.

Brennen fucks me, with deep forceful strokes. Both of his cocks only add to the pleasure and I can't wait until they both fuck me again. Every time he thrusts into me, I moan around Ta's cock. Ta leans forward and strokes a finger, tenderly down my face. "You have no idea how beautiful you look, right this second. Being fucked by your mates. We love you, Araline. Never doubt our feelings for you."

I stare up at him, obviously unable to answer him as my mouth is somewhat full with his gorgeous cock. But my eyes widen with shock as I feel the heat of Brennen's dragons flame. Ta pulls his cock free which is probably a good idea. As I buck, the dragon's flame licks around my labia and I feel it fleetingly across my clit. I stare at Brenn, his eyes are black and he's breathing the white flame down onto my stomach.

"Fuck!" I scream, "Too much." I try and pull away but Ta

holds onto my shoulders, keeping me in place. Brennen circles his hips, his pubic bone grinds into where his flames have just marked me again and it pushes me headlong into another release. My back arches and I can't hold the scream in, my heart is racing, while my brain can't quite process all the sensations I'm feeling. Brennen gently eases my legs off his shoulders, as I have no control over them, and they flop open in the shallow water.

"Fuck me, Araline, when you come it's like a vice around my cock." He slips free from me, pulling me up until he's lying down, and I'm sprawled across his chest. He kisses me soundly before Ta drips water into my mouth. I greedily swallow.

"More." I gasp and he cups his hands to deliver the refreshing water that revives my body and soul. I sit up and move off Brennen's chest to sit in the water. Wow, I blush as what we just did flashes in my mind, it was amazing, and I know it's only the beginning. I watch them, taking in their beauty as they drink, its thirsty work, obviously. I chuckle and Ta winks at me before they walk off, but they don't go far. It's so they can give me more of the flowers. I take them and the scents are just as they were before, of dark erotic spices. The essence of each male, my males. I know I'm expected to get them some as well so, standing I walk off to find my ruby red flowers.

They devour them, just as they had the first time. The look of desire they give me makes me tremble. After I have swallowed the last petal, I feel heat wash over me as my own need starts to rise again.

Brennen picks me up, walking into the second pool. This

one has tiny golden bubbles popping on the service, which reminds me of frothy champagne and feels delicious as they burst against my skin. It's hotter than the last and it takes a while to become accustomed to the extra heat. I float on my back in the middle, looking up at the thousands of twinkling gems that give off just enough light so we can still see each other.

"Araline, I need to be in you." Ta says as he pulls me towards him.

I kiss him, wrapping my legs around his waist and I feel his cock slip into me. Staring into his eyes, I start a slow easy ride. The golden bubbles pop and fizz against our skin as I lean down to kiss him. Our tongues tangle and my hands grip his shoulders when I feel Brennen move in behind me.

I feel his lips on my shoulders as he kisses from one to the other shoulder blade, nipping his sharp teeth against my skin. His fingers stroke down my spine until they come to my bottom.

"I love how you look when Ta fucks you." He tells me as the naughty man slips a finger into my ass.

I turn my head, and he stares at me while Ta slows his hips so he's barley moving.

"How do I look?" I ask huskily. Ta's hands are holding me still so I'm unable to rise up and down. It's frustrating only because I can feel the flowers effects starting to make my blood heat with erotic need. But they are such dominant males that I have no choice but to obey.

"You look good enough to eat. I love when you're made to come by either of us, your skin blushes and your screams of pleasure only has us both hardening for you." His wicked fingers now buried deep in my ass scissor and my eyes cross.

"Move, please, I have to move." I beg them, feeling the need coiling within me dying to be set free.

Ta frees my hips, and I can't keep still any longer, I ride him, hard. Brennen follows us with his hand and teeth biting the tender skin on my neck. I have a feeling that I'm going to be marked in more ways than one come morning.

I'm just about to come when Ta says, "Drink, Araline." He cups his hands and scoops up some of the fizzing water and I swallow greedily.

As I swallow, I'm jolted with awareness. I can feel what they feel. I feel how they view me.

"What's happening?" I whisper trying to compute what my mind is showing me. I see flashes of myself, through their eyes. I feel the love, the tenderness the scolding desire they both feel for me. I feel how their bodies harden, how they've kept back some of their darker desires because they didn't want to scare me away. I can feel my body encasing theirs and how it excites them beyond measure. "Fuck! You feel this way?" I groan as my own body begins to move, up and down on Ta's cock.

"Yes, Little Flower. You can feel us as we can feel you. Only and forever for you." Brennen tells me, as his hand with his fingers buried in me still follows me up and down. "We will never stop feeling this way for you."

I can feel another release building and I don't know how long I will be able to last. I'm not a multiply orgasm girl. Once or twice if I'm lucky, and that's on a good night.

"You will lose count of how many times you come for us

tonight." Ta says as he grips my hips and slams into me. "And you will take it." he brings my head down and takes my cries as my body crumples and I come for them again. "Fuck, Araline feel how you make me feel." Ta cries as he joins me, his thrusts uncoordinated now as his release washes over him.

All I can do is hang on, until he slows and kisses me.

"That was amazing." I whisper against his lips. "And this pool, it made me see and feel things from both of your points of view." I groan when Brennen removes his fingers and dives into the pool. We both watch as he swims deeper and deeper and then it's the black dragon that shoots out of the pool. Water droplets cascade over us as he flies over our heads. The frightening tail flicks more water over us making us laugh.

CHAPTER FORTY-EIGHT

"Tell me more about this place, Ta." I ask, my eyes track the dragon, while I languish in Ta's arms. The bubbles from the pool still fizzing and popping over my sensitive skin. For something so large it was utterly graceful in the air.

"The story goes, the first King of Mertier found this place by chance. He'd been out hunting and had got himself lost. Anyway, he somehow managed to communicate with the dragons and they struck up an accord. To live in harmony each species would share the body of the royals, as they were the strongest of all the males on the planet. That's how Brenn's family are now the dragon keepers. He was said to have lived with the dragons for many years until they felt he was worthy of their gift. Everyone had thought he had died, until he walked back to the royal palace with a dragon in tow." He saw my quizzical look, "Don't ask me how it all works; I've no idea. But isn't he amazing?"

We both turned to watch the aerial display Brennen's dragon was treating us to. Then a thought struck me and my whole body stiffens.

"Ta," I murmur, not sure how to continue, "Um, do I have to do anything with the, um," I stumble a bit. "You know with the dragon?" I feel my skin heat up with embarrassment. I can only pray he says no as I'm really not into fucking a dragon. I'm all up for trying different kinks but that… no way!

Ta lets out a bark of a laugh, and it echoes throughout the cave. Brennen flies over to re-join us landing in the pool and shifting effortlessly back into a man.

"What so funny?" he looks at me for an answer as Ta's still doubled up laughing.

I glare at Ta, "It's not that funny." I grate out, rolling my eyes.

Holding his sides, because obviously it was that funny.

"She thought," laughter overcomes him, and he falls back into the pool. Brennen glances at me and I shake my head. When Ta finally resurfaces, he continues, "Araline thought she would have to get down and dirty with your dragon." He chuckles, seeming to gain a little control of himself.

Brennen moves towards me, lifting me into his arms. I wrap my legs around his waist as he nuzzles my neck, my sensitive nipples peaking as they rub against his chest. "Little Flower, I'm sure he would love to, but it's just not practical."

I can see Ta trying not to break out in laughter while I feel outraged!

"I didn't want to!" I feel my skin heating as I blush. "I was only asking Ta because it flashed in my mind and I was worried I'd have to." I mumble. I keep holding onto him as he steps out of the pool and jumps with me into another one. I only have a moment to hold my breath before we are under water. I splutter as we float to the top.

It's freezing! "Fuck, g-g-get me out!" I shiver as he laughs before walking out. "I don't like the-the cold!" My nipples have beaded with the cold and I'm covered in Goosebumps. I'm still shivering as he heads to another one. "This one better be warm." My teeth chatter as we sink into the water. It's hot; in fact, it's steaming hot. Literally I can see the steam rising off my cooled skin, but I enjoy how I start to thaw. I've never been in water as cold as that pool had been.

"Better?" Brennen asks and I nod, looking around for Ta. "He's gone for food. He'll be back soon."

I nod, I wasn't feeling particularly hungry but as soon as he mentioned food, my stomach gave a very unladylike growl, he grins. This pool is quite shallow, standing on my own I look down my body in wonder at the new markings that Brennen's dragon has branded on me.

"He's nowhere near finished with you Little Flower." He tells me, walking towards me; I see his dragon scales shimmer just under his skin.

I reach up and stroke his chest, it's almost hypnotising how his scales follow where I touch. It reminds me a bit of those cushions you could buy on Earth in sequins. You brush them one way and a picture appears; brush them another way and it's something else.

"Hope your both hungry?" Ta calls out. He is pushing a loaded cart that is hovering just off the floor. It's overloaded with food and drinks and it all smells delicious.

"I know I am." Brennen heads towards him and holds his hand out for me to join them.

We pile our plates and sit on some rocks that look to have been moulded into comfortable seats. People must have sat here for centuries, and I have to admit I'm awed by the history of this place. I still have no idea what I'm eating, but it's brightly coloured and tastes so good.

"You'll have to explain to me what we are eating, one day." I tell them, popping a mushroom shaped thing into my mouth. So far though, I've not eaten anything I don't like.

"We will, we have so much to show you. But we have a few lifetimes to do it. There is no rush." Ta smiles at me.

After we've eaten our fill, I close my eyes, leaning back against the rock. You'd think rock would be cold, but I touch it and it feels warm. I relax thinking about what we have done so far tonight. God these men have turned me into a nymphomaniac. I've never in my life had sex like I've had here. It's been mind boggling.

I open my eyes to see both Brennen and Ta are watching me. They've picked their flowers, which they are holding, offering them to me once again. My body responds immediately. I glance around for my bright red flowers and once I spot them, I walk off to pick a couple. I walk back and already my body is heating up, becoming wet and ready for them both.

"We have only two pools left, Little Flower." Brennen says softly as he hands me a flower and I offer him one of mine.

"Yes, I know," I reply softly, while biting my lip. I've no idea how long we've been here, it could be the following day to when we arrived for all I know. I keep eye contact as he devours my flower. I turn to do the same with Ta. I take his and he takes mine, then we join Brennen and eat our flowers.

Holy hell, sexual need blossoms in every cell, it's like a tidal wave rushing over me until I'm moaning. My eyes drift over their bodies as they stand there, proud and strong. "I want you in me! Now!" My hands go to my breasts, cupping them, needing their mouths on them, sucking on the hard tips.

Brennen moves fast and has a nipple in his mouth before I can process that he's even moved. Ta walks over in a slower prowl to stand behind me. The feral look of ownership in Brennen's eyes as he drops to his knees, almost have my own giving out.

I'm lifted by Ta, until my legs go over Brennen's shoulders, opening my body up for him to gaze in wonder at. Ta's arms are under mine keeping me in place while his hands massage my breasts, tweaking my nipples.

My head is resting against Ta's chest as I watch Brennen lick his lips, he has a lascivious look on his face, and he looks as if he's deciding on how best to eat me. As if I'm a tasty morsel served on a silver platter and he's a starving man.

"I love how pouty your lips are. Your clit is swollen, and I need it in my mouth." He moans, before he moves a little closer, and I shudder when I feel his heated breath caress my clit.

"Please." I beg while Ta's draws lazy circles around my nipples, which seem super sensitive from Brennen's dragon's brands.

"Please what?" Brennen growls, kissing the inside of my thighs.

The naughty man is going to make me beg! "Please suck my clit, Brenn."

He nips the tender skin of my thighs, "Is that all that you desire Little Flower? You don't want my fingers inside you, fucking you?" he sucked one of my labia lips into his mouth and I can't contain the moan.

The exoticness of what the two males are making me feel is like nothing I could have comprehended before being brought to this planet.

"Yes, yes." I shriek, rolling my hips, trying to entice him to giving me what I desire. "I want everything, please Brenn."

"I don't know. What do you think, Ta? Does she seem to want it enough?" he glances to Ta, over my shoulder.

"Yes, I do! I do!" I moan. My hands are free, and I run them down my body, until I can rub my clit.

"Fuck, Ta. You should see this." Brennen gasps.

"Is our woman being naughty?" Ta asks while leaning over my shoulder trying to catch a glimpse of my finger pleasuring myself.

"Oh, yes she is so naughty."

My eyes flutter open and I watch Brennen as he avidly watches my finger as I strum my clit.

"It feels so good." I whisper. "But your mouth would be so much better. Please Brenn."

Brennen leans in and removes my fingers and I watch while he sucks them into his mouth, swirling his tongue around them.

"You taste so good." Just before he swoops in and sucks my clit. Brennen's tongue wreaks havoc sweeping into my cunt and latching onto my swollen clit with unnerving accuracy. Some men couldn't find it even if it was painted bright red.

My hips dance provocatively under Brennen's talented tongue, silently demanding he gives me everything he has, but Ta holds me securely in place, while he nuzzles my neck, using his teeth to nip the oversensitive skin.

I'm not going to last long. I was already on the edge with my own fingers. My thighs are trembling and my stomach quivers as the release starts to build and like a tsunami it's going to be devastating.

"I need to come! Oh fuck, please." I beg, breathlessly.

"Make her come Brenn," Ta orders.

Brennen listens and I feel two fingers enter me, crook, and find my G-spot.

"Argh!" I moan as he expertly rubs it. My ex, Giles, the pig spawned from hell, insisted the G-spot was a myth. Obviously, it's not!

My whole body locks up and my eyes are wide with shock as I come and come. I also feel liquid leave me and I'm mortified. Have I just wet myself?

"Oh fuck, Araline, you just squirted all over my face."

I watch, helplessly as Brennen wipes his face then licks his fingers. He looks up at me with utter devotion etched on his face.

CHAPTER FORTY-NINE

Squirted? I struggle to get free, I'm so embarrassed. Never before has that happened to me.

"No Araline. That's a wonderful thing. I can only wish it was on my face!" Ta whispers in my ear.

I watch Brennen lower my legs, which are crazy unstable. I'm thankful Ta is still holding me otherwise I'd be on the floor. I'm still embarrassed but I take in how Brennen seems to have enjoyed it.

"You need to do it on me someday." Ta turns me and takes my mouth in a savage kiss. He wades through the pool, and I wrap my legs around his waist as we enter the last pool.

This pool is surrounded by our chosen flowers and other greenery that makes it look as if we have stumbled upon a hidden pool in a jungle. I pluck a couple of flowers and hand them to my males, I love the way their nostrils flare as they breathe in the scent of the flowers. As soon as they can pull away from smelling them, they pick theirs and I copy them, breathing in the unique scent that is both of them. We quickly eat the flowers and I once again feel the rising sexual need.

The water is silver in this pool, like the bathing pool we have in our home. I duck my head under and come up to find them watching me. I smile, biting my lip as they both walk towards me. I have a feeling they won't be holding back, not that they have, but this pool will be where this night sadly ends and I have a feeling they will both be taking me and I'm excited to feel them both again.

Brennen pulls me into his arms, winding his arms around my waist, pulling me in close to his hard body. My lips brush against his as I feel Ta kiss my nape. "I want to feel you both." I whisper.

"And we need you." Brennen's hands lift me in the water, and I gasp as when I'm lowered his cock slips into me. His smaller extra cock is pressed tightly against my clit. He's large, and I take a moment for my body to become used to his girth. But desire soon whips through me as he circles his hips, making his smaller cock rub my clit.

He walks backwards until his back hits the side of the pool and he rests his elbows on the edge. It's shallower here and Ta picks a flower, rubbing the lube substance provocatively as it drips over his cock. I'm left in no doubt about what they intend to do, and I crave it.

"Are you ready for us, Araline?" Ta's voice is low, guttural, as he leans over and rests one hand by Brennen's elbow on the side of the pool. His other hand guides his cock and I feel the pressure as he slowly thrusts inside me. Turning my head, he kisses my lips until he is fully inside.

OMG! That kiss. It makes my blood sizzle.

Both males are buried balls deep in me. My eyes flutter closed and I'm panting as Brennen's smaller cock has been rubbing my clit all the while Ta was slowly entering me.

"Fuck, she feels so tight, Brenn." Ta moans as he pulls back and starts thrusting into me at a slow lazy pace.

"Yes, she is, she is perfect." Brennen says as he joins Ta in slowly entering me and pulling almost all the way out, all the while, his smaller cock is deliciously rubbing against my clit.

My mouth finds Brennen's and my tongue slides against his. His breath is hot, and he tastes of fire and everything I've ever craved.

"Please…" I whisper against his lips. "I feel you both. Your cocks are making me feel so full. I've never felt this. You two are mine! I love you so much." I finally admit. I do, I love them so damn much. It's taken longer for me to allow my feelings to grow for them both. For months I wanted to escape, but I slowly realised there wasn't anything left for me on Earth. My life will be infinitely better here with my two males.

Brennen kisses my neck and I feel his fire against my skin again, making his patterns along both sides of my neck and the lobes of my ears. The bite of pain makes me scream out as it pushes me straight into my release. I'm screaming as Ta holds my hips still in a biting hold. His hips grind against my bottom and I feel his cock bob as he shouts out his release. Brennen isn't far behind him as he pulls his face back and stares into my eyes as he comes.

"You are ours and I love you, you will never be alone again." His wide grin shows me that my telling them that I love them has delighted him. He kisses me so softly before turning my head so Ta can kiss me.

"You've made my life utterly complete. I love you so much Araline, I never dreamt my mate would fulfil me as you do. I want to be a better male for you." He whispers against my lips before kissing me.

As we kiss, I feel them leave my body and the water works its magic and sooth my tender bits. I have never, ever, had a night like what we have shared, and I know I can have it whenever I want. This new life will be exciting, and I will be fully sated with my two males and a dragon.

EPILOGUE

A year later

"Araline," Alish calls out as she walks up to me. I am in the shopping District looking for some presents for my males.

"Alish, it's wonderful to see you." She pulls me into a hug, and I laugh as my parcels drop to the floor. We both bend to pick them up.

"And you, lass." She links her arm through mine and leads me over to the indoor water feature that I sat at when I first arrived with Brennen and Ta. "Have you heard?" she asks, brushing her mane of hair off her shoulder. She still hasn't had any of the glorious length cut off.

"Heard what?" We do love a good gossip whenever we are together. Alish has become one of my best friends here on Mertier.

"The vortex is open!" she whispers, her eyes wide with

excitement.

"So soon?" I've been taking history lessons, as I would one day be queen here I thought it was a good idea to learn about the planet I was now living on, and was told it only opened every hundred years or so.

"I know. The Court is all a flutter, I've heard, though I don't know how true it is. But Talon is meant to be going down to Earth and bringing his mate here." She looks somewhat shocked, as am I.

"Wow, that will go a long way to make it up to him as to how he and his brothers have been treated," I whisper to her.

She nods in agreement. "There's more." Her eyes widen. "During his time out of the family, he's decided to have two males instead of the one to share his mate with, So whoever they bring through will have three mates."

I fan my face, "Oh my god. I can just about handle two, never mind three…" Last night flashes in my mind. The way I had crept up on Ta and ended up having my wicked way with him on his desk. While I had been lost in sexual pleasure, Brennen walked in and joined us. I can feel the heat tinge my cheeks and laugh when Alish gives me a knowing grin and wink.

"I know what you mean. Oh, and Simone has been in talks with one of Talon's brothers. Apparently, he had been the one to look after her whilst she was in their camp, and he's also got two males he's chosen. So, Simone might have three mates. Which I expect will be much more acceptable than five for her. Though, I do have a few friends outside of the court that have five mates. I must introduce you to them. They seem very happy."

"I will go and see Simone soon, once she is settled. Perhaps she will become one of our friends now?" I wonder aloud, smiling. I'm happy Simone will get her dragon after all.

"I will come with you. Now I must hurry home, Steel is away at camp. So, it's just me, Hunter and Brogan at home. We want to make the most of it and I know that you will understand that, lass." She winks at me before kissing my cheek.

"Oh well, enjoy." I grin as she hurries off with a wave. I think of the gossip she's just told me. A new female will be arriving soon, and Simone will get her happy ever after. It's funny how life turns out sometimes.

I sit there for a few moments longer, taking in the sights, until I spot Ta and Brennen walking towards me. Bloody hell, they are something to behold. I am so thankful I was in that church and Brennen brought me here to my new life.

I stand just as they reach me. "Let's go home. I want to spend the rest of the day showing you both how much I love you."

They each take a hand and lead the way. I will follow them wherever they go. We have a few lifetimes to love the hell out of each other and I intend to do just that.

THE END

ABOUT THE AUTHOR

Now a bit about me.

Sorry, but I'm not half as interesting as my characters. But here goes. I grew up in the county of Hampshire, in southern England. I was incredibly lucky in that my childhood was with the most amazing parents you could wish for. I wanted to be a dancer, nothing more, nothing less, and as an only child, I enjoyed dancing lessons, which I think taught me a little discipline or maybe the tenacity to finish what I start.

I have a son who is my pride and joy, and to me, he's pretty darn perfect. But DON'T tell him that!

I live with my partner and our cat, who is spoiled rotten, which often leads to him thinking he rules the house! I was always told that

I had a somewhat fanciful imagination—and thank God for that! So here I am, doing something I love: writing.

I have had many jobs, doing all sorts of things to make ends meet, but fell into writing after copious amounts of reading and wanting to escape the daily grind. I needed to get these stories out of my head. I have a love for all things paranormal and the erotic and wanted to incorporate the two. I hope you've enjoyed the first book in my Royal dragon series as much as I have writing it, I have a feeling these dragons will be keeping me busy for many, many books!

I'd love to hear from you. I don't bite... well, I do sometimes but only if you ask me nicely. If you want to follow me, please find me at the following.

Hope to hear from you soon!

facebook.com/HelenJohnstonwriter

twitter.com/HelenJohnstonIL

instagram.com/authorhelenjohnston

Printed in Great Britain
by Amazon